OPERATION DEVIL'S VENGEANCE

MJ JAVANI

Operation Devil's Vengeance is a work of fiction. The people and events depicted in this story are a product of the author's imagination. Any resemblance to actual events, or persons, living or dead is purely coincidental.

Published by:

UNIT 81 PUBLISHING

United States of America

E-book ISBN: 978-1-7330093-2-4
Print book ISBN: 978-1-7330093-3-1
Learn more about the author at www.mjjavani.com

In Loving Memory of Roz

CONTENTS

1. RESIDENCE OF DR. RAY SIMMONS, LEESBURG, VIRGINIA

September 21

I t was time to move. They stood in darkness among the trees wearing tactical uniforms and matching ski masks. Only four of them had orders to enter the house. The fifth man waited in the home next door. They were trained to perfection for maximum lethality. Night-vision goggles covered their eyes as they waited for thirty minutes. At 11:30 p.m., Dr. Ray Simmons and his wife, Connie, shut the bedroom lights. The assault team crept slowly toward the house. The bushes surrounding the pool provided an extra layer of cover. The decision to attack Dr. Simmons at home was taken after learning the large estates in this section of Leesburg, Virginia, a suburb of Washington, DC, were built a significant distance apart from one another. The assault team rented the house in the adjacent property. For the past four months, their pattern of life indicated that they were technology entrepreneurs.

When the assault team commander put his fist in the air, pulling down an invisible cord, all four men ran in unison up the stairwell and onto the back deck. Their movements were synchronized to perfection, like the Swiss watches on their wrists. The commander bit his lip, catching himself before tripping over a garbage can lid. One wrong move would destroy months of preparation. He gently pushed the lid aside and motioned his team forward. In front of them, four floor-to-ceiling windows opened into the living room from the back deck. As expected, one of the windows was ajar. They removed the external screen and walked in one after the other. It was no accident the team had chosen this method of entry. Connie Simmons had posted photos of the living room on her public Facebook page. The pictures had revealed that alarm sensors did not protect these windows.

From the living room, the commander and two others cautiously walked through the kitchen toward the front of the house. A winding staircase led to the bedrooms upstairs. One assault team member was responsible for preparing the kitchen sitting room for the ghastly task ahead. Upstairs, the rest of the men proceeded to the master bedroom in silence. *The corrupt scientist and his wife deserve what they'll get; these Americans have too much space for just two people,* the commander thought.

As soon as Dr. Simmons opened his eyes, duct tape was used to cover his mouth, along with his hands and feet. Dr. Simmons frantically turned to his side. His wife had fared no better. Moments later, husband and wife were dragged through the hall and down the stairs. Their legs hit every single step of the stairway. Two wooden chairs from the kitchen table faced each other. Dr. Simmons was tied to one while his wife was tied to the other. The assault team, navigating the darkness with goggles, kept the lights off.

The four men stood in silence to create fear. Connie shook nervously in her seat. Finally, the commander spoke out. His voice sounded ominous in the dark.

"Dr. Ray Simmons, do you vant to live or die?" the commander asked.

The question hung in the air without an answer. The commander moved forward to yank the tape covering Dr. Simmons's mouth. The scientist let out a quiet gasp.

"Damn it, what's the meaning of this? I'll tell where we keep all our jewelry and valuables."

"Are you Dr. Ray Simmons vith the US Army Medical Research Institute of Infectious Diseases at Fort Detrick, Maryland?"

After a long silence, the commander continued. "Perhaps that question was too difficult. Are you a microbiologist?"

"Yes."

"Ve're not here for your jewelry."

"What is it you want, then?"

"Ve've heard you've been doing some dangerous research. Ve vant you to teach us vhat you've learned."

Dr. Simmons remained silent.

"Ve need to talk about your new veapon."

"I don't know anything about a new weapon," Dr. Simmons said.

"You're so modest, Doctor. You're the world's top expert in this field. Ve're eager to learn from you."

"Please, you've made a terrible mistake. Yes, I'm Dr. Simmons, but I develop vaccines, that's it."

After a brief pause, the commander raised his voice. "Please don't lie to me. Ve've followed you every morning driving north on Route 15, all the way up to Fort Detrick. Ve know vhat happens in Fort Detrick."

"Okay, okay. I work for the US Army at Fort Detrick. So what? The army needs vaccines to protect our soldiers. I'll tell you all I know to protect yourself from influenza, if that's what you want."

Seconds later, the lights in the kitchen came on. The assault team stood silently around Dr. Simmons and his wife. Their goggles were now holstered, and their masks came off their faces. One of them removed a twenty-centimeter serrated combat knife from inside a pant leg while the others watched.

"*You* guys! I've said hello to you every morning for the past few months. What kind of sick joke is this?" Dr. Simmons said.

"Maybe everything is a fucking joke to you Americans but not for us. This is serious business," the commander said.

"No. God, please no."

As Dr. Simmons pleaded, one of the men drove the combat knife straight into Connie's uncovered thigh. Blood squirted out around the metal blade, then slid down her leg and trickled to the floor. Connie squirmed, trying without luck to jump out of the chair. Her efforts to scream were muffled by the duct tape as her eyes pleaded for help. The man who stabbed her thigh took the knife out while another placed a pad over the wound, applying pressure to stop the bleeding.

"Next ve take out her eye unless you cooperate," the commander said.

"Okay, you sick bastard, but my research is sensitive, and my notes are all inside the lab. You can drive me over to Fort Detrick, and I'll get what you need," Dr. Simmons said as tears welled up in his eyes.

"Nice try. You'll tell us everything you know right here in this house. I brought this for you." A notepad and pen were placed in front of Dr. Simmons. "If I think you're giving me shit information, I'll kill your wife."

"What exactly do you want to know?"

"Everything. Vhat do we need to duplicate your new veapon?"

As Dr. Simmons wrote, one of the men slammed the doors of the kitchen cabinets one by one.

"Do you have any tea in this house?" the man asked.

Dr. Simmons stared for several seconds. His eyes were now filled with hate. "There are Lipton tea bags in the top shelf of the cabinet next to the fridge."

The man calmly filled a kettle with water before placing it on the stove. Although the men were used to brewing their tea, they were stuck with the American tea bags for the moment. As the water came to a boil, the commander walked over to Dr. Simmons to check his progress. Within seconds he shouted, "Ve need to know the primary instrument of delivery. How do you keep it alive outside the body?"

The assailants took turns drinking their tea. One of them remained behind Connie at all times, with a knife under her throat. At 2:30 a.m., Dr. Simmons put his pen down.

"You're finished?"

"Yes, I am finished," Dr. Simmons replied mockingly.

The commander ignored the slight. He walked over to review the notes. After ten minutes, he proclaimed his satisfaction. "Very good, very good. I hope you're not lying to me. I know vhere you live. I also know vhere your kids live."

"I'm aware," Dr. Simmons said.

"Okay, ve're done here," the commander said while putting the notepad inside a small bag.

"Are you going to let us go now?" Dr. Simmons asked with a quivering voice.

"Not exactly," came the terse reply. The commander maneuvered behind Dr. Simmons, watching the hairs rise on the back of his neck. The American seemed surprised as the commander grabbed his ear. A split second later, Dr. Simmons shook his head, still clearly oblivious of what had happened.

"Are you pissing on my neck, you sick bastard?" Dr. Simmons demanded, still in shock, as an earlobe landed on his lap. The American was suddenly aware that the warm liquid on his neck was blood. The expression of horror on Connie's face served as confirmation. As he suddenly writhed in pain, Dr. Simmons pleaded, "Why are you doing this? I gave you everything you wanted!"

"You don't understand, ve need to make it look like a robbery. The police vill think you didn't tell us vhere the money was, so we had to kill you."

Seconds later, commands were given in a language Dr. Simmons was not expected to understand. Two assault team members ran upstairs.

"It's time to pay for the crimes of your government, Doctor," the commander said while placing duct tape over Dr. Simmons's mouth once more. A minute later, Dr. Simmons's other ear was chopped off. The American was almost unconscious, but the nauseating stench must have brought him back. It was burning flesh. One of the men pressed a lit cigarette against Connie's thigh. Seconds later, the commander gave the order to put her out of her misery. One of his men placed a suppressed Colt pistol over Connie's left temple and pulled the trigger.

His bleeding wife was the last thing Dr. Simmons saw before his own demise. The shell casings were picked up as the scene was sanitized for evidence. The house was sacked, and the jewelry was taken. Sofa cushions were overturned as cookie jars were emptied. When the commander was finally satisfied, he gave the order to retreat. It was now 3:15 in the morning. They had to catch a 6:00 a.m. flight to Toronto. The assault team gathered its equipment and exited the house the same way it had entered. They ran past the pool and through the tree line to the adjacent property.

Inside the garage, the fifth member of the assault team was waiting in the car. They locked the equipment and fatigues in the garage storage closet. The driver headed toward the Toll Road, arriving at Dulles Airport at 4:00 a.m. No one would search for Dr. Simmons until Monday morning. An hour and a half later, the commander boarded the plane with his men. His superior was anxiously waiting for the precious notes.

2. RESEARCH CENTER FOR EMERGING AND REEMERGING INFECTIOUS DISEASES, AKANLU, IRAN

September 22

D r. Roozbeh Navabi adjusted his stance to ease the pressure on his legs. He'd been standing for fifteen minutes. Beads of sweat dripped out of every pore on his body. It was the sensation of countless insects crawling under his skin, taking tiny bites of his flesh. Addressing the itch was completely out of the question. The pipette in his right hand contained a culture of the SARS virus. The deadly strain had recently infected several individuals in the capital city of Tehran. It was essential to develop a vaccine. Roozbeh pressed the button under his thumb and inserted the SARS culture into the small tube. After closing the cap and placing it on a rack, he released the pipette tip into the proper receptacle before walking over to the tube rack. The SARS culture had to be analyzed, the DNA extracted, then sequenced for further study.

The Research Center for Emerging and Reemerging Infectious Diseases, or RCERID, was considered Iran's premier center for epidemiological research. A division of the Pasteur Institute of Iran, RCERID was located in the remote village of Akanlu, surrounded by mountains. Far from urban populations, it provided Tehran authorities a safe location to study deadly infectious diseases. Founded in 1952, the center was the most well-funded biological laboratory in the country. It was one of Iran's best-kept secrets, and that's the way the authorities liked it. Roozbeh approached an incubator that held the strains of different pathogens. A telephone at a nearby desk lit up. He picked up.

"Roozbeh, they're ready for you in lab five."

"What about the rat, have you administered the sedative?"

"Yes."

"How long ago?"

"I'm not sure."

"That's not good enough, the rat must be properly sedated. Otherwise, we'll have a serious problem."

"I understand."

Roozbeh hung up. After exiting the lobby of the main building, he walked across the courtyard. Labs 5 and 6 were both located in a building resembling a large house. Roozbeh scanned his badge, opening the main entrance. All along the walls, ceiling-mounted cameras monitored the activity of the scientists around the clock. The two labs in this building had a ventilation system that generated negative pressure, allowing air to flow in but not to escape the rooms. After scanning his badge a second time, Roozbeh entered an anteroom that separated lab 5 from the main hallway. There were two doors in this room perpendicular to each other. The doors interlocked to prevent them from being opened at the same time. The anteroom provided space for changing into a biohazard suit before entering lab 5.

After tightening his suit, Roozbeh punched in a code that opened the steel door. The light display turned green as he walked in. There were three other men already present, Dr. Iman Vakili and two assistants. The others wore the same suit as Roozbeh. Unfortunately, these were not the positive-pressure suits he had requested for work with biosafety level-4 (BSL-4) pathogens. This experiment required the injection of a lab rat with a live strain of the Crimean-Congo virus. The virus caused a hemorrhagic fever with a thirty percent fatality rate in humans. After a three-day incubation period, infected individuals exhibited flulike symptoms including high fever. Similar to Ebola, Crimean-Congo made victims bleed out of various orifices. It also made them experience mood changes, becoming irritable and at times overly aggressive. Still others became confused, exhibiting symptoms of amnesia. Even worse were the nosebleeds, bloody stools, and vomiting.

Roozbeh observed as a technician, Peyman, carried the sedated rat for injection. No matter how many times they practiced this scenario, the risk remained high. A positive-pressure suit with a coiled air hose dangling from the ceiling would have reduced the risk considerably. Given the denial of additional funding, their boss had been unable to purchase these suits.

Everyone was ready. Iman's breathing quickened while his chest moved rapidly. Roozbeh stared at the beads of sweat forming on Iman's forehead. Peyman held the rat with both hands as Iman shakily maneuvered the syringe containing the deadly virus. Roozbeh wanted to delay the procedure. His colleague was bound to make a mistake. He decided not to diminish Iman's authority in front of the others. Iman closed his eyes in an attempt to focus. Once his eyes were open, the young scientist pointed the tip of the needle toward the rat. As soon as the syringe made contact with the furry rodent, all hell broke loose. The rat came to life with a burst of energy. The events that followed flashed by at light speed.

Before Roozbeh gathered his thoughts, the rat jumped away, dashing across the table. Iman continued to insert the syringe, straight into Peyman's left hand. No longer concerned about the furry creature, all four men froze in place. The needle punctured Peyman's glove as well as the skin. A small drop of blood was visible on the white glove. Peyman was likely infected with the deadliest pathogen in Iran.

"Quick, get him to the sink and apply the disinfectant," Roozbeh yelled as Iman stood frozen in place. There would be hell to pay with their boss, but that would come later.

"Iman, don't just stand there. Call for a helicopter to Vali-Asr Hospital. Peyman must be isolated immediately."

As they scurried about in panic, the rat disappeared under a table.

"Find that rat at once. It's the only living creature inoculated with our experimental vaccine. Without the rat, we won't know if our vaccine works," Roozbeh shouted at them.

One of the assistants pressed the emergency alarm on the wall. The warning went out to the entire facility about the contamination. The siren pierced their eardrums as the strobe lights flashed on and off. During the ensuing commotion, a wall-mounted phone several meters away came to life. He walked over to read the caller ID. It was the director's office.

"What the hell is going on down there?" the director growled.

"We've experienced an accidental infection in lab five. We're following protocol." It was a lie. Roozbeh could think of nothing else to say.

"Never mind that. There's a matter of utmost importance I need to discuss with you."

"But, sir, we've got a crisis down here. I need to—"

"Roozbeh, are you listening to me? Stop wasting time and come to my office at once!"

Roozbeh hung up. Without saying a word, he made a beeline to the steel door separating the lab from the anteroom. After going through the decontamination showers, he dried himself off and put on his clothes. Several minutes later, Roozbeh entered the office of his boss, Dr. Javad Ahvazi. The man had been appointed as director of RCERID two years earlier. During that time, he had managed to double the funding of the facility while firing most of those who'd worked there before his arrival. He was not a man to be crossed or disobeyed.

"I got here as fast as I could. There was chaos at the lab. As I mentioned—"

Dr. Ahvazi, already annoyed, cut him off with the wave of his hand. "Forget about the lab for now. We've been assigned a top secret project."

Roozbeh's ears perked up. RCERID worked for the Pasteur Institute, which was part of the civilian Ministry of Health. There had never been a classified application for his research.

"This particular project, *ghoolp*, is of special interest to the supreme leader. The man in charge is Major General Vahid Kalantari. Does that give you a hint of the importance of the project?"

Dr. Ahvazi had a bad habit of making disruptive noises when he spoke. Roozbeh's thoughts transitioned away from the debacle in lab 5. General Kalantari was chief of Iran's Islamic Revolutionary Guard Corps Qods Force, known as QF. The QF was responsible for the external operations of the Revolutionary Guards. Its mandate included providing supplies to proxy militias, training foreign militaries, sabotage, and all forms of terrorism. There was little good that could come of this.

"Sir, the QF is a military organization. What could they possibly want with us?" The rhetorical question was meant to show Roozbeh's moral objection, not his lack of understanding.

"Roozbeh, you know as well as I do, the QF is the most well-funded organization in this country. Times are tough with these economic sanctions. The QF has promised enough money to quadruple our funding, *khhhh*." Dr. Ahvazi took a second to clear his throat before continuing. "This could mean complete independence from the home office in Tehran. We'll become our own autonomous facility directly under the QF." Sensing that Roozbeh was not convinced, Dr. Ahvazi elaborated.

"We'll still be able to research infectious diseases for civilians, except we'll also have 'special projects' for our military sponsors as needed. This is a dream come true, don't you agree?"

For you, perhaps, Roozbeh thought before speaking up. "Dr. Ahvazi, what's this project about anyway?"

"I'll fill you in on the details as necessary. For now, we're being asked to choose five scientists and ten technicians in addition to me. I'm putting you in charge of selection. Ask Iman to help you."

"What about the others?"

"General Kalantari has asked us to let the others go. Sixteen remaining individuals will undergo stringent background investigations for a top secret clearance. As of this moment, our facility is dedicated solely to this task."

Roozbeh felt nauseated. "When do we start?"

"That too is something I don't know. We're awaiting a team to procure a sample."

"A sample of what?" Roozbeh said incredulously, trying hard to hide his disdain.

"That'll be all, Roozbeh. Dismissed."

As Roozbeh left the room, he was plotting his next move.

3. ARLINGTON MEMORIAL HOSPITAL, ARLINGTON, VIRGINIA

September 26

He exited the elevator and walked down a long hallway. Around the corner was the reception desk. He showed his driver's license and waited for the receptionist to make the call.

"Your father's in surgery. He requested that you wait for him on the third floor."

"Thank you," Janusz Soltani said before walking back toward the elevators. Farhad Soltani was head of the oncology department and its best surgeon. The old man had graduated at the top of his class from the University of Virginia Medical School. Farhad had encouraged Janusz to follow in his footsteps, but Janusz chose a different path after the death of his brother in Italy. That single event continued to reverberate throughout his life. Recently, he had made a habit of visiting his father after work every Wednesday afternoon. They usually headed down to the cafeteria, where they chatted over food and coffee. On the third floor, Janusz took a detour through the snack room before entering the waiting area. He checked the messages on his phone. A young boy, around eleven years old, and his mother sat across from him.

The mother was trying to calm her son about an upcoming surgery. Janusz tuned in and out. He had been to this hospital hundreds of times over the years. As far back as he could remember, there was always a shortage of staff. Patients constantly had to endure long waits before being called in to see a doctor. On top of that, there was the horrible food at the cafeteria. He contemplated bringing sandwiches from outside on his future visits.

That's when the shouting began. A man was screaming to see a doctor. The growing intensity of the sound indicated that the commotion was moving in Janusz's direction. He tried to block out the distraction, to no avail. After several minutes, the shouting turned into obscenities and direct threats against the staff. Janusz wondered when security would put an end to the charade.

Several minutes later, a nurse came by to take the mother and son to see the doctor. The screaming man was much closer now, standing in the hallway outside the waiting area. As mother and son got up to follow the nurse, all hell broke loose. The irate man grabbed another individual by the collar and threw him against the wall.

"You fucking bastard, where is Dr. Stephens? He killed my wife," the man screamed as froth trickled down the side of his mouth. He looked to be in his mid-thirties, short brown hair and a scruffy beard. He was wearing a blue sweatshirt with jeans and combat boots.

"Sir, calm down. Dr. Stephens is out today. I'm his colleague here—" The doctor was cut off and pinned against the wall. Two assistants, most likely nurses, stared with trembling hands. Janusz whispered for one of them to call security, but they could not move.

"He killed my wife. Stephens killed my wife during that botched operation. I'm holding all of you personally responsible."

"Sir, let's just sit down and talk about this calmly. Sometimes there is nothing we can do—"

"I'm through talking with you people. I want blood. Someone has to pay for what happened to my wife." As he said these words, the assailant reached into his bulging pant pocket to pull out a gun. He used the 9mm Ruger-57 to pistol-whip the doctor over the head several times, sending him crashing to the floor, blood running down the side of his face. The hate in the assailant's eyes indicated he was not finished. Seconds later, he lunged forward to grab the boy standing with his mother only a few feet away. Like everyone else, they were frozen in place by the unfolding scene. The angry assailant pushed the protesting mother to the floor before pointing the gun at the boy's head.

"Now that I have your attention, someone get Dr. Stephens down here at once. I have some unfinished business I need to discuss with him."

At that exact moment, two security guards arrived. They immediately drew their weapons but seemed unsure how to proceed.

"Drop your guns, or I'll shoot the boy. I mean it. All I want is to speak with Dr. Stephens. I'll let the boy go when he comes down to see me."

One wrong move and the boy would not live to see another day. The security guards were obviously out of their league.

"I'm only going to say this once more. Back away, or I'll spill his brains all over the carpet." The way he handled the Ruger, his haircut, and his self-assurance indicated that the assailant had military training. The situation called for extreme care.

"It's all right, brother. I think there's a way to do this honorably," Janusz broke in before the security guards had a chance to make a mistake.

"Who the hell are you?"

"Just a soldier like you who knows what it feels like not to be heard."

"Who told you I was a soldier?"

"It takes one to know one, brother," Janusz lied. He figured his service with the CIA was close enough. "You can take me if you let the boy go." As Janusz spoke, the boy stared at him with pleading eyes. He desperately wanted out.

"Who put you in charge? I determine who stays and goes around here."

"I'm not arguing with you. You're doing this because you've

been ignored and you want to speak with Dr. Stephens. What better way to prove your honorable intentions than to let the boy go?"

"What do I get in return?"

"You'll still have me as a bargaining chip. No nonsense, I swear!"

The man's brow furrowed while he contemplated the proposition. Janusz motioned for the guards to move back. They obviously sensed his commanding presence and complied. The armed man surged forward with the boy before letting go to grab Janusz by the arm, placing the Ruger against the back of his head.

"Okay, what now, wise guy?" The assailant pushed Janusz's head forward with the pistol.

Janusz looked at the nurses in blue scrubs. "Can someone get Dr. Stephens here at once?" he yelled as one of them made a call. Janusz took a furtive glance around in all directions. The boy was dragging his mother down the hall in the opposite direction. The pistol-whipped doctor was sitting against the wall, tending to his injured head with his hands. The doctor's next move was a surprise.

"Are you happy now, you bastard? You cut my head open. I hope you spend the rest of your life in jail!" This was not going to end well.

"Shut up, shut the fuck up before I shoot you."

"Go ahead, shoot me. You think you're such a tough guy, let's see you shoot me."

Janusz was not happy with the needless display of bravado. Without warning, the assailant let go of Janusz and pointed the gun at the doctor. The injured man immediately crouched into the fetal position. That's when instinct took over. Janusz grabbed the extended arm of the assailant at the wrist and in one motion, forced him to drop the Ruger. He quickly kicked the weapon out of reach before being tackled from behind by the assailant. Janusz tightened his grip around the man's arms, then ducked to lift him over his back and body-slam him against the floor.

Not wanting to hurt a man who had already lost his wife, Janusz placed him in a choke hold and squeezed. Within seconds, the man passed out. Janusz stood vigilantly over him until the police arrived.

That evening Janusz came home and went straight to his study. He was in no mood to eat. He grabbed a book off the shelf and threw himself into the plush leather chair perched against a wall. He was in no mood to read either but needed a distraction. The book was about the fighting tactics of the Iranian Revolutionary Guards Corps, known as IRGC. After twenty minutes, Janusz flipped the page to start a new chapter. As soon as he placed his feet on the ottoman, his eyelids grew heavy. His head snapped up as his wife cleared her throat. Drool trickled down the side of his mouth.

"Hey, how long have you been standing there?" Janusz said groggily.

"You were supposed to be home for dinner. Another long day at the office?"

"Actually, I left early to spend the afternoon at the hospital."

"Oh, I forgot it was Wednesday. How's your father?"

"I didn't get to speak to him much. There was an incident at the hospital."

"An incident?"

"Don't want to talk about it."

"What were you doing before you fell asleep?"

"Reading a book about the IRGC's fighting tactics. Didn't realize how tired I was."

"You still can't get enough of the fight, can ya?"

"This is not the time for this conversation."

"All I'm saying is that you should write more and let others do the fighting."

Janusz closed the book and placed it on a nearby table. He motioned for her to come closer. "Is there something you'd like to discuss?"

She stared at him coldly with her arms folded under her chest. "Oofta, what's the point?" Her Minnesota accent always came through when she got excited.

"Come on, out with it, let's go."

"We just celebrated our first wedding anniversary. You're still jumping from mission to mission. Don'tcha think you've done your part?"

She was obviously upset. He didn't have the bandwidth to deal with it now. "Nonsense, you know as well as I do how risk-averse our government has become. My work is more important than ever now."

"You can't change the direction of our country no matter how much ya give. If you push too hard, you'll go right over the edge. Excessive risk taking, that's your outlet."

"Not fair," Janusz said, raising his voice. "I went to therapy for gambling. I swear I'm cured!"

"Your problem was never gambling. Your pain is much deeper. Ya need to figure oot what drives ya to push so hard. It's only a matter of time before—"

The ringing of his phone cut her off. *Why is he calling now?*

"Tony, please tell me you drunk-dialed me?"

"Good, you're awake. Listen up, I need you at the office on the double. We got work to do."

"Can't this wait till the morning?"

"Actually, pack a bag while you're at it. You're going on a trip in the morning," Tony said before hanging up.

"What was that aboot?" Jennifer asked.

"I don't know. I gotta pack a bag and show up at the office."

"Ya see, this is exactly what I mean, you're addicted to the fight. You need ta ask yourself why."

He stared at the floor in quiet contemplation. As he exited the study, she grabbed his arm.

"Oh, and, Janusz."

"Yes?"

"You have a wife now. You hafta make a change in order to

keep her."

He peeled her arm away as he went upstairs to pack.

The meeting was informal. The only others in the room besides himself and Tony, the director of the Unit, were Stan Roth, Tony's deputy, and Bill Turner, head of operations. Tony sat behind a desk, while the other two stood nearby.

"You guys look like hell. You should get some sleep," Janusz said.

"Maybe later. We have a situation on our hands," Tony said.

"Let's hear it."

"There was a news conference earlier today in Brazil. An Iranian defector, Roozbeh Navabi, claimed his government is developing a new biological weapon," Tony said.

"The defector claimed to be a microbiologist," Bill said.

"What kind of biological weapon, and who is the target?" Janusz asked.

"Both excellent questions. The defector didn't address either one. That's where we come in," Tony said before continuing.

"The news conference was a local affair in Brasília. No foreign journalists for some odd reason. Jason Osborne, chief of staff of the SSCI, speaks Portuguese. He saw the conference by chance during lunch before informing Senator Patrick, who then came to us," Stan said.

Senator Donald Patrick was the chairman of the Senate Select Committee on Intelligence or SSCI. He was a staunch advocate of Unit 81, also known as "the Unit," a private alternative to the risk-averse US government.

"What about the CIA?" Janusz asked.

Tony quickly broke in. "You know the drill. By the time this thing makes it through the layers of bureaucracy to the seventh floor, it'll be too late to stop the Iranians."

"Can't argue with you on that," Janusz said.

Bill turned to Janusz as he spoke. "Senator Patrick thinks we should jump on this before it's too late. We happen to agree."

"Any limitation on our ability to act?" Janusz asked.

"None! You have an open budget. It's all gloves off on this one. Just remember, time is not on our side as the Iranians have a head start," Tony said.

"Lovely, when do I leave?"

"I've arranged a Gulfstream to fly you and Kim to Brasília in the morning. You can sleep in my office before your flight," Tony said, dismissing the group.

On his way out the door, Janusz reflected on what Jennifer had said. What would taking this assignment mean for his marriage?

4. ENTEBBE INTERNATIONAL AIRPORT, UGANDA

September 27

One by one, the members of the assault team walked through customs. Each of the five men carried a diplomatic passport. Outside the terminal, they drove a rented Range Rover to the Iranian embassy in Kampala. The forty-three-kilometer drive took them just over two hours. The road had only one lane in each direction. Along the way, the driver expressed annoyance with the local rules.

"How am I supposed to drive here? Everything is on the wrong side, including the steering wheels and the—"

"No one asked for your opinion. Keep driving," his commander snapped.

There was silence as the men mentally prepared for what lay ahead. They disembarked outside the gates of their embassy on a leafy road named Kololo Hill Drive. Once inside the compound, they ate a quick lunch before receiving a threat briefing by the QF intelligence officer for Uganda. No one at the embassy dared ask about their mission. It was a strictly need-to-know operation ordered by Supreme Leader Mashhadi. After the briefing, the assault team collected its tailored weapons, hazard suits, and medical kits. Their weapons had been snuck in utilizing the diplomatic pouch. They packed everything inside the Range Rover.

The two-hundred-forty-kilometer drive to the village of Bumbo, near the Kenyan border, took over ten hours. Most of that time was on the A109, a two-lane highway. This part of Africa was much different than Iran. The countryside was lush, full of trees and green grass in all directions. It was hard to imagine what awaited them. As soon as they passed the town of Tororo, the Range Rover was mired in mud. The roads in this part of the country were not paved. It had rained the previous day, making the trek to Bumbo treacherous. The road had turned mushy with crater-sized pools of water as a bonus. As the assault team approached the hot zone, local military vehicles dotted the landscape. In rapid succession, they encountered checkpoint after checkpoint. Military convoys and cargo vehicles were everywhere.

They arrived at the outer reaches of Bumbo after dark. The Range Rover suddenly stopped dead in its tracks. It was a roadblock. The area beyond this point was under quarantine.

"What are you folks doing here? This area is closed off," a uniformed soldier, black as night, declared with a distinct local accent.

"Closed off? Vhat for? Ve're part of a humanitarian mission to deliver medical supplies. Please let us through," the driver said with an accented English of a different kind.

"That's not possible."

"Vhy not?"

"We have orders."

"Vhat orders?"

"Haven't you heard the news?"

"Vhat news?"

"The Ugandan president issued a decree. This region is under quarantine. No one can enter, no one can leave."

"Yes, but ve came a long way to deliver medicine. Ve're members of a relief organization."

"I'm sorry. No exceptions. No one gets through," the soldier replied, bringing the AK-47 closer to his chest.

The assault team commander was used to such situations. He calmly reached over to count a wad of American currency.

The soldier smiled, with a newfound eagerness to be helpful. "The work out here is dangerous. We haven't been paid in weeks."

"How about fifteen hundred dollars for your troubles?"

"I'll see what I can do."

The commander handed over the cash and was promptly waved through. They were blind without lights in this part of the world. The commander decided they should rest for the evening right there and then. It was not an easy decision. Surrounded by alien jungle on all sides, with the sounds of crickets and unfamiliar animals, the men found it hard to sleep. They took turns guarding the vehicle by the side of the road. When the sun finally reemerged, it was not a minute too soon.

Driving through the town of Bumbo, the driver navigated the muddy streets with great care. The villagers had vanished from the face of the earth. As soon as the assault team spotted the first of the dead bodies along the side of the road, they disembarked. They huddled around the commander for a prayer and their instructions.

"This is exactly why we came here. Put on your suits, masks, and gloves. We'll move forward in formation to search for dead bodies. Load your weapons, and don't hesitate to shoot at anything that moves."

The assault team proceeded to walk from house to house. Without warning, a loud shriek thundered through the sky. A group of gigantic birds was fighting above their heads.

"What the hell are those things?" one of the men asked.

"Those are vultures!" the commander said.

The men moved together to investigate the commotion up above. As they approached, the sound of the screeching vultures grew more intense. There were several houses separating them from a large clearing up ahead. When they made it to the other side, it was obvious what the vultures were screaming at. The commander's heart sank at the horror. Hundreds of corpses were piled on top of one another in a large heap. Vultures dove to fight over the choicest pieces of human flesh. The biggest prize of all, the eyeballs.

One of the men started heaving. He immediately removed his mask despite the objection of the commander. It did not take long for his breakfast to end up on the muddy ground below his feet. The rest of the assault team crept forward ever so slowly. It was as if they were expecting the dead bodies to rise and attack them. When they reached the pile, the grisly details were more distinguishable. The corpses had empty eye sockets. It was like a horror film, except this was all too real. A sudden gust of wind blew the stench of rotting flesh through their masks. The unmasked man lost his cool. He began convulsing in place as he dropped his supplies to run. The commander grabbed him by the shoulder.

"No, I must go back. I can't take it anymore. I can't," the delirious man shouted. This sort of panic could be infectious if not stopped.

"Soldier, you have until the count of ten to get a hold of yourself. We're on a special mission for the supreme leader. Weakness will not be tolerated."

The commander took out his Colt .45 sidearm while counting off. "One, two, three …"

Before he reached ten, his subordinate stiffened. "I'm good, sir. I'm good!"

"You sure?"

"Yes, sir."

"Anyone else feeling weak? Anyone? Anyone?" the commander shouted.

His men stared back coldly through their masks. He was certain they understood his willingness to eliminate anyone exhibiting cowardice. "Let's collect our samples and leave. The Ugandan Army will be here any minute to burn these bodies."

Every single one of these men knew what the invisible monster surrounding them could do to the human body. The worst part, they had to accompany the samples all the way to Tehran.

"Sir, these bodies have been here for a while. Do we still have to go through with this?"

"It doesn't matter. The agent survives in the body several

days after death. That's why the locals are not allowed to bury them. These bodies will be burned to prevent transmission to others," the commander replied.

Facing each other, they must have all secretly hoped the biohazard suits were sufficient. Each man opened his bag to take out a syringe and tube for the suction of blood. As they approached the pile, they knew they were face-to-face with death itself. The corpses had bled out from every orifice. The virus had liquefied their internal organs. Some of the mouths were still open with their tongues swollen. Blood oozed out of the ears. Each member of the assault team prayed to Allah before inserting his needle. *"Besmillah Rahman-e Rahim,"* they chanted in unison, *In the name of God, the merciful.* This had to be the handiwork of *Sheitan,* the devil.

Visibly shaken, they each grabbed an arm. The skin felt soft to the touch. When the syringe went in, a suction pump was used to suck out the hardened blood. They applied a blood thinner to make the suction easier. They each collected ten vials before wrapping several layers of adhesive tape around the tubes. They then put the tubes in a temperature-controlled container for the trip home. The containers were locked up as the assault team made its way toward the vehicles. They stripped off their bloodied gloves, suits, and helmets and ditched them along the side of the road. It was obvious that none of the hardened QF men felt comfortable sitting next to the vials of the contaminated blood. Few words were exchanged during their trip back to Entebbe Airport. Their government had chartered a private Iranian Air Force C-130 for the ride home. They could not afford an accidental outbreak on a passenger plane. General Kalantari had other plans for the contaminated blood.

5. RESEARCH CENTER FOR EMERGING AND REEMERGING INFECTIOUS DISEASE, AKANLU, IRAN

September 28

D
r. Ahvazi leaned back against the executive leather chair and took another sip of hot tea. Deep in thought, he studied the RCERID's finances on his desktop computer. More money was needed from the Ministry of Health. Maintaining a comfortable lifestyle in his country was not easy. One son was enrolled at Oxford University in the UK, the other at the University of Paris. His house, the leather sofas, the Mercedes, all these things cost money. His salary was determined by the total budget of the RCERID, so he needed to justify a larger budget. The solution, as always, was to take liberties with facts and figures. Last quarter he'd requested additional funding for the purchase of positive-pressure suits from abroad. The extra money had paid for a well-needed vacation. The vaccine trials on the Crimean-Congo fever had been unsuccessful to date. It was time to give the bureaucrats in Tehran false hope to keep the money flowing in. Once his team discovered a vaccine, no one would ask for the accounting of every penny.

Dr. Ahvazi opened the source documents for printing. He put the printouts on his desk, deleting the chosen figures with a whiteout marker before entering new numbers. Walking over to the office safe, he destroyed the original copies in the shredder. With that out of the way, the results of the vaccine trials for the Crimean-Congo fever showed great promise with further funding. *Now for the most important part,* he thought. He felt the cheeks of his melon-shaped face parting as he smiled. Why had he allowed himself to balloon in this way? It was the stress of this damn job. Things were so bad he could no longer stand his own reflection in the mirror. His face was not the only body part that needed work. His egg-shaped torso was that of a cartoon character. When he was younger, some of his schoolmates referred to him as Humpty-Dumpty. These days he was fond of comparing himself to an American congressman from New York whose name he could never recall.

With a whiteout, he deleted his own signature on the consent form authorizing the vaccine experiments. After months of practice, he forged the signatures of Roozbeh and Iman in place of his own. The ringing phone on his desk caused his hand to mangle the last signature. *Fucking whore, who could this be?* He checked the caller ID. The forged signature would have to wait

"Good morning, Haj Kalantari," Dr. Ahvazi said, using the honorific "Haj" for the QF chief. It meant that General Kalantari had made a pilgrimage to Mecca. It was also the way everyone referred to him.

"*Ya'Allah,* how is the staffing issue coming along?"

"I've picked fifteen individuals as you requested, five scientists and, *ghoolp,* ten technicians."

"Praise be to Allah, as soon as my team returns from Uganda, I'll have them deliver the samples directly so you may begin at once."

"Sir, *ehhem,* I don't know how exactly to say this, *ehhem,*" Dr. Ahvazi said.

"Get on with it. I don't have all day for your rambling."

"To tell you the truth, I feel the need to reemphasize the contagious nature of this deadly disease. The smallest mistake and we'll have a national crisis on our hands."

"Praise be to the hidden imam, we're taking all the precautions you requested. I don't know what else to tell you."

"Very well. Sir, there is one other thing." He hated delivering bad news.

"What now?"

"One of my men is missing."

"What do you mean missing? Who the hell is it?"

"Roozbeh. Roozbeh Navabi. An accomplished researcher, but, *ghoolp*, I'm not sure if he's cut out for this type of work. He may become a liability."

"How much have you told him about our project?"

"Unfortunately, I had to tell him everything. He was my deputy. Should I inform our security staff?"

"No, I'll handle this myself. We're working with the Ministry of Intelligence on this project. Send me this man's file. *Ya'Allah.*"

Dr. Ahvazi cleared his throat. "As you wish, Haj Kalantari, *khhhh.*"

With Roozbeh out of the way, Dr. Ahvazi was taking RCERID in a new direction.

6. COCO DELICIA RESTAURANT, BRASÍLIA, BRAZIL

September 28

Roozbeh played with the glass of mojito as the intense Brazilian sun beat down on his forehead. He was forced to crank open the outdoor umbrella over his table. Despite the heat, he preferred the outdoors with its calming views of Lake Paranoa. Coco Delicia Restaurant was highly recommended by his contact for its waterfront views and delicious food. The only problem, the local reporter who had contacted him had not yet arrived. Finishing the mojito grew increasingly difficult as Roozbeh strained to keep his eyes open. He'd barely slept since making the fateful decision to expose his country's clandestine bioweapons program. For the time being, it was best not to return to his wife. His head fell forward as fatigue overpowered him.

Without warning, he found himself inside a dark windowless room. The search for a light switch came up empty. What's worse, he was paralyzed. He could not move no matter how hard he tried. The odor of damp mold and unwashed feet overpowered him. He tried his best not to scream as the light hit his eyes. A bearded man wearing an olive uniform appeared in front of him with no shoes. Roozbeh stared at his feet as the man wiggled his toes.

"So, are you going to talk, or do we have to do this the hard way?"

"Who are you? What am I doing here?"

"We're going to teach you a lesson you won't forget. I just got through raping your wife. Now it's your turn." The man laughed from the bottom of his heart.

Roozbeh stared at the dirty toes with thick hair growing below the nails. "Where am I, and why are you not wearing shoes on your nasty feet?"

"Section 2A of Evin Prison is your new home. Pull down his pants," the man shouted as Roozbeh felt powerful hands grab his waist. With his pants down to his ankles, he was bent over a table. The interrogator spread his cheeks as others tied him down to the table. The distinct sounds of a zipper coming undone ricocheted through his ear. Roozbeh tried to break free, but it was no use. He was frozen in place.

"Let's see how much you enjoy being treated like a woman."

"No, please! Someone help me. Please, please, please!" he screamed at the top of his lungs.

"Senhor Navabi?"

Roozbeh jumped up. Sweat poured down his face as his heart pounded.

"I'm sorry, Senhor Navabi, are you okay?" the man asked in English.

"Yes, I'm just tired. I fell asleep," Roozbeh replied.

"Please forgive me for being so late. I got held up at work, a last-minute story."

"No problem, I can use the rest. Please sit down."

The two men sat across a round wooden table facing each other.

"Senhor Navabi, as I mentioned after the conference, my name is Alberto De Souza. I'm with *Notícias de Brasília*, the largest newspaper here in the capital," Alberto said while flashing his press credentials. "It's not every day that an Iranian scientist defects to our country."

"I have an uncle who lives in Brazil. I'll stay with him until I figure out my next move."

"Do you mind if I take notes while we speak?"

"Not at all. I want the world to know what the Iranian government is doing. I'm upset that none of the international media was at the conference."

"When you contacted our office about your story, we only informed our local affiliates. Perhaps after this interview there'll be more global interest," Alberto remarked while scribbling on his notepad. "Before we begin, why don't you tell me a little about yourself? Our readers will have more empathy for you if they're familiar with your story."

"Well, I'm married with two children. A seven-year-old boy and a ten-year-old girl."

"And they're accompanying you?"

Roozbeh stared at the lake as he pictured their faces. "Yes, I took them out of Iran to be safe."

"Are you planning to approach the Americans for asylum in exchange for information?"

He stared at the Brazilian intently. "No, I don't have plans to seek asylum in the US."

"Very well, Senhor Navabi. I assume you've been working on biological weapons for your country for a number of years. What made you decide to leave all of a sudden?"

Roozbeh clenched his teeth. "I'm a virologist focused on vaccines and treatments. I've never worked on biological weapons."

He adjusted his chair before continuing in a lower voice. "The QF hijacked our facilities for their program. I was not willing to cooperate."

"The QF?"

"Revolutionary Guard Qods Force."

"What kind of weapon?"

"A very deadly virus. One for which there is no available vaccine or treatment."

"Forgive me. This is difficult for me to believe, senhor. Why would they do that? They're not crazy, after all."

"No, they're not crazy. But they're fanatics. No one was willing to provide an explanation as to why this new weapon was necessary. Under the circumstances, I felt it was best for me to warn the world," Roozbeh replied as he squirmed in his chair.

"I'm sorry if my questions make you uncomfortable. But I must establish your credibility."

As soon as lunch arrived, Alberto steered the conversation to football. "You know, I began my career covering the Brazilian national team. I'm a friend of Ronaldo."

Roozbeh's face immediately lit up. Alberto took out his cell phone. He opened a cache of photos that included several shots of him standing next to the Brazilian soccer legend.

"Here I am with Kaka. We were all at a nearby bar with Ronaldo."

"Wow, do you still stay in touch with him?"

Alberto grinned from ear to ear. "I tell you what. You look like you could use a break. Why don't you come with me? I'll get the check. Afterward, we'll take my van to Amazon Bar up the street. I'll ask a couple of friends, including Ronaldo, to join us."

"Really, is that possible?"

"Of course. I'll call them now."

Alberto dialed a number shortly after, speaking in Portuguese. Roozbeh had no idea what he said.

"We're set. Everyone's on their way. You ready?"

"I should call my wife and let her know what I'm up to."

"Call her from the bar. Let's get going. Did you bring a car?"

"No, I took a taxi."

"Perfect, I'll drive."

Alberto paid for the meal as they left the restaurant. "After you, my friend. The van is at the end of the parking lot."

Roozbeh placed his cell phone in a small backpack he wore over his shoulder. As they made their way outside, Alberto pointed to the blue minivan.

"There it is. That's my van," Alberto said casually. As they got closer, a man emerged out of nowhere beside the van. His head was shaved, and he wore several earrings on both ears. His short-sleeved shirt revealed muscular arms covered with tattoos. His face was scruffy and mean. Roozbeh froze in place, staring back at Alberto.

"What's the matter? Go on. That guy is not with me. I don't know what he is doing he—"

Before Alberto could finish, Roozbeh was in full stride. Alberto tried to hold on to him by grabbing his backpack. Roozbeh wiggled free to make his escape.

"I told you not to get out of the van before we reached the door. Come on, go after him," Alberto yelled in Arabic, a language Roozbeh had learned in school.

"What if he calls the police?"

"I grabbed his backpack. His cell phone and wallet are in there. He won't get far," Alberto replied, only a few steps behind him.

Roozbeh heard them closing in as he ran down the boardwalk toward a small pier.

"There's no use, you've got nowhere to run," Alberto shouted from behind.

At the end of the pier, Roozbeh jumped into a small motorboat miraculously docked with the keys in the ignition. He started the engine in a futile attempt to maneuver away from the dock. He fumbled the rope with trembling hands as two shadows fell over him. The rope came undone as the boat took off. Alberto fell in the water as Mr. Tattoo stared from the dock. Roozbeh headed for the other side of the lake, wondering if he'd live to see another day.

7. PENINSULA LAGO SUL, BRASÍLIA, BRAZIL

September 28

J anusz rang the doorbell again. He was getting frustrated. Footsteps finally approached on the fifth ring. An attractive woman in her thirties opened the door. She had shoulder-length black hair. Her brown eyes were tired. Her nose was the only feature on her face not characteristically Middle Eastern. It had become custom for women in Iran to undergo rhinoplasty to resemble Europeans. Her somber appearance was his first indication that something was wrong.

"Hello, madam, my name is John. I'm with Interpol, the international police." He shoved a badge in front of her face.

"Hi, I'm Marjan."

"Do you speak English?"

She opened the door farther, motioning for him to come inside. "Fluently! I was educated at a private school in Tehran," she replied, beaming with pride.

Janusz took inventory of his surroundings. The spacious house, the opulent furniture, and the upscale neighborhood. "Lovely house. Yours?"

"Oh dear, not at all, it belongs to my husband's uncle."

"I see. Is your husband Dr. Roozbeh Navabi?"

"Yes," she replied with a tremor in her voice.

"Well, I'm here to discuss an important matter with him."

Her expression turned to shock. "That's not possible."

"And why is that?"

There was an awkward silence as she stared into his eyes. He fidgeted with his pocket keys before breaking eye contact. Her chin quivered as her eyes filled with tears.

"My husband has disappeared."

Her answer caught him by surprise. "What do you mean disappeared? He gave a press conference on Wednesday!" *It took too long to find this address.*

"You mean you don't know? I've already informed the local police that I can't get a hold of him. His uncle is out looking for him. I should be out there too, but I have to stay here with my children now."

Janusz had barely arrived in Brazil and was already behind the curve. "I'm sorry, this is news to me. I was going to follow up with your husband about Wednesday's press conference."

She closed her eyes and briefly lowered her gaze, trying to calm herself. "Do you think this is related to what he said? I told him not to say those things on TV. Do you think the Iranian government has got him?"

Janusz placed a hand on her shoulder. "Please try to remain calm. We don't know anything yet. He might be lost. How long has he been out of contact?"

"Oh dear, let me think. Since after the press conference on Wednesday."

"I'm sure he has a lot on his mind. Perhaps he needed time to think." Janusz did not believe a single word coming out of his own mouth. "Has he talked to anyone from the Iranian embassy or to friends from back home since you arrived?"

She shook her head furiously.

"I want to help you. Can you think of anywhere he could be, perhaps a park to clear his mind?"

"I don't know. This is all crazy. We shouldn't have come here now."

She was becoming hysterical. It was no use pushing her harder at this point. He wanted to comfort her, but time was short. Without Roozbeh Navabi, he had nothing. He reached into this pocket to pull out a pen and piece of paper.

"This is my local cell number. If you hear anything, don't hesitate to call me, day or night," Janusz said, feeling uneasy while pressing the paper into her hand. "In the meantime, I'll search for your husband myself."

8. VIA S3, BRASÍLIA, BRAZIL

September 28

R oozbeh ran down the street as fast as he could. He had maintained this pace for the past hour. His legs felt as though they weighed a ton while his breathing grew increasingly more difficult. He scanned the horizon without luck. Not one police station in sight. How ironic. For the first time in his life, he wanted nothing more than a man in police uniform. In Iran, the police were dreaded like the plague. Now what he wouldn't give to run into one. The damn cell phone was in the backpack Alberto had swiped off his back. Roozbeh was petrified to approach a stranger in this town. If the Iranian government has agents inside the local media, who else could be working for them? He was afraid of going home. If someone was on his tail, they would find out where he lived. Perhaps it had been a mistake to leave Iran. He had a great job with benefits at the RCERID. He had been next in line to succeed Dr. Ahvazi. Perhaps his country had every right to build biological weapons for itself. After all, didn't the Russians and the Americans have their own stockpile at some point? Why shouldn't Iran have them too? Of course, who could forget the Halabja chemical attack?

Years ago, Iraqi President Saddam Hussein had punished Kurdish militias working with the Iranian regime. In those days, the Kurds were fighting for autonomy from the central government in Baghdad. In the spring of 1988, Saddam Hussein ordered the use of mustard gas, in addition to some other chemicals, against the civilian population of this town near the

Iranian border. As a result, five thousand people were killed with an additional ten thousand scarred for life. It was a brazen act of genocide in front of an international audience. Dr. Ahvazi's current project was magnitudes more dangerous than Halabja in comparison. The release of a deadly pathogen, for which there was no vaccine or cure, unto an unsuspecting population could spread rapidly around the world. Millions might die before the outbreak was contained. There was no way he could facilitate such a program and still be able to live with himself. Roozbeh sought a place to rest and think things through. The rumbling of an engine caught his attention. The approaching noise grew louder. People screamed all around. A blue van careened down the sidewalk at full speed. Pedestrians scattered to and fro to escape the onslaught.

Roozbeh dove instinctively out of the way as the van flew by, fractions of a centimeter to his side. It continued down the sidewalk before the brake lights came on. Studying the van carefully, Roozbeh recognized it as the same vehicle Alberto had had waiting in the parking lot of Coco Delicia. He rose to his feet as quickly as possible and looked frantically around to make his escape. A leafy divider adorned with trees separated the street. On the other side were several buildings where he could hide.

Roozbeh made his move, rushing head-on into traffic. Several cars came to a screeching halt with blasting horns. The sounds of obscenities in a foreign tongue were strangely familiar. Roozbeh held out his hand on his way to the median. The blue van turned and came straight at him. Its tires spun as it closed the distance. Roozbeh lost his balance for a brief second. His heart pounded as time stood still. Of all the places to die, why this Brazilian street whose name he did not know? He ordered his legs to move faster. He ducked just in time to miss a thick protruding branch. Two seconds later, he changed course to miss another obstruction. Suddenly, he was back in traffic, making his way to the other side of the large boulevard. Most drivers had stopped to stare at the unfolding scene. A loud crash thundered from behind.

Roozbeh turned. The blue van was stuck in the median, smashed against a tree. The same tree whose protruding branch he had narrowly avoided moments ago. He breathed a sigh of relief. Seconds later, the occupants of the van opened their doors to chase after him. The driver was Alberto De Souza. There was a hilly embankment paved over with tiles. It led to another street up above. Roozbeh ran toward it, crossing a narrow side street to get there. The distinct voice of Alberto came from behind as he ran. Roozbeh pushed with all his might. His head was dizzy as he reached the top.

Regaining his balance, he stepped over a short railing as a man on a red Vespa scooter drove by. Roozbeh was not about to miss this chance. One hard shove threw the Vespa and its occupant toward the ground. Roozbeh pushed him out of the way and jumped on the scooter. A quick glance over his shoulder revealed that his assailants had stopped to shout into a cell phone. Roozbeh gained a few seconds to decide his next move.

He walked down the alley in mortal fear of the unknown. What if someone was waiting for him? What if someone had observed him turning the corner? What if they had been watching him the entire afternoon? Roozbeh had dumped the Vespa and was on foot once again. Was that Alberto and Mr. Tattoo by the gas station next to the bus stop? Or perhaps it was them staring at him at an intersection down the road? Earlier in the day, he could not wait for the sun to set. Now he felt even more vulnerable in the darkness of this alien city. Roozbeh walked cautiously down the alley. Not only was he cognizant of the sounds of his own footsteps, but he was also convinced another set of footsteps were approaching from behind. He quickened his pace. As he stepped over a glass Pepsi bottle a *click, click, clang* noise hit his ear. A metallic garbage cap fell over. There it was, a large brown rat, the size of a gofer, making a beeline for his feet. As

Roozbeh prepared to kick the galloping rat, it changed course in midstride, grazing his leg on its way down the alley. He breathed a sigh of relief at the false alarm.

He could no longer trust his own mind. No one was following him, as no one knew he was in this alleyway. He caught a glimpse of the flashing lights. The red beam grew more intense until he was nearly blind. A loud voice barked orders in Portuguese. The only word he understood was *policia*. Roozbeh raised both hands to indicate his surrender. What a relief, he was finally in police custody. He stood frozen in place until the dark figure emerged from behind the veil of flashing lights. Roozbeh was only able to pick out a silhouette as he strained his eyes.

"*Qual é o seu nome?*" *What is your name?*

"English, I speak English," Roozbeh said.

"Okay, your name?"

"Roozbeh, I'm Roozbeh Navabi."

"Passport?"

"No, it was stolen."

"*Quis?*"

"I don't have it."

"Okay, come with me."

The policeman guided him toward the cruiser. Roozbeh was ready to enter the backseat. Before he was put inside, another officer emerged. The second man frisked him while the first spoke into a radio. Roozbeh was startled by a *clickety-clang* noise. A pair of metallic cuffs shackled him from behind.

"Senhor, is this necessary?"

His head was shoved into the backseat. The two officers sat up front before driving off. Would they take him to his embassy? That was tantamount to a death sentence. No use worrying about that now. Roozbeh rested his head against the back window. A wave of calmness washed over him. He was no longer being hunted. He could finally quench his parched throat once they made it to the station. After that, he would call his wife to let her know he was alive. As the vehicle took a sharp turn, he was thrown out of his seat. The cruiser sped up as Roozbeh tried to figure out where they were. Several more turns down bumpy streets. The streets kept getting narrower while the headlights grew sparse.

Outside the window, Roozbeh could see they were back in an alley. A chill ran down his spine. The front doors opened simultaneously as the officers stepped out. They closed their doors and walked into the darkness until they disappeared. After several minutes, Roozbeh tried to escape. He turned his back toward the door while slowly maneuvering his cuffed hands in search of the handle. After clumsily fumbling about, he found what he was looking for. He pulled on the latch. It was no use, the door was locked. Roozbeh turned on his back to kick out the windows. His tired legs were not up to the challenge. As he fidgeted nervously in the back, he was alarmed by the approaching voices. Three silhouettes emerged from the darkness. One of them walked over to open the back door. As soon as he stepped out, Roozbeh recognized the third man. It was Alberto De Souza.

"*Obrigado,*" Alberto said to the officers before turning to Roozbeh. "Senhor Navabi, we've found each other once again."

A few moments later, the police drove off, leaving Roozbeh alone in the alley with Alberto.

9. RESEARCH CENTER FOR EMERGING AND REEMERGING INFECTIOUS DISEASE, AKANLU, IRAN

September 29

Dr. Ahvazi sat comfortably in his chair as his benefactor explained what was needed. General Vahid Kalantari had just flown by helicopter from his office in the Firuzyeh section of Tehran. The QF chief was in Akanlu to inspect the RCERID and meet its employees. General Kalantari was not easily swayed by flattery, seldom engaging in chitchat. A man of average height and weight, the QF general had piercing brown eyes that cut through the toughest man. Originally from the southern city of Kerman, the general had a dark tan in contrast to his silver hair.

General Kalantari was considered a superb organizer and leader of men. He had risen quickly through the ranks of the IRGC during the bloody Iran-Iraq War. His assignments were always with special forces. Secretive by nature as he was, most Iranians had not read about his association with the QF until the Western press had exposed his role. He was the primary organizer of Shia militias fighting the American occupation in Iraq. The general was responsible for the deaths of hundreds of American combatants. His trademark was the armor-piercing improvised explosives, known as IEDs, that had maimed so many infidels.

"Praise be to Allah, we're going to punish the Americans. What you don't know is they sabotaged our missile program," the general declared to Dr. Ahvazi.

"Wait, I thought the explosion at Malard was an accident."

"That's what we wanted everyone to think."

"*Khhhh*, you mean the Americans are responsible for the death of Dr. Esfehani?"

"Indirectly, yes."

Dr. Ahvazi stared at him in confusion.

"No need to concern yourself with the details. What's important is that the Americans always stick their snouts where it doesn't belong. May Imam Hossein give us the strength to teach them a lesson. How soon can you weaponize the virus?"

"The notes you provided are a good start. We just need time to procure a treatment."

General Kalantari raised his voice, catching Dr. Ahvazi off guard. "Nobody asked you to find a cure for this scourge. When can you deliver a weaponized form of the virus?"

Despite his better judgment, Dr. Ahvazi felt compelled to object. "Forgive me, Haj Kalantari, but we can't release such a virus without some way to mitigate its effects. If for no other reason than the possibility the disease may wipe out our own people."

"Your concern is understandable. We're considering an attack against a small isolated town to limit the damage. However, you may pursue a treatment as long as the development of the weapon remains your top priority."

"You have my word, Haj Kalantari. I'll handle the details with your staff. Have you decided on a method of attack?"

"May Allah bless me with patience, that's what I need *you* to figure out."

Dr. Ahvazi paused before opening his mouth once again. "Based on the notes you gave us, we need to spray a liquid from an aerosol can. The main question is the quantity of virus per drop of liquid."

"The notes didn't spell this out?"

"Not exactly, *ghoolp*, some details were left out. No need to worry, my team can figure out the rest."

"How long do you need?"

"At least four weeks." Sensing the general's annoyance, Dr. Ahvazi elaborated. "We must test the effectiveness of our agent. By that, I mean we must know exactly what type of liquid best preserves the virus. We also need to figure out how long the intended target must inhale the viral mist. The closest thing to a human we can experiment on is a chimpanzee. If the chimps in our experiment become infectious, we know we've succeeded. I'm currently awaiting the arrival of a group of chimps from Africa. *Achuu.*"

"What's the matter, are you sick?"

"No, why do you ask?"

"Very well. I expect a progress report from you on a regular basis. Notify me of any, and I mean any, delays."

"Yes, of course."

General Kalantari walked out of the room without saying good-bye. Dr. Ahvazi was already busy concocting a story for his team. Without their cooperation, the program was doomed.

10. SHAHRAM SABETI'S APARTMENT, ASA SUL, BRASÍLIA, BRAZIL

September 29

He turned off the lights to wait in the darkness. His entry into the secure seven-story apartment building was courtesy of a friendly tenant. Janusz was tense after thirty minutes. He had not found a single clue during his search. The resident of this apartment, Shahram Sabeti, was the Iranian cultural attaché in Brazil. It seemed Shahram did not spend much time here. His fridge was empty, along with his shelves.

The sound of keys turning a lock brought him to attention. Strangely, he was hoping for a physical altercation due to a lack of exercise. The lights came on in the kitchen. Keys were dropped on a counter followed by the sound of approaching footsteps.

"Lovely, there you are. You know how long I've been waiting?" Janusz said in Persian.

Shahram jumped up, moving back toward the wall. "I'm sorry, I wasn't expecting anyone. Did you just arrive from Tehran?"

"Not exactly. To be honest, I flew in from Washington, and I'm very tired. The faster you answer my questions, the faster we can both get some rest."

Shahram stared at Janusz, confusion plastered over his face. His next move caught Janusz by surprise. Shahram grabbed a book from a nearby shelf and hurled it at him. The projectile landed straight on his nose.

"Motherfucker," Janusz cried out in English this time. The Iranian picked up a lamp from an end table next to the love seat. Running toward Janusz, he swung his weapon with reckless abandon. Janusz ducked, immediately punching the cultural attaché in the right kidney. The Iranian roared as he promptly dropped the lamp. Janusz grabbed him by the waist, picked him up, and slammed him against the nearest wall.

The Iranian immediately brought his face up against Janusz, opening his mouth to bite his ear. Pain shot through Janusz's skull like a bolt of electricity. He jumped away from the wall, still holding Shahram by the waist. He hurled the Iranian toward the floor, body-slamming him while he remained on top. Shahram's body went limp instantaneously as he cried out in pain. Janusz maneuvered to finish the job by placing him in a choke hold. Within seconds, the Iranian passed out. Janusz brushed himself off. He then threw the Iranian over his shoulder and made his way up the back stairs toward the roof.

As soon as his eyes opened, Shahram Sabeti flailed his arms. His entire world must have seemed inverted as he stared up into the courtyard below. Shahram shot his eyes up toward his ankles. He was held upside down over the ledge of a building by a pair of powerful arms.

"We need to cut to the chase very quickly, dear friend. My arms are getting tired."

"Who are you? What do you want?" Shahram replied, slurring his speech.

"I already told you, I'm an American. I have a few questions about the activities of the Iranian regime here in Brazil."

"Fuck your mother," came the terse reply. Shahram swung back and forth in a vain attempt to grab on to the ledge.

"Perhaps you don't appreciate the full *gravity* of your situation, dear Shahram," Janusz said before letting go of the left ankle.

"I'm sorry, I'm sorry! I'll tell you everything you want to know," Shahram said. His breathing grew heavier as he closed his eyes while clenching his fists.

Janusz grabbed the left ankle once again. "That's better. What's the role of the cultural attaché's office in Brazil? I'm particularly interested in your efforts to recruit spies for Iran."

Shahram kept his eyes closed as his face grew red from the rush of blood to his head. "Everyone works through the Islamic Culture and Relations Organization, the ICRO. Cultural and religious activities are used to build sympathy for our views. Once that happens, we recruit individuals to work for us as cultural ambassadors and intelligence sources."

"What else? Think hard."

"Our recruited agents help us circumvent international sanctions. The agents set up front companies or banks, allowing us to purchase spare parts, technology, and anything else we need without the use of Iranian names. If an American company is selling airplanes, computers, or GPSs to a Brazilian entity, they have no way of knowing the entity is under our control."

"Good, I knew this already, just wanted to hear it from you."

"Thank you," Shahram said with a sigh of relief. "Please bring me down."

"Not just yet. Tell me about Roozbeh Navabi. He gave a press conference three days ago about a new Iranian bioweapon program. What did you do with him?"

Shahram stared at the courtyard below once again. Several beads of sweat fell from his forehead into the abyss as he clenched his jaw while speaking. "I didn't do anything. It's the ministry guys. They're responsible."

"What ministry guys? Don't lie to me. Foreign operations are assigned to the QF."

"The Ministry of Intelligence divides its tasks with the QF in many of the embassies. The ministry usually handles the counterintelligence operations. They're handling all the business with the Navabi case."

The Ministry of Intelligence, known as the MOIS, had been the Iranian government's premier foreign intelligence organization. In the late 1990s, many of their responsibilities were handed over to the rival QF. The MOIS was not happy with the new arrangement. They had no say in the matter, however. Iranian Supreme Leader Mashhadi weakened them by transferring their responsibilities to a more trusted organization, the QF.

"I need names. Who in the MOIS is in charge of all this?"

"I don't know, really. I don't know any names," Shahram cried hysterically.

"Nonsense."

"Please, I beg you."

"My arm is getting tired, Shahram." Shahram tried several times to pull his body up toward Janusz. The American began to swing him violently back and forth in response.

"Okay, okay. His name is Morteza Karami. He's in charge of everything related to this Roozbeh Navabi bastard. Are you happy now? Let me down."

Janusz was suddenly struck by a distant memory. As Shahram hung perilously over the edge, Janusz remembered reading about the Iranian cultural attaché in Brazil years ago. His name had been mentioned in a news article. It was in relation to a disturbing incident.

"I know you. You're the guy from that party," Janusz said while clenching his jaw.

"What party, what are you talking about?" Shahram said, desperately flailing his arms for something to grab on to.

"The Mandarin Hotel in Brasília four years ago. It was a summer pool party in honor of foreign diplomats. The guests brought their children to play in the pool. A group of twelve-year-old girls swam in the deep end. That's when you went underwater and fondled them."

"You have me confused with someone else," Shahram shot back.

"Spare me, the papers mentioned your name after the arrest. They let you go when your president intervened with an offer to invest in a Brazilian mining company."

"That was a misunderstanding."

"Yes, I remember that. That's exactly what your embassy called it, 'a cultural misunderstanding.' I believe now is a good time for a cultural reckoning."

There was nothing Janusz hated more than the abuse of children. A terrorist had murdered his own brother at a young age. Justice could no longer be delayed in this matter.

"Your embassy can't help you this time."

"What do you mean?" Shahram asked as he tried to pull himself up again.

"Do you know what the penalty is for child molestation in Iran?"

"You can't be serious? Please, sir, please!"

"Say hello to *Sheitan*."

The fading scream reverberated through the evening air as Janusz let go of both ankles. Within seconds, the explosion below shook his eardrums. It looked like someone had spilled ketchup. How long before the police would arrive?

11. PENINSULA LAGO SUL, BRASÍLIA, BRAZIL

September 29

Not five minutes had passed after the Iranian fell before his cell phone rang. It was a local number. The faint whimper of her sobs was the first thing he heard.

"It's Marjan. Please hurry, something terrible has happened."

"On my way," Janusz replied without asking questions.

Half an hour later, he rang her doorbell. Marjan greeted him with puffy eyes and watery cheeks. She walked to the kitchen table, where she sat in silence staring at a wall. He sat next to her, giving her space to speak when she was ready. What she said did not surprise him.

"I got a call from the police. Oh dear," she said, holding back tears.

"Go on."

"They found Roozbeh." She brought her shaking hand toward her mouth. She was not able to stop the quivering of her chin as tears poured down her face. "He was in an alley outside Brasília, shot in the back of the head. His wallet and passport were missing. The police say it's a street crime."

Janusz was skeptical. It was more likely an execution.

"Roozbeh's uncle is still out looking for him now. I haven't yet been able to reach him. The kids are sleeping upstairs. They want me to identify the body. I didn't know who else to call."

Janusz gently placed a hand over hers. He let a moment pass

before speaking. Luckily, Kimberly Jennings had accompanied him.

"I'll call my colleague, Kim. She can stay with the kids while we go to identify the body."

Not long after he'd made the call, an attractive blonde rang the doorbell. Marjan stared intently as Kim entered the house.

"Don't worry, she's worked with me for years. She knows how to handle the kids if they wake up."

Kim walked inside without saying a word.

Janusz and Marjan drove to the city morgue for the grim task of identifying a dead body. The place was empty as they checked in at the reception. Moments later, Captain Eduardo of the Brasília Police Department greeted them. The captain explained that no one, besides Marjan, had yet been informed of the tragedy.

"Would you like me to come with you to the viewing room?" Janusz asked.

She gently nodded as she wiped her nose with a crumpled tissue. They walked down a long hallway before turning left. A large man in uniform opened the door to a cold-storage room. A chill ran over Janusz as soon as he walked in. The scent of formaldehyde overpowered his nostrils. The bodies were kept in this room before the final disposition. Captain Eduardo nodded to the uniformed assistant to pull out the body. When the zipper was open, exposing his face, Marjan's cry shook the room like an explosion. She lost her balance and fell straight into Janusz's arms.

"Oh dear, what have they done to him?" Marjan cried on his shoulder for a while before getting back to the grim task of identifying her husband's body.

"Son of a bitch," Janusz mumbled softly to himself as he examined the body.

The disfigured face was similar to the one Janusz had seen

on TV back in Virginia. It appeared as though the man had been beaten savagely about the head. The potential new source was dead, while the lives of countless others hung in the balance. Marjan was his best hope at the moment. It would not be an easy task to debrief her after this.

They made their way back down the hall and out toward the parking lot. Neither one said a word during the somber drive to the house. When they walked in, Kim was sitting silently at the kitchen table. It was past midnight, and the kids were asleep. Realizing Marjan needed time to rest, Janusz made arrangements to return later. After inquiring if she wanted anything, he left the house with Kim.

Janusz visited Marjan several hours after daybreak. He was not sure what to expect from the grieving widow. Was it wise to question her so soon after the fact? He had no choice. After opening the door, she invited him into the living room. She sat on a sofa across from him staring off into the distance. Several minutes passed in silence. She must have sensed the urgency in his eyes.

"I know you wanted to speak with my husband. I'll do my best to help you."

He studied her in quiet contemplation. "My superiors are concerned about your husband's recent press conference. We want to prevent a possible terrorist attack against innocent lives."

"You're not with Interpol, are you?"

The accusatory tone of the question was to be expected. He had a ready reply. "No, I'm not. I represent the interests of the United States."

She gazed at him intently before calmly declaring, "You're CIA."

"Like I said, I represent the interests of the United States," Janusz repeated with a smile.

She rolled her eyes before Janusz picked up where he'd left off. "Marjan, do you know who your husband worked for?"

"Of course I do. He was a research scientist with the Pasteur Institute of Iran. He worked in a laboratory near Hamadan, a town by the name of Akanlu. We lived in Tehran."

"So you lived apart?"

"Oh dear, no, Roozbeh drove home to be with us every Thursday night. He drove back on Sunday morning. I must admit that it was difficult for us not to be with him during the week."

"Are you sure he was not working for the military? Perhaps the Artesh or the IRGC?"

"Absolutely not. Roozbeh took me to his lab in Akanlu several times. Why do you ask?"

"It's usually the military that works on biological weapons in every country," Janusz said.

"I don't think my husband was working on any weapons."

"Then why did he make those allegations at the press conference?"

"Because he wanted out. I'd been pressuring him to leave Iran. Life there is difficult now. We were both opposed to the regime."

"So you're telling me your husband lied to the world? There is no new Iranian biological weapon program?"

"I don't know about the Iranian government as a whole. It's certainly possible. As far as my husband's work was concerned, definitely not."

"How can you be so sure?"

"Let me see, what is that word? Oh yes, he was a pacifist. If they'd asked him to build weapons, he would have said no. Roozbeh told me everything!"

Who was telling the truth here, the husband or the wife? Was it possible he never told her?

"Were you aware of the type of projects Roozbeh worked on?"

"He researched vaccines and treatments for infectious viral diseases. The last one he discussed with me involved research on a vaccine for the Crimean-Congo fever."

"Was he successful?"

"I'm not sure now. We had to leave before he could finish his work."

Janusz asked her about Iran and her family to see if anything else would fly out of her mouth. She added little to her previous comments other than to convey the financial difficulties of her parents. Janusz thought it best to change the subject.

"Where are the kids? They're awfully quiet."

"Roozbeh's uncle came by this morning and took them to Rio. They needed a break from this craziness."

Janusz suddenly stood up. "I need to get going, but I want you to know that your life is in danger. Whoever killed your husband might come after you and the children. I can talk to my people to arrange asylum for you in the US if you're interested."

"Who would want to hurt us? My husband only helped people."

"Are you willing to risk your children's lives on that?"

His last sentence made her brow furrow. On his way out, he took out a business card from his wallet and handed it to her. "These people work with me. Call that number if you change your mind."

There was no telling what Iranian intelligence would do to tie up the loose ends.

12. ROYAL TULIP HOTEL, BRASÍLIA, BRAZIL

October 01

He took another sip of coffee, images from the morgue still racing through his head. Janusz rested against a large sofa in the lobby of the Royal Tulip Hotel. Kim sat next to him as they contemplated their next move. To add to their troubles, the local papers were full of stories about the Iranian cultural attaché who had fallen to his death in the parking lot of his apartment.

"It's only a matter of time before they start narrowing their list of suspects. Do you think Marjan will stay in Brazil?" Kim asked.

"I'm hoping she'll seek asylum in the US. We need her to provide more details about—" His cell phone rang before he could finish.

"Switch your phone to secure mode," Bill, head of operations back in Virginia, demanded. Janusz pressed a button before placing the phone against his ear.

"What do you have for me, Janusz?"

"Two dead bodies, Roozbeh Navabi and the Iranian cultural attaché. At this point, I have more questions than answers."

"Perhaps I can help *you* out. There's been a break that might spark a new life into your mission," Bill said.

"Let's hear it."

"One week before Roozbeh's press conference, there was a

double murder here in Virginia. Dr. Ray Simmons and his wife, Connie."

"Oh yes, I heard about that. They were killed at their house in Leesburg. Police announced it as a robbery."

"That was a cover story. The Pentagon withheld vital information about Dr. Simmons. He worked for the US Army at Fort Detrick, Maryland. Mostly classified projects. He was their lead expert on the Marburg virus. You ever hear of it?"

"Yes, it's similar to Ebola if I'm not mistaken?"

"You're not. Its effects on the human body are just as gruesome, if not worse. Marburg has been known to kill up to ninety percent of infected victims. The army was researching Marburg's viability as an offensive weapon to see how an adversary might utilize it against us."

"Jesus, you can't be serious!" Janusz said as Kim listened intently.

"Wait, it gets better. The army believes the people who killed Dr. Simmons knew about his work on Marburg. His body showed signs of torture," Bill said as Janusz raised an eyebrow.

"Son of a bitch! Roozbeh's wife told me he was a pacifist and would never agree to work on a biological weapon. He must have defected when he got his new assignment."

"We think Roozbeh worked for a man named Javad Ahvazi."

"Javad who?"

"The SSCI just faxed over new phone intercepts from the NSA. Their computers were programmed to pick out conversations coming out of Iran for the words 'Ray Simmons.' Dr. Ahvazi directs an infectious disease research facility in—"

"A town named Akanlu?"

"How did you know?"

"Roozbeh's wife."

"Anyway, Dr. Ahvazi mentioned Ray Simmons during a phone conversation with a subordinate named Iman Vakili. Iman is headed to a World Health Organization conference this week about—"

"A treatment for Marburg?" Janusz jumped in.

"You don't miss much. We'll arrange your tickets for pickup at the airport," Bill said before hanging up.

"Grab your bags, Kim," Janusz said.

"Where are we headed?"

"I'll tell you on the way to the airport."

13. RESEARCH CENTER FOR EMERGING AND REEMERGING INFECTIOUS DISEASE, AKANLU, IRAN

October 01

Mohsen Salehi and Omid Reyshahri faced each other in sheer terror. Which one was going to risk his life on behalf of the program? Since they could not reach a consensus, they settled it like schoolkids. Rock, paper, scissors. After five rounds, the matter was decided. Mohsen would have to bite the bullet.

"You're responsible for my wife and kids if this test goes to shit," Mohsen declared.

"Don't worry, I'll go next time. Let's call the boss."

"Dr. Ahvazi, the animals are ready," Omid declared over the receiver.

"*Khhhh*, very well, I'll be down shortly," Dr. Ahvazi said.

Across the courtyard from Dr. Ahvazi's office sat three numbered buildings. Each held two labs, numbers 1 to 6. A fourth building was not numbered. It was called the hot chamber, where the most dangerous biological experiments took place. The animals that entered this room were subjected to vicious experiments. It was the result of a complete lack of accountability. The Iranian regime did not abide by international standards for the ethical treatment of animals. In case anyone ever dared to question the regime's methods, Tehran quickly accused its detractors of exhibiting anti-Muslim sentiments. At that point, the accusations would magically disappear. It was amazing how useful Western liberals had become for the Iranian government.

Dr. Ahvazi scanned his card to open the door to the hot chamber. Inside, there was a small viewing room with a variety of measuring equipment. The viewing room was separated from the chamber by a thick layer of glass. The building used a specialized ventilation system to generate negative air pressure. Today there were exactly four rows of metal tubes inserted into the ground. Each row contained three tubes placed three meters apart for a total of twelve tubes in the chamber. A ten-centimeter metal chain was attached to the tubes, the end of which held a leather strap collar. At the moment, the leather collars held twelve male chimpanzees against their will. Their hands were tied behind their backs as they cried out in anger. It was obvious that they sensed something terrible was awaiting them.

"Is the IRGC really going to use this stuff against our enemies?" Mohsen asked.

"Nobody said anything about that. We're building a capability for deterrent purposes only," Dr. Ahvazi said.

"This is insanity. Why can't we douse them using the Henderson apparatus like normal scientists do in the West?" Omid asked Dr. Ahvazi in frustration.

"Because the IRGC is a military organization, and this is how they may use it. They've instructed us to test this method of attack for viability."

"Can't we at least sedate them? It's obvious the chimps are extremely agitated. That's a dangerous way to administer this," Mohsen said.

"I agree, but the IRGC is paying for this, and that's the way they want it. Now suit up and get in," Dr. Ahvazi said.

"What about the positive pressure suits, sir?" Omid asked.

"*Ehhem*, we don't have any funding for that in our current budget. We're under a strict deadline to produce a working weapon. We can't wait around for the funding approvals."

"But—" Omid tried to interject.

"Not buts, they've asked us to do this using exactly the same methods they might use in the field."

"I don't get it, who is going to apply a Marburg tainted aerosol with—"

"That's enough, Mohsen. It's time to do your job. Has the solution been transferred to the aerosols?"

"Yes, sir, they're inside the chamber by the door," Omid said.

"Very well, let's get started," Dr. Ahvazi ordered.

Mohsen walked over to a nearby changing room to suit up. He wore a full-body yellow biohazard suit and blue gloves, along with a white headcovering and a breathing apparatus around the mouth. The chimps cried raucously in unison as soon as he walked in. On a small table near the doorway, four cans of aerosol spray were placed next to each other. He picked one up as the chimps jumped up and down. To relax, Mohsen visualized his children. He'd never signed up for this. He was about to walk back out when he remembered his government insurance policy. As long as he performed his assigned tasks, his family was guaranteed a salary for the remainder of their lives, in the event of his demise in the line of duty.

He picked up a can and walked cautiously toward the nearest chimp. A wave of calm came over the primate as he approached. The hairy ape brought its face forward as if it were expecting Mohsen to feed it. It was inhumane to infect these defenseless creatures. But then who was going to support his own children? As the chimp opened its mouth in anticipation of food, Mohsen pointed the can at its face. He sprayed directly into the eyes and nostrils. The chimp instinctively winced before lunging at Mohsen in anger. The metal chain held it back. Mohsen fell several centimeters behind, trying to escape. His heart pounded as his goggles fogged up. He could not afford to take them off. There were now particles of the Marburg virus floating in the air. He breathed heavily while surveying the rows of chimps. One down, eleven to go.

"Very good, Mohsen. You're doing great, *ghoolp*. Carry on," the voice came through the speakers. The show must go on. The instructions were clear and simple. Spray the chimps in the first row by pressing the nozzle for one second. Two seconds for the second row. Three seconds for the third row. The objective was to figure out the minimal time of exposure, equivalent to a pre-determined amount of virus particles that would cause a fatal infection in a chimp. They would then extrapolate for the height and weight equivalent of an average man. They had to find out how long and at what distance to spray a human target for a fatal infection. It was a crude method of delivery, but it was what Dr. Ahvazi wanted.

Mohsen readied himself for the next target. This chimp was not going to cooperate. It understood the human in the suit was not its friend. It yanked on its chain, trying to escape. This was bad news for Mohsen. His target was looking away from him. Mohsen tapped its shoulder. The chimp screamed wildly as it lunged at Mohsen and knocked his goggles to the side. Mohsen pulled back to regroup. The chimp screamed again, showing its teeth, as he approached. Keeping track of the spray time under these conditions would not be easy. He brought the can forward and sprayed the chimp in the eyes and nose for a total of one second. Two down, ten to go.

After an hour, Mohsen's entire body was drenched in sweat. His stomach growled as he felt the acid churning. He was tired and ready to call it quits. There were only two chimps left to infect. He pushed on without requesting assistance. The chance of accidentally infecting another technician was too great. Dr. Ahvazi had given explicit instructions that there should only be one technician in the chamber at any given time.

The second-to-last chimp was thrashing about insanely. Mohsen extended the can in his right hand. The chimp grabbed the spray can with its mouth, refusing to let go. He punched the chimp with his left hand, only serving to provoke the hairy primate even more. The chimp finally let go of the can as Mohsen found himself seething with rage.

"Two can play this game," he said out loud before spraying the chimp in anger. He pressed the nozzle for a full five seconds. The droplets of mist dripped down his gloved fingers onto the floor. The chimp suddenly shrieked. Mohsen should have pulled away earlier, but he was too tired to think straight. The chimp opened its mouth, this time grabbing three of Mohsen's fingers with its teeth. The chimp bit hard as Mohsen cried out.

"Help me! Someone please help me!"

"For the love of Imam Hossein, we need to get in there," Omid pleaded as Dr. Ahvazi just stood there expressionless.

"No, no! No one goes in there now!"

"But he needs our help!"

"There are only fifteen cleared individuals in this program now. If Mohsen goes down we can't afford another infection. He's on his own, *ghoolp*," the RCERID director proclaimed to the incredulous Omid.

Pulling with all his might, Mohsen was finally able to extract his fingers. Blood seeped out from the tip of his glove.

"Sir, I think he's bleeding," Omid said frantically.

"Yes, since his gloves were wet with the agent, chances are Mohsen is infected with Marburg," Dr. Ahvazi said in a calm voice.

"What do we do?"

"He needs to be isolated and sent to Tehran for treatment. *Khhhh*, his fate is in the hands of Allah now," Dr. Ahvazi declared coldly before walking out of the viewing room.

14. VALI-ASR HOSPITAL, TEHRAN, IRAN

October 01

Mohsen arrived at Vali-Asr Hospital by helicopter. He was quarantined on the roof while the staff prepared a second isolation room across the hall from Peyman. The infectious disease ward on the top floor of the hospital was crawling with men in IRGC uniforms, Kalashnikov rifles slung over their shoulders. Nurses ran frantically to and fro, their heads covered with the mandatory hijab for women. No one knew exactly what was going on, not even the doctors. They only knew that an employee of the Pasteur Institute had been infected with a deadly virus. Two men infected by a deadly pathogen within a week. Everyone was frightened. What was the government hiding? Was Iran involved in dangerous experiments?

After hours of waiting on the roof, Mohsen was finally wheeled into his specially prepared room. The nurses were reluctant to attend this victim. They had not been told the name of the pathogen. They were given a short briefing by the attending doctor that their latest patient had a highly infectious disease spread through bodily fluids. They were each issued thick rubber gloves, a rubberized white suit, and a face mask. The suit was to be taken off each time they left the rooms and sent to the hospital's decontamination room. Their imaginations filled in the rest.

◆ ◆ ◆

When Mrs. Salehi finally arrived at the hospital, she was sent to a special waiting room where another woman was sitting with her children. The woman facing her appeared tired. Teardrops hung between her eyelids. Mrs. Salehi spoke up to break the tension.

"I wonder how long they'll keep us waiting."

The crying woman wiped her nose and chuckled. "Don't hold your breath. You'll be here for a while."

Mrs. Salehi did her best to ignore her comment. "My husband just arrived from a government lab. Our situation is different."

"If you're in this room, it can only mean one thing. Your husband is infected with a deadly pathogen for which there is no cure."

Mrs. Salehi stared at her intently. "And how do you know this?"

"Because this room was set aside for our family after my husband arrived from Akanlu. We were told that in the event there are other victims from the RCERID, they would be sent to this room. The kids and I have been coming here since last week without updates. We've only been able to see Peyman once."

Mrs. Salehi impulsively stormed out the door. To alleviate her anger, she ran up the stairs to visit her husband. Panting when she reached the top floor, she took a handkerchief out of her purse to wipe her face. She walked through several corridors before coming to a halt. She made a beeline toward the armed guard at the end of the hall. The IRGC man put his arm out as she approached.

"Lady, this is a private military wing. You don't belong here. Please go back in the other direction."

"Go back in the other direction? You go back in the other direction! God only help you if you make me angry."

"Lady—"

"What have you done with my husband?" she screamed at the top of her lungs. Her voice reverberated through the entire floor. The IRGC guard froze in place, unsure how to react. In response to the commotion, a doctor ran down the hallway.

"Dear lady, this is a hospital, and there are sick patients in these rooms. You can't scream like that."

"This man won't let me see my husband," she shot back.

"She tried to walk into the infectious disease rooms. When I told her to leave, she screamed at me," the IRGC guard explained.

"It's okay, it's okay," the doctor said as he waved the guard away. The uniformed IRGC sentry walked several meters in the opposite direction. The doctor put his arms around Mrs. Salehi and walked her toward the nearest wall. He seemed to know whom she wanted to visit.

"Your husband was flown here earlier today from the RCERID. There was a tragic accident at the lab. It's possible he may be infected with a contagious virus."

"What kind of virus?"

"We don't know yet. RCERID has not informed us. What we do know is that your husband was researching treatments to help people in Africa. Iran is doing great things to alleviate suffering around the world. I'll come to see you as soon as I learn more. Please go back downstairs and wait—"

"Like the other lady who's crying because she's been waiting since God only knows when? She told me she has not been able to see her husband in quite a while."

"Now, now, everyone's situation is different. An attractive woman such as yourself should not concern herself with the affairs of others."

"But—" Mrs. Salehi tried to object.

"Peyman's wife has already seen her husband several times. She is difficult and definitely not distinguished like you. Please go back to the waiting room." The doctor walked her to the elevators and pressed the down button.

"What's your name, Doctor?" Mrs. Salehi asked as the doors opened.

"I'm Dr. Nader. Feel free to come see me whenever you need an update on your husband."

Once inside, Mrs. Salehi stared at Dr. Nader, who stood there with a smile. She could tell he was hiding something, and she was determined to figure out what it was.

15. ARTHUR'S RESTAURANT, GENEVA, SWITZERLAND

October 03

What would it take to grab her attention? The attractive brunette with the blue eyes could have stepped out of a magazine. He knew it was rude to stare, but he could not help himself. If only the women in his own country were allowed to dress this way publicly. Then he could avoid shameless ogling when given the opportunity to travel abroad. She wore a navy-blue blouse and a short white skirt. Her shoes resembled the footwear of a ballerina. Around her wrist, he recognized an IWC watch with a black leather strap. He had gifted a similar piece to his wife years ago. The brunette's long, flowing hair was tied in the back, accentuating her delicate face. He had been waiting twenty minutes for a table in the back of Arthur's Restaurant, along the bank of the Rhone River. The hostess finally approached him with a forced smile.

"Monsieur, your table is ready," she said uncomfortably. A table for four had opened up right next to the water. She seated him there away from everyone, probably just to get rid of him. He took stock of his surroundings. An emerald-green river below, a clear blue sky above, and an abundance of attractive women all around. Technically, it was not Iman's first trip to Europe. He had traveled to Greece for his honeymoon. But he considered that country to be Middle Eastern. Geneva, on the other hand, was in the heart of Europe. As luck would have it, the traitor, Roozbeh, had defected to Brazil. Otherwise, it would have been Roozbeh sitting here in Switzerland instead. He took a quick glance at the menu. Every item was written in both French and English. He had not bothered to take French in high school. Another thought suddenly entered his mind. He turned impulsively from side to side; the coast was clear. Iman knew exactly what he wanted. The waiter finally arrived to take his order.

"What would you like, sir?"

"I'll have the pork chops with potatoes," he said, still turning from side to side. Pork was *haram*, forbidden, in his native country with its Islamic laws.

"Anything to drink?"

"Whiskey on the rocks." *Another forbidden item.* "Oh, and a glass of water." He planned to savor every sip and every bite of the forbidden fruits of the West. It was a well-deserved respite after the morning session. The conference participants included some of the world's top Marburg researchers. The American pharmaceutical company Merck had made great advances, while the British GSK was transferring its research to a nonprofit in Washington, DC. It was, however, a smaller company that had just declared success in clinical trials with guinea pigs. The company's top Marburg researcher was an Iraqi man who worked in the US and was attending the conference. Iman was planning an excuse to meet with him for possible avenues of collaboration. If that did not work, Yahya, a QF officer, had expressed readiness to help with the extraction of information from the assembled group of scientists.

Geneva was so different from the godforsaken village of Akanlu. He was deep in thought when his food arrived. After the meal, he watched the ferries sail by on the river as he sipped slowly on his whiskey. A chocolate tiramisu was the perfect way to finish things off. There was something else he wanted. He had promised his wife, but she was not around, and the timing was perfect. He pulled out a pack of Marlboros, leaning back while lighting one in his mouth. It was so good to be free. Like those days long ago at the University of Tehran, when he drank and smoked without anyone nagging him.

Just then something caught the corner of his left eye. He straightened his back as the smoldering cigarette almost fell to his lap. She wore high-heeled shoes, no stockings. A tight skirt came down way above the knees. Her striped blouse had sleeves rolled up to the elbow. An elegant belt brought the entire ensemble together in the middle. Her hair was yellow and straight, going below the shoulders. There were several empty tables nearby, as the restaurant had quieted down. He could not believe his luck. There was only one empty table separating him and the blonde. He wanted to say something but was at a loss for words. His English was not that fluent, and Allah only knew what language she spoke.

She stared at her menu for a strangely long time. Her hands seemed soft and delicate as he watched her turn each page. Her fingernails were colored pink. The little blond hairs on the back of her milky white hands glistened in the sunlight. Iman's pants grew tighter at the crotch. He made a quick adjustment, moving his eyes back where they wanted to be so badly. A sudden breeze carried a whiff of perfume to his nostrils. Somewhere deep inside, instincts refined by millennia of evolution stirred wildly. He could not take it any longer. Iman lit another Marlboro to drown out the scent of the perfume. *What can I say? She'll probably laugh at me with my stupid accent.*

"Excuse me, sir? Hello? Can you hear me?" came the soft-spoken voice. There was no mistaking it. She was speaking directly toward him.

"Hi, do you mind if I borrow one of those?" She made a gesture with two fingers. He quickly reached for his pocket.

"Yes, of course, no problem." He raised the Marlboros in front of her as she leaned over to take one. She placed it in her mouth and stared at him in anticipation. He immediately picked up the lighter and leaped at the opportunity. She took a few drags before the smoke wafted out of her nostrils.

"Thank you," she said.

He was not about to let the moment pass. "Are you English?"

"No, American. What about you?"

This was the part he hated about traveling. His country did not have the best reputation around the world. He had to think about his answer. "I'm Persian."

She smiled. "Oh, like the cat?"

"Yes, yes, like the cat." He hoped she would not connect the dots with Iran.

"Are you here on business?"

This was also a tricky subject, given his mission. He had to tread lightly. "Yes. I'm a scientist. I'm here for a conference."

"About what?"

The sweat trickled down his armpit toward his elbow. He took another sip from the glass of whiskey.

"About what?" he repeated. "About viruses. I study viruses."

"Oh," she replied with little interest.

He did not know whether to be happy or disappointed with her lack of enthusiasm. Suddenly, the bulb went off in his head. *What harm could it do?* "I conduct research on AIDS. I'm very close to a cure."

"Really?" Her eyes grew wide, along with her mouth. "That's so exciting. When will you announce your discovery to the world?"

"Very soon, very soon," was all he could think of in response. "Would you like to join me so you don't have to sit alone? We can order some drinks and smoke." He held up his packet of cigarettes.

"Sure." She picked up her leather purse and walked over to his table. She sat in front of him and extended her right hand. "I'm Elizabeth, nice to meet you." Her bright red lips parted to reveal a mouthful of perfectly aligned white teeth.

He shook her hand. "Very nice to meet you, Elizabeth. Please order anything you like. I'll pay."

The drinks arrived one after the other. Whiskey on the rocks for Iman, along with martinis for his new companion. Before long, the glass ashtray was full of cigarette butts, half of them decorated with red lipstick. The more he drank, the more confident he grew. This was going to be his lucky day. He would place his manhood inside this blond infidel, and there was nothing anyone could do about it. The stories he'd heard must be true. Western women were whores. An Iranian woman would never act this way with a man she'd just met.

"You're so funny, Iman. Perhaps I should visit you in your country?"

"Oh no. That's not a good idea."

"Why not?"

"My country is not good for women. They would force you to cover. You're too beautiful to be covered." He did not know where that came from. It was mainly the whiskey talking now. After another round of drinks, the check finally arrived. Eleven hundred Swiss francs. He had no idea how he was going to explain this expenditure to his wife. But that was a problem for another day. By the time he covered the check, the sky had grown dark.

"Wow, how time flies. I should be going back to my hotel unless you want to accompany me to another restaurant?" Iman said.

"Actually, where is your hotel?" Elizabeth replied.

"My hotel? I'm at the InterContinental on Chemin du Petit-Saconnex. Why?"

"Oh, that's a great place. I'll grab us a taxi."

Iman followed her out toward the street. Could this be his lucky night?

16. RUSSIAN NAVAL FACILITY, TARTUS, SYRIA

October 03

General Anatoly Zelnikov sat back in his chair, listening to the Iranian through a translator. Although he was not particularly fond of Muslims, or Iranians, they served their purpose for the Kremlin. Russia had forced defeat on Iran with the Treaties of Gulistan, 1813, and Turkmenchai, 1828, taking the territory from the Northern Caucus Mountains to the Aras River. Unlike some of his countrymen, Zelnikov was not threatened by Moscow's budding alliance with Tehran. The Iranians were pawns to poke the Americans in the eyes. They were also useful for maintaining Russia's influence in Syria as well as the Middle East writ large. For all these reasons, Zelnikov was willing to sit down with General Kalantari of the QF at these planning sessions. Today's discussions in Tartus were about a joint offensive. The objective was to help Assad's forces consolidate their control over the last parcel of rebel territory in Syria. The Russian Air Force orchestrated the aerial bombing, while the Iranian QF led the ground troops.

After years of intense fighting, President Assad finally had the upper hand thanks to the cooperation between Zelnikov and General Kalantari. The QF chief told the meeting participants that morale was high among his men and an assault could move forward as soon as the Russian side softened the rebels from the air.

Zelnikov leaned forward to speak. "The Salafists in Idlib are particularly troublesome. They murdered eight Spetznaz advisers when they overran our outpost near the city last year. I want to punish them more than you can imagine."

"What are you proposing, General Zelnikov?"

He pointed to a map on the wall. "A chemical attack on these targets. Specifically, an attack using sarin gas. In addition to killing everyone on the battlefield, it'll lower morale among the jihadists."

"But there is a large civilian population nearby, not to mention my troops on the ground." General Kalantari did not seem to be as keen on killing his fellow Muslims.

"We'll provide your troops with the proper equipment to protect themselves."

General Kalantari stared at the map in silent reflection for a few more seconds. "Perhaps there is an alternative. Instead of a chemical attack, just carpet-bomb the region with your bombers. You can use our airbase at Hamadan. This way your planes don't have to travel too far, saving you the extra cost of fuel and maintenance."

After thinking it through, Zelnikov agreed to the arrangement. "That sounds reasonable. I'll have my people contact yours to hammer out the details."

As everyone in the room gathered their belongings, General Kalantari moved closer to grab Zelnikov's wrist. "There's another matter. Can I see you in private?" The QF chief motioned for the translator.

"What is it?" Zelnikov said.

"Some of our scientists are working on a new virus to deter our enemies, *Inshallah*." *God willing*. "We're hoping to get your assistance with a treatment."

Zelnikov cleared his throat while straightening his tie. "After our last conversation, I brought this up at a national security meeting with Defense Minister Shoigu and Secretary Patrushev. I'm sorry to report the Kremlin is not interested in cooperating with your government on this project."

"Are they aware of the level of assistance Iran is providing to the Russian Federation here in Syria?"

"Yes, they're very much aware and appreciative of your assistance. However, biological weapons are forbidden by international treaty. Moreover, Moscow wants to stay away from anything having to do with viruses. I'm afraid I can't help you!"

"Very well, I ..."

"Yes, what is it?"

"I ... On second thought, I've got a better idea about Idlib. Instead of carpet-bombing the town, you can provide close air support while my men take the town on the ground."

"You said you didn't want to risk more troops, that you've lost enough men already. Make up your mind. Do you want us to pummel this town for you or not?"

"Close air support will suffice. My troops will take the town house to house with Syrian militias and the Afghan Zeinabyoun fighters."

"Why the sudden change of heart?" Zelnikov asked.

"I'm worried about the infrastructure problem afterward. If you carpet-bomb the place, it'll take much longer to get the town up and running when the war is finally over."

"Suit yourself, it'll be your boys dying on the ground. I'll have my air commander talk to yours regarding the use of Nojeh Air Base in Hamadan."

"*Spasiba*, General Zelnikov." *Thank you.*

The sudden about-face to take Idlib house to house could only mean the Iranians had plans for something they wanted to hide.

17. GENEVA, SWITZERLAND

October 03

Jennifer stepped off the elevator into the white-marbled lobby. She was wearing a tight black leather dress several inches below the waist with black stilettos. To say the dress was revealing was to put it mildly. She carried a small leather purse in her left hand, which was missing a wedding ring. She ordered a martini and made her way to the piano lounge above the main entrance of the Mayflower Hotel in Washington, DC. Her long tan legs were freshly shaved. She checked her watch. It was twenty minutes past nine. She was early. She sat back, enjoying the sounds of Chopin's nocturne on the piano while sipping on her drink. At exactly 9:35 p.m., a tall man walked over toward her. He wore a tailor-made gray suit, a white dress shirt, and a black tie. His body was chiseled, his eyes green, his hair finely combed, and his complexion olive. Not only was the man handsome; he exuded confidence from every pore. He smiled warmly as he extended his hand to greet her. There was only one problem. This man was not her husband.

"Ah, there you are. I thought you'd forgotten about me fer sure," Jennifer exclaimed.

"I got caught in traffic. I hope you won't hold it against me," the dark stranger replied.

She squeezed his hand as she gazed coquettishly into his eyes. "We'll see about that. You'll hafta earn my favors tonight."

"Shall we get going?"

"Don't be silly, I've got a suite upstairs. A chilled bottle of champagne is waiting for us."

"Let's not waste any more time down here, then," the stranger whispered as he patted her on the bottom. Their eyes flirted all the way to the elevator and up to the room. When they arrived, Jennifer slid the key card into the slot and opened the door.

"Here we are."

"Wow, this room must cost a fortune."

"Not to worry, my husband is a savvy investor. It's time ta enjoy the fruits of his investments."

"Won't he be upset if he finds out about us?"

"Don't worry about him; he's off fighting the QF."

"The who?"

"It's not important. He's fighting a battle against his demons."

"And what about me?"

"You're the designated pinch hitter. Tonight you're fucking his wife," she said as she unzipped his pants.

"Well, then," he said with a smile.

"Your turn?" she said after pulling out his manhood.

The man stripped her down to the waist. She slapped his hand away so she could push the dress down to the floor herself. She stood naked except for a pair of black thong panties. She gazed at him invitingly.

"What about the champagne?"

"That can wait for now," she said as she loosened his tie and unbuttoned his shirt. A moment later, the bare-chested man removed her panties with his muscular arms. He immediately picked her up and threw her on the bed. She was laughing now as if already intoxicated.

The dark stranger hesitated. "I'm not sure about this. Your husband will kill me."

"Stop talking," she said, pulling the man on top of her.

◆ ◆ ◆

"Motherfucker," Janusz screamed as he jumped up from the

bed. The room was completely dark. He was drenched in sweat. He reached for the bottle of water by the nightstand.

Damn, what the fuck was that? It was the first time he had dreamt about Jennifer being unfaithful. Her words the evening before the trip to Brazil were haunting him. He was still angry after drinking an entire bottle of water. Even a hot shower did not help. The Paquis, Geneva's seedy bar district, was only a few blocks away. He got dressed, picked up his passport, and walked out the door of his hotel room.

He left the bar ten minutes after he had arrived. Janusz was restless the whole time. Still on edge about the dream, he went for a walk. Her words reverberated in his head. "You still can't get enough of the fight" and "You need to figure out what drives you to push so hard." She had said these things before. This time her words had struck deep inside his psyche. Had his career choices always been for purely patriotic reasons? He told himself he wanted to save American lives. Perhaps there was more to it than that. He could not go back to the hotel now. He needed to assist someone, anything to erase the helplessness. Observing the pimps and drug dealers coming in and out of bars all around, he knew he'd get a chance to do some good this evening. Around the corner, something caught his attention.

Two young men speaking in American accents came out of a bar. They smoked cigarettes while making their way down the street. Janusz was far enough back to avoid detection. Suddenly, four others surrounded the Americans. The assailants took out knives, forcing the young men against the wall. Janusz hid behind a shadow, listening to their conversation. The four assailants sounded Albanian. A large wave of Albanian migrants had entered Switzerland in the late 1990s. Like immigrants everywhere, they were mostly families in search of better opportunities. Some of these Albanians were part of criminal networks. The rise in illegal activity by the Albanian Mafia had transformed Switzerland into a more dangerous country than before. Janusz's nightmare was an omen, calling him to this spot.

Things did not calm down after the two Americans turned over their wallets. On the contrary, it seemed the Albanians were just getting warmed up. They pushed the Americans against the wall and punched one of them in the stomach.

"Having fun?" Janusz said as he emerged from the shadows.

The largest Albanian, about his own height, was acting as the leader of the group. "This does not concern you. Turn around and get lost."

"On the contrary. These two are Americans. It concerns me very much."

The big guy laughed, pulling out his own knife. "Then perhaps you'd like to join them?"

Janusz stood his ground like a samurai warrior. The Albanian leader ordered the others to continue what they were doing. The large man made his way toward Janusz. Less than a foot away, he tried to stare down Janusz. The Albanian could not hold his gaze.

"I told you to get lost before—"

A fist caught him in the throat before the Albanian could finish his sentence. Janusz struck with maximum force. The Albanian dropped his knife and collapsed to the ground. Janusz was certain the windpipe had been crushed as the Albanian struggled to breathe. Janusz proceeded to walk over him like a speed bump in the way. The injured man's comrades were clearly not expecting this turn of events. All three clenched their knives while facing Janusz. Behind them the two Americans ran away, leaving their rescuer to fend for himself.

Janusz stood there as the Albanians shouted at him. It took a while for one of them to muster the courage for a charge. When he did, Janusz ducked to avoid the knife jabs that cut through the air. A sharp pain above the eye sent him into a fit of rage. He grabbed the knife-wielding arm and twisted it backward in one quick motion. He used his open hand to strike down at the man's elbow like a karate master breaking a block of wood. The forearm flopped down like a snapped twig as he cried out at the top of his lungs. His two buddies froze in horror at the sight of their friend's dangling arm. They dropped their knives and ran as fast as they could in the opposite direction.

Janusz brought his hand to his face to check for the source of the pain. "Son of a bitch!" he shouted, staring at the blood on his fingers. He had not ended the fight fast enough. He placed a hand over his eye, keeping pressure on the cut as he walked back to the hotel. His demons were beginning to get the best of him. It could only have a negative impact on the mission.

18. INTERCONTINENTAL HOTEL, GENEVA, SWITZERLAND

October 03

Iman jiggled the door several times. It would not open.

"Let me see that. I think you're just excited," she said, taking the room key. "You have to be gentle. You can't just ram it in like an amateur." She giggled playfully.

"Here we are," she said before opening the door. She proceeded to throw her purse on a side table.

He picked her up and placed her in an empty chair by the bed. "I think there's alcohol here somewhere. I'll search the bar." He grabbed the handle of the minifridge, pulling so hard it almost came off the hinges. He frantically surveyed the options before picking one.

"How about some vodka?" He showed her two tiny bottles of Absolut.

"That's perfect. Get us a couple of glasses." As he made his way to the other side of the room, she opened her purse, keeping a constant watch over him. She quickly grabbed the pills, deftly placing them in between her fingers, before dropping the purse back on the table.

"I'm back, darling." He handed her a glass. "Let's have a drink." He laughed as he tried to open a bottle while holding the other glass in the opposite hand.

"Let me help you with that." She took the bottle and glass away from him. "Why don't you sit right here?" She situated him on the bed and placed the glasses and bottles on the nightstand while keeping the pills hidden in her hand.

"I think you should take off some of these clothes," she said, clutching Iman's shirt as he sat on the bed. "What's the matter, are we feeling a bit shy? Perhaps I should start?"

With the pills still in her hand, she unbuttoned her blouse and threw it on the floor along with her bra. Next came her shoes, her belt, her skirt, and her panties. Iman's eyes popped out of their sockets as he stared at her crotch. She playfully brought his face close to her bush for a few seconds before pushing him down on the bed. She poured the drinks and quickly dropped the pills in one glass.

"How about now, are you ready to play?" she asked. Iman nodded without saying a word as she helped him undress. When he was fully naked, she handed him a drink and plopped herself beside him.

"*L'chaim!*" she said in honor of an old boyfriend who was Jewish.

"*L'chaim!*" he parroted dutifully without noticing the irony.

She took a sip from her glass as she watched the Iranian guzzle his concoction in one gulp.

Iman then threw his glass to the floor before maneuvering himself on top of her. She let him kiss her neck and breasts until the sedative took over. Ten minutes later, he was snoring like a banshee. She pushed him to the side to walk toward the cell phone in her purse. She stood there naked, staring out the window at the city below. *Come on, come on. Pick up.*

"What took you so long? The target is ready," she said before hanging up.

19. INTERCONTINENTAL HOTEL, GENEVA, SWITZERLAND

October 04

"**W**here the hell were you?" Kim asked.

"I had to deal with this," Janusz said, pointing to the cut above his eye.

"What happened?"

"I had an accident. Where is our boy?"

"He's on the bed," she replied.

Janusz spotted Iman on the bed. "He's sound asleep and naked. Great job, Kim. Let's get him ready."

She helped Janusz to prop the Iranian scientist in a sitting position. Janusz proceeded to take a variety of compromising pictures of Iman with Kim. He turned to Kim when he was finished.

"It's time to get our new friend talking," he said while placing a few drops of liquid inside Iman's mouth. After fifteen minutes, Iman came to. He was confused but conscious.

"Okay, repeat after me, 'My government has sent me to conduct research on a biological weapon to use against our enemies,' " Janusz said.

"My government has sent me to conduct research on a biological weapon to use against our enemies," Iman repeated dutifully. Janusz spent the next hour coaching the drugged Iman before putting him back to sleep.

"Okay, that's a wrap. We'll let him sleep this off. Let's go."

Janusz and Kim gathered their equipment before wiping down the room for fingerprints. They walked out of the room as if it were theirs.

Fifteen minutes after noon, the phone came to life in room 1013. It rang over and over again. A groggy voice finally answered.

"Hello."

"Iman Vakili?"

"Yes?"

"I thought you'd never wake up. The drugs should've worn off by now. Anyway, we need to talk."

"Who is this?"

"I'm John King," Janusz answered.

"Who?"

"I'm your new best friend, and I want to help you."

"Listen, I've got a huge headache. Can we talk later?"

"I'm afraid not. There is something very important I need to share with you. I must see you immediately in the lobby of your hotel. It's about the virus."

"Okay, okay. Let me take a shower. I'll see you downstairs in twenty minutes."

Forty minutes past noon, Iman entered the lobby. The Iranian walked aimlessly around. Janusz raised a hand, prompting Iman to walk straight to his table.

Janusz immediately extended his hand for a shake. "Lovely day, sir. Thank you for coming."

"I'm very sorry. I had too much alcohol last night. My head still hurts."

"Happens to the best of us," Janusz shot back.

"You said something about being my best friend and a virus. Have we met before?"

Janusz waved to grab the attention of the waiter. "I'll have a tall glass of orange juice and a coffee for my friend here. Make it black."

"Thank you. How do we know each other?" Iman persisted.

"Instead of taking the time to explain the nature of our friendship, I'll just show you?"

Janusz proceeded to place a plain cream envelope in front of the Iranian scientist. Iman stared at it in silence. He finally picked it up, opening the flap with a table knife next to his plate. It took a few seconds for Iman to remove the contents. He instinctively jumped back. Within seconds, Iman's entire body tensed while his face grew red.

"Seems the drugs finally wore off. Perhaps you won't need that coffee after all," Janusz said sarcastically.

"Where did you get these? I met this girl yesterday. Were you hiding in my room?"

"I don't think you understand, Iman. Perhaps this will help you." Janusz proceeded to play an audio recording of Iman talking under the influence of drugs.

"What is the meaning of all this?"

"It's very simple. I plan on sending these pictures and recordings to your embassy unless you help me."

"Who are you? Whom do you work for?"

"That's not important. What's important is that you work for me now, in service to the United States, of course."

"Is this some sort of joke?"

"You'll do everything I tell you unless you want your government to get proof of your extracurricular activities," Janusz said without missing a beat.

The waiter arrived with the tray of orange juice and coffee. Iman could not bring himself to drink.

"It's very simple really. If you cooperate, there'll be financial compensation for your troubles."

"And if I don't?"

"I think you already know the answer."

"Very well. What do you want?"

"I need to know about your research at the RCERID. Why are you here in Switzerland? Are you helping Dr. Ahvazi develop a new biological weapon for the Iranian government? Who is the target of your weapon? I have several more, but these will do for now."

Iman poured sugar and cream into his coffee before raising the mug to his lips. "The Marburg virus. We're developing the Marburg virus as a potential deterrent. It's not that different from you Americans. We need credible weapons for our defense."

"Who is the target?"

"What target?"

"The target of the virus. Who are you going to use it against?"

"I just told you we're not, the research is purely for defensive purposes."

"Then why did Roozbeh give his life to warn the world?"

"Wait, Roozbeh is dead?"

"I'm afraid so. His body was found in Brasília."

"Who killed him?"

"I don't know for sure. I have my suspicions."

Iman sat there in silence, sipping his coffee. He was clearly surprised by the news. "Well, Roozbeh was a traitor to his country. I don't know why he said those things at the press conference."

"He said the Iranian government was developing a new biological weapon."

"He was obviously lying. Perhaps he wanted to sell a story for money."

"So there is no intended target for these weapons? Your government just decided to develop them for fun?"

"For the last time, it's for deterrent purposes only. I'm here to find out if scientists from other countries have found a treatment or a vaccine for Marburg. Obviously, we would never weaponize a virus for which there was no available cure."

"Very well, who is in charge of this effort besides Dr. Ahvazi?

The Pasteur Institute and the Ministry of Health are civilian organizations. They have no use for such a program."

Iman sat silently without a reply.

"Let's hear it, I don't have all day," Janusz said impatiently.

"Dr. Ahvazi reports to …" He stopped to take a deep breath. His eyes darted back and forth. "… reports to General Kalantari these days."

Janusz leaned back in his chair to take it all in. "The QF? The QF never builds anything for deterrence. I've got bad news for you, Iman. There's more to this program than you've been told."

"So, what do you want me to do about it?"

"Have you identified anyone with useful information for your mitigation efforts at the conference?"

"I have one or two people in mind."

"Who do you report to regarding such matters in Geneva?"

"Dr. Ahvazi instructed me to speak only to a man named Yahya. I don't know much about him other than his affiliation with ICRO at our Geneva consulate."

"The conference itinerary indicates a cocktail party for the participants at the Four Seasons Hotel tomorrow night. You need to be there. Make sure to bring Yahya with you. Tell him you met me at the conference, and I represent one of the American pharmaceuticals on the brink of a cure."

"But—"

"No buts, just do it. I'll contact you with a prepared story for Yahya. Before you go, I need Yahya's contact information."

Janusz placed a blank piece of paper and a pen in front of Iman. The Iranian took out his wallet and scribbled a few lines.

"I'll be in touch. You've already missed half a day at the conference. If anyone asks, you had a migraine and needed rest. Don't do anything stupid," Janusz said, pointing to the envelope. He placed a ten-franc note on the table for the juice and coffee before walking away with the envelope. His stomach felt uneasy, and it was definitely not from breakfast. Iman was not a reliable asset, but Janusz had no other choice. There was no telling when the QF would carry out their attack.

20. RECEPTION ROOM, FOUR SEASONS HOTEL, GENEVA, SWITZERLAND

October 05

J anusz stood in the middle of the grand ballroom holding a glass of champagne. He was surrounded by an eclectic group of scientists from around the world. A plump Russian man tried to start a conversation but was rebuffed. Several of the women in the room also tried to engage with him in idle chit-chat. He got rid of them all. There was no telling which of these people worked for an intelligence agency. Fifteen minutes later, Iman arrived wearing an ill-fitting navy suit with a bright yellow tie. The Iranian virologist made a beeline for him.

"Glad you could make it, Iman. Where's Yahya?"

"He should've been here by now. He was eager to meet you after I relayed your story."

"Perfect. Don't say anything stupid when we find him. I'll do the talking."

Iman nodded his agreement before picking up a small crab cake from a passing tray. As Janusz examined the room, a rather portly man with glasses approached.

Iman abruptly walked over to introduce himself. "Dr. Abdullah, I've been following your work closely. Absolutely amazing what you're doing with the Marburg treatments. I'd like to congratulate you personally." Dr. Abdullah worked for Nanogen Scientific, one of the largest pharmaceuticals in the world. After the fall of Saddam Hussein, he had spent several years in jail for his role in the Iraqi bioweapons program. Upon his release, Nanogen had hired him.

Janusz was annoyed by Iman's unexpected move. They had work to do.

"Congratulations are premature. We're still in early clinical trials with guinea pigs. *Inshallah*, we'll have the same success during the human trials," Dr. Abdullah declared.

"*Inshallah*, I'm very proud of your work," Iman reiterated.

"And what do you do, Mr. ...?"

"This is Dr. Vakili, a microbiologist with the Iranian Pasteur Institute. They're also quite busy with viral research these days," Janusz interjected sarcastically before introducing himself. "Please forgive me, I'm John King, lead attorney and corporate representative for Vaccigen."

"Vaccigen! You're located in northern Virginia if I'm not mistaken. I didn't know you had a presence at the conference," Dr. Abdullah observed with surprise.

"Not officially, I'm the only one from our company. Mostly observing the competition if you will."

"Competition? I thought we were all in this together."

"We are, which is why we need to be aware of the opportunities for mergers and acquisitions," Janusz said as he scanned the room once more.

From over the top of their heads, Janusz spotted a short man wearing a gray suit like his own. The man wore a collarless shirt without a tie, a dead giveaway for an Iranian government official. He had broad shoulders, a thick neck, and a wide forehead. He reminded Janusz of Neanderthal man dressed in a suit.

Janusz grabbed Iman by the arm. "Is that Yahya over there?" Iman nodded.

"Will you excuse us, Dr. Abdullah?" Janusz said.

"Certainly," came the quick reply.

Janusz shoved Iman toward Yahya. He then walked back to Dr. Abdullah and squeezed his arm firmly as he whispered in his ear, "Consider this a warning. Stay away from Dr. Vakili and all other Iranians at this conference. They're here to collect information for their bioweapons program. Do you understand?"

The Iraqi scientist froze in place and said no more as Janusz turned to find Iman and Yahya standing behind him.

"Mr. King," Iman said, "I'd like you to meet my colleague Yahya. He also works at the Pasteur Institute."

"A pleasure to meet you, sir," Janusz said with a forced smile. He grabbed two full champagne glasses from a nearby tray. He offered one to Yahya just to make him uncomfortable.

"I'm sorry, I don't drink. It's against my religion," Yahya declared.

Janusz offered the second glass to Iman, who also refused under the watchful eye of Yahya.

"Cheers," Janusz said as he emptied both glasses before placing them on a passing tray.

"Iman tells me Vaccigen has made a breakthrough with a Marburg treatment. What's it called?" Yahya asked.

"We don't have a name for it yet. We've made great progress with the M-191 monoclonal human antibody during our animal trials."

"How long before you sell on the market?" Yahya asked, sounding eager.

"That depends on a number of factors. We're just starting our human clinical trials. If all goes well, we'll need FDA approval for the consumer market. Lots of red tape, you know how that is."

Yahya stared at him with an inquisitive expression. "Does this mean you give bribes to get necessary approvals in America?"

"Bribes? Oh no, not at all. We prefer to call it lobbying. That's right. In America, we lobby to get approvals."

Yahya grinned from ear to ear. "I bet Vaccigen is good at lobbying as well?"

"Oh yes, of course. That's the only way to get things done in Washington."

"In that case, your country is no different from mine," Yahya said. As much as Janusz hated it to admit it, Yahya was correct on that point.

"Do you have a card, Mr. King?" Yahya asked.

Janusz handed over a freshly printed business card. "Here you go."

"Since our governments are so similar, perhaps you'd consider a joint venture in Iran. We have eighty million people who need a variety of drugs. Marburg is just the tip of the iceberg. We need all kinds of medicines. We're seeking a partner for our Pasteur Institute that has a monopoly on the Iranian vaccine market," Yahya said.

"Well, I don't know. Your government is currently under sanctions."

"There is an exception for medicine. You can use a foreign subsidiary to conduct business in our country if you're worried about the sanctions."

Yahya was trying hard to cut a deal. Janusz had him right where he wanted him.

"Mr. King, what kind of car do you like to drive?"

"Is this some kind of test?" Janusz replied.

"Not at all, I'm very serious. What's your favorite car to drive?"

Janusz grinned. "In that case, I'd say I'm particularly fond of German engineering. The Mercedes-Benz is the first car that comes to mind."

"I tell you what, here is my business card. Come visit my showroom tomorrow after the conference."

Janusz took the card. It was for a Mercedes dealership in Geneva.

He stepped into the showroom, not knowing what to expect. The Unit did not have any background information on Yahya, if that was his real name. Janusz was not even certain what organization in the Iranian government Yahya represented. All he knew was that Iman reported to this man on security-related matters. The showroom was clean. Pictures of Michael Schumacher and Lewis Hamilton covered the walls. There were four other customers inside. Janusz stared at a black Mercedes SUV. He then sat inside the vehicle to fiddle with the instruments. Across the showroom, the same model was available in white. As Janusz got out to walk around, a voice caught his attention.

"Mr. King, I'm glad you're here. I'll close the store and join you in a few minutes."

Janusz turned to find Yahya standing behind him. After acknowledging his host, he scanned the room for clues. A set of framed pictures in the back of the showroom caught his eye. Janusz walked closer for a better look. Four pictures spaced perfectly apart, all with one thing in common. Yahya was at the center of all of them. In each image, he was surrounded by a group of men, all of them taller and more muscular. It appeared Yahya was the leader of this group.

"You like my photos, Mr. King?" Yahya whispered from behind. This was the second time the Iranian had snuck up on him. The showroom was empty now.

"Lovely, friends of yours?"

"No, they work for me here in Geneva. They're salesmen."

Janusz said no more, although he was certain the men in the picture had a military affiliation.

"Please come to my office."

"Certainly."

They walked toward another office on the opposite end of the showroom. An assortment of Iranian military insignia covered the room. There were numerous pictures of Yahya with high-ranking QF officers whom Janusz recognized immediately.

"Who are these guys?"

"I was in the Iranian Army. Please sit down."

Janusz took a seat facing his host on the other side of a large mahogany table.

"I made a few phone calls to friends in Virginia before we met. It seems you have a great reputation at Vaccigen," Yahya said.

Janusz was not surprised. The CEO of Vaccigen, located across the street from the Unit's headquarters, was a close friend of Tony, the Unit's director. "I'm curious why you invited me here today."

Yahya opened a cabinet on the right side of his desk and took out a wooden box. He placed the ornately decorated container on the table between himself and Janusz. Yahya opened the lid to reveal a set of hand-rolled cigars, Cohibas to be exact. Janusz's father liked to smoke them from time to time.

Yahya extended the box toward him. "Cigar?"

"No, thank you. I don't smoke."

Yahya smiled before taking one for himself. He cut the tip with a golden cigar cutter on his desk. "I love these things. I get them from our Cuban friends in Bern. I drive out there once a week."

"You seem to be an important man around here. A showroom in Geneva, friends at the Cuban embassy, facilitator of joint ventures for your government."

"I'm a good negotiator. People hire me to make deals," Yahya said as he lit the cigar. He took several drags before the cigar came to life. He blew out eight large smoke rings to prove his proficiency. Although he had a thick accent, Yahya's command of English was not in doubt. Janusz remained quiet. He was certain that this power display was meant to convey a point.

"I'm in demand because I get things done. I don't have fancy cigars and a beautiful showroom because of luck. I always deliver for my friends."

"Is that why you invited me here? You want to be my friend?" Janusz said sarcastically.

"I invited you here because you told me you like the Mercedes-Benz. You seem to be particularly fond of that Black SUV." Yahya pointed toward the showroom. "You tell me how much you want to pay for it and it's yours."

"You're kidding, right?"

"Not at all, give your price."

"Okay, ten thousand dollars."

"It's a deal, but that's not all. If you like beautiful women, I have some Albanian friends that can get any lady you like. Tell me your hotel room number. The girls will be there before you get back."

"That's very generous," Janusz said.

"You see, I'm always working to make my friends happy. Yes, I want you to be my friend too. As friends we can help each other," Yahya said before pausing to blow out a few more rings.

"You can also make me happy by talking to your executives about opening a viral research facility in Iran. We're particularly interested in a joint venture to produce a treatment for the Marburg virus."

"I don't understand. Marburg is not really a problem in Iran to my knowledge," Janusz said.

"Yes, but our joint venture could become very lucrative down the road. My government wants to improve its reputation in Africa by eradicating the next outbreak. Vaccigen will also be mentioned in our press release, of course."

Janusz chose not to mention the limited number of Marburg outbreaks even in Africa.

"There is one other thing that might persuade your executives," Yahya added.

"What's that?"

"You remember our conversation about red tape in your country?"

"Yes, of course."

"Well, you don't have to worry about approvals in Iran. You can start human trials for any of your vaccines and treatments right away. How does that sound?"

The thought of unregulated human tests with a lethal virus sent a chill down Janusz's spine. He tried his best to feign excitement. "That sounds very tempting. I'll do my best to convince our people."

Yahya took the cigar out of his mouth and placed it in the ashtray.

"About that Mercedes. Can you get a deal for a friend of mine?" Janusz asked.

"Certainly, how many do you need?"

"You can get more than one? I find that hard to believe."

Janusz was curious to find out what kind of scam the Iranians were running. Yahya studied him for a few seconds before answering.

"I handle all import/export work for my government in Switzerland. As a diplomat, I don't have to pay taxes on these vehicles, and I get a special rate from the manufacturer in Stuttgart."

Everything suddenly fell into place. The Iranians were using diplomatic courtesies to sell German vehicles at discount prices to raise cash for their terrorist operations around the world.

"What about the other dealers, don't they mind your unfair advantage?"

"They don't know. We list our automobiles at the same price as everybody else. When customers come into our store, we ask them, 'What is the best price someone else will give you?' Whatever that number, we go a little bit lower."

Janusz's blood boiled. The Iranian regime was manipulating diplomatic law to gain an unfair market advantage. What happened next was not part of the plan. "You run this shop on your own, or do you get assistance from others?"

"I have a few friends who help me."

"How many?"

"What do you mean?"

"How many people help you? Do they also work at the Iranian consulate?"

Yahya tightened the grip around the pen in his hand. He squirmed in his chair, trying to regain his composure. "I'm sorry, Mr. King, this is none of your business."

"Iman tells me you are in a bit of a hurry to get your hands on a cure for Marburg. What if I were to tell you Vaccigen has what you're looking for? How quickly do you need to deploy the first batch in the field?"

Yahya's body tensed as he sat upright. His eyes grew tense as a grimace appeared on his face. "I think it's time for you to leave, Mr. King. You have overstayed your welcome."

There was no turning back now. Yahya was onto him. "Is this what happened to Roozbeh Navabi? He overstayed his welcome too, so you had him killed?"

Yahya's brow furrowed, and he shouted obscenities in Farsi. He reached under his desk and opened a drawer before pointing a small .22 Beretta Bobcat pistol at Janusz.

"Okay, let's not get carried away," Janusz said, realizing that his anger had ruined this opportunity.

"Get moving. We are going to take a ride, you son of a bitch," Yahya said.

"Oh yeah, where are we going?"

"Shut up!"

Janusz moved back cautiously, facing Yahya the whole time. He was not about to turn his back on a man who was ready to kill. He noticed the bookcase full of trinkets. Janusz stood still.

"Keep moving," Yahya ordered.

"Iman tells me General Kalantari is in charge of a program to weaponize the Marburg virus. Is this why you need a cure? To protect yourselves if the virus gets out of hand?"

"*Khafeh Shoh, Madar Jendeh,*" Yahya shouted, *Shut up, you son of a whore*, as he closed the distance to strike Janusz with his pistol. Having anticipated the move, Janusz grabbed the bookcase and pulled with all his might. A shower of trinkets rained on Yahya before he could react. A shot rang out. The debris had forced Yahya's arm downward. Yahya fell to the floor as the bookcase came to a rest against his desk. Janusz moved the obstruction out of the way to grab Yahya. The Iranian raised his arm again, still holding the pistol. Janusz grabbed his wrist and pushed the Beretta toward Yahya's face.

"Relax, Yahya. I just want to talk to you."

The Iranian kept pushing back with an unusual amount of force that came as a surprise to Janusz. He had another trick up his sleeve.

"Yahya *Jan, dasteto shol kon*," Janusz said in Farsi. *Dear Yahya, please loosen your hand.* Yahya slackened his arm for a split second in confusion. Janusz was able to turn the .22 toward Yahya's forehead.

"Let go, Yahya," Janusz said in English. Yahya maneuvered his index finger over the trigger as he tried to shoot Janusz. His finger tensed as Janusz pushed the weapon back toward his head. *Bang.* The noise reverberated through the showroom. The bullet entered between Yahya's eyes. The blood trickled down his face and was absorbed by his white dress shirt.

"Son of a bitch!" Janusz shouted.

Janusz had to make sure he was dead. He shot Yahya twice more. The Iranians would surely pull Iman out of Geneva now. On top of everything else, there was no telling how quickly the Swiss would come looking for him.

21. LUFTHANSA AIR FLIGHT, ABOVE THE ATLANTIC OCEAN

October 08

Morteza Karami opened his eyes to the sounds of a crying baby several rows back. A throbbing pain shot down his neck as he struggled to find a new position for his head. He wiped the drool on his beard, smearing it below his seat. He then placed a hand under his chin to prevent his mouth from opening inadvertently. Morteza hated traveling coach, especially on a foreign airline. More than anything he needed sleep, but that was impossible with the crying baby. He had not slept well in weeks. Not since his reassignment to the dreaded virus project. It was another QF project, after all. General Kalantari would take all the glory for himself once again when all was said and done.

After years of neglect, someone let the MOIS get a piece of the action. Except Morteza and the MOIS would do the dirty work while the QF got the credit. As always, General Kalantari's men would benefit from a larger budget while he was stuck flying coach. So what else was new? The damn baby was still crying as more passengers woke up. He finally gave up, sitting tensely upright. He played with the in-flight entertainment system to busy himself. Staring at the screen, he had a flashback from his first mission for the MOIS.

The graduation ceremony at Imam Bagher University, the training academy for the MOIS, seemed like yesterday. He was

immediately assigned to Geneva as a counterintelligence officer accompanying the Iranian nuclear delegation. It was a tense
negotiation between Iran, the US, Russia, and the European
powers. He had thwarted an attempt by an American to recruit a
member of his delegation who was later executed. Here he was,
all these years later, going back to the city where it all began.
Things were worse this time. Someone had killed a decorated
QF officer in Geneva. The QF officer, known as Yahya, was also
responsible for the procurement of supplies for the Iranian government's clandestine virus project. After all these years, he had
been forced to become a glorified chaperone for another QF-
led operation. He had just finished cleaning up their mess in
Brasília; now this. One of these days he'd have the opportunity to
turn the tables on the QF. Perhaps not today, but someday soon.
Morteza tried without success to fall asleep.

Striving hard to stay awake, Morteza stepped through customs at Geneva Airport with a scowl on his face. His suit was
slightly wrinkled while his shirt hung partially over his trousers. He was a man of average height and build, with an indistin-
guishable face. He had not bothered to comb his thinning hair
or straighten the drooping glasses on the bridge of his nose. He
was the textbook definition of a tired hapless traveler, exactly
the image he wanted to present. Two colleagues waited for him
near the baggage claim. They were subordinate MOIS officers
stationed in Switzerland. One of the men grabbed his luggage,
before all three walked toward the parking lot.

"*Rooz khosh Ghorban, be Genev Khosh Amadid,*" the man holding the luggage said. *Good day, sir. Welcome to Geneva.*

"There is nothing pleasant about this day, you buffoon. Now,
what the hell is the latest development down here?" he replied
tersely.

"We're trying to learn more about Yahya's contacts. He met
all kinds of people as the QF procurement chief for Europe. His

Mercedes dealership in Geneva is also a front for drug smuggling."

"I know all this, you imbecile. What else?"

"The Swiss are upset. They claim this was payback for Yahya's involvement in criminal activity. They filed a démarche with our ambassador. They said that if we don't clean up our act, they'd sever diplomatic relations."

"The Swiss and their problems are not my concern. What else have you learned that can help *my* investigation, you cretin?"

Once they reached the consulate vehicle, Morteza sat in the back of the black Mercedes SUV. It was part of the fleet procured for the consulate by Yahya.

"The only other item is Yahya's meeting with an American at the Four Seasons Hotel three days ago," the man said before pausing to gauge interest.

"What the hell are you waiting for, the return of Imam Mehdi? Continue."

"According to Yahya's notes, the American is a representative of Vaccigen, a pharmaceutical company on the verge of a Marburg cure. Yahya met with him about a joint venture."

"Do we have pictures of this American?"

"Sir, Yahya had a hidden camera in his room. I can show you the image, but we believe the American was wearing a disguise."

Morteza clenched his jaw as he stared out the window.

"Sir, there is one other thing."

"What's that?"

"One of our scientists, Iman Vakili, is in Geneva for a week-long conference about the Marburg virus. But—"

"But what, you miserable ass kisser?"

"Well, sir, no one informed us about his arrival or mission. We only found out about it by reading Yahya's notes during the investigation."

"And?"

"The day before Yahya was killed, Iman visited his showroom to discuss something. Iman's name is in Yahya's logbook.

We don't know what they discussed, but the whole thing is kind of strange."

"So you think Iman is somehow connected to this incident?"

"I don't want to raise alarms," the man said guardedly as if expecting another invective.

"Relax, I'm way ahead of you. It just so happens that I had to arrange the elimination of another scientist tied to this wretched program in Brazil. I don't know what kind of operation the QF is running here, but it seems to have lots of holes," Morteza said with a sour taste in his mouth. "Gentlemen, it appears we've been tasked to plug a leaky ship."

His subordinates nodded.

"Sir, I thought we'd stop by Iman's hotel and pay him a visit. We haven't had a chance to question him yet."

"No! Absolutely not! If Iman is involved in all this, I don't want to tip him off. Take me to the consulate now. There is another way to do this."

22. CONSULATE OF ISLAMIC REPUBLIC OF IRAN, GENEVA, SWITZERLAND

October 09

"You don't remember the name? Well, what company did he say he represented?" Morteza asked the MOIS source over the phone.

Morteza followed up. "Yes, and a physical description?

"How old would you say he was?"

The source was only able to provide a guess.

"What was he wearing that night?"

The source's information was of little use, despite his fancy science background. That was the problem with intelligence work in general. One had to gather a mountain of information, sifting through it for countless hours, before finding the golden nugget.

"Very well, thank you for your—" As Morteza was about to end the call, his ears perked up once again.

"Interesting. Are you sure he wasn't just making that up?" Morteza wrote down the first and last name in capital letters and underlined them.

"Thank you, let us know if we can be of assistance with your research. I'm sorry I didn't get a chance to contact you sooner," Morteza said, and hung up. An assistant walked in with a tray full of refreshments. Morteza popped a sugar cube into his mouth, slowly sipping hot tea while reading over his notes. He made the call to a MOIS subordinate as soon as he finished with the tea.

"Where are you?" Morteza's face burned hot after he was told that his subordinate was on a lunch break.

"Stop wasting time, you miserable cretin. I've got an assignment for you."

Iman adjusted his pillow for the tenth time in as many minutes. He could not get comfortable on the small couch. The nudity on Swiss TV had lost its initial appeal. The more he switched channels, the more he longed for his own language. To add insult to injury, there was no substance to the programming on Western TV. Just shiny objects catering to the most primal instincts. As he flipped the channels, he finally identified the root of his frustration. He had been trapped by his own libido. Now he had to pay the price. It should have been obvious the beautiful blonde, whoever she was, was just using him. Why had he not been skeptical, questioning her motives earlier?

How easy had he made it for her to place him under the complete control of the Americans? What would his wife think about those pictures? What would his government do when they found out? He shook his head to erase the images from his mind. The thought of being tortured at Evin Prison was unbearable. The *tap, tap, tap* on the door caught his attention. Perhaps the Americans had sent another prostitute to bury him deeper. Iman stood up to answer. He would send her back, whoever she was.

A cheerful man with green eyes was standing outside. He wore a leather jacket with jeans.

"I have something for you," the man said in English. Iman stared as the man handed him a sealed plain white envelope.

"You need to open that immediately," he said before walking down the hall toward the elevators.

"Excuse me. Excuse me. What is this about?" Iman shouted,

chasing after him.

The man entered the elevator and disappeared. Iman walked back to his room staring at the envelope. There were no markings. His mind raced at a million kilometers an hour. Was it another extortion attempt? Perhaps the contents of the envelope were laced with anthrax. Perhaps it was laced with Marburg, the very virus he was here to understand. Iman opened the envelope, consequences be damned. He cut a small hole on the side and opened it with his index finger. He pulled out a single sheet of white paper. The following message was written in the middle of an otherwise blank page.

Meet me in Trembley Park at 10:00 pm. I've got another assignment for you.

John King

He shredded the paper into four little pieces, using a lighter to burn each piece in the bathroom sink. He quickly got dressed for the short walk to the park. Along the way, he pondered killing his American handler when they met. That would only further exacerbate his problem. The American had pictures and audiotapes. His only choice was to defect and request asylum. What about his wife and children back in Iran? There was no telling what the authorities would do to them.

Iman glanced nervously around as soon as he arrived at Trembley. It was fairly dark, despite the park lights. He was the only one there. A light wind blew over him. Minutes later, the sound of footsteps could be heard. Was there someone waiting in the shadows? Was there someone waiting to kill him? His options were limited. Iman could not approach the police or his own consulate. He had no choice but to play this out.

He checked his watch; it was 9:55 p.m. His mind was transported once more into the dark musty rooms of the notorious Evin Prison. Sodomy was a form of torture used to exact confessions in Iran. So was flogging the soles of the feet with copper cables. The possibilities of inflicting pain were endless. A noise came from behind. *Yyeeeeooouuu.* Iman jumped, his heart pounding out of his chest. A stray cat ran across the narrow walkway in front of him. He breathed a sigh of relief before another noise caught his attention. He turned faster than a bobble head. It was the rustling of leaves over the walkway. He checked his watch once again at 10:15 pm. He paced back and forth to calm down. Another twenty minutes went by. Still no sign of his contact. He could take no more. He walked back toward the hotel. The American knew where to find him if he wanted to talk.

Iman checked his rear one last time. A young couple walked hand in hand, but no sign of the American. He went straight to bed upon reaching his room. The next morning, Iman sent a text to John King.

I want to meet somewhere crowded this time. Meet me at the Studio Twenty dance club tonight at 11:00. I'll be at the bar.

The techno music blasted from speakers all around. The multicolored lights illuminated the gyrations of the scantily clad women. He adjusted his fake nose and eyebrows in the mirror before turning back toward the revelry. The scene transported Janusz to the college parties of his youth. The music had not been so loud in those days. Maybe his ears were extra sensitive now. Maybe, *oh, perish the thought,* age was starting to catch up. Janusz pushed the dread of aging out of his mind as he walked straight up to the bar. The skinny-faced bartender with the big tits approached after several minutes.

"Qu'est-ce que vouz voulez?" she asked with flirty eyes. *What do you want?*

"Give me a Grey Goose straight up."

"You got it."

Janusz scanned the room for Iman. Five minutes later, someone tapped his shoulder.

"You showed up this time," Iman shouted over the music.

"Why did you want to meet here? It's impossible to talk," Janusz said.

"Last night."

"What about last night?"

"Why didn't you come?"

"Come where?"

"To our meeting."

The men stared at each other. For a moment, the club stood still. As Iman's eyes widened, Janusz realized they had been double-crossed. Janusz grabbed the Iranian by the arm and dragged him to a quiet corner. Revelers bumped into them from every direction. There was little room to maneuver. Janusz pushed dancers out of the way to clear an opening. The cry was unmistakable. Someone yelled, "*Allahu Akbar*." Janusz's arm jerked back as Iman's grip tightened around his elbow. It was the iron grip of a gorilla. Blood poured out of Iman's mouth. The Iranian's eyes were wide-open as he held on to Janusz.

The music blasted his ears. He pulled Iman forward, placing an arm around his back. That's when he felt the knife handle. Iman's back was drenched with the warm liquid. Janusz tried to stop the bleeding, but there was nothing he could do. Pulling the knife out could make things worse. Iman fell forward, his limp body now resting on Janusz. Several dancers gathered in a circle around them. Amazingly, the rest of the club was oblivious of the unfolding drama. Dancing continued with reckless abandon to the hypnotic music. Janusz gently placed Iman's head on the floor before standing up. He grabbed a skinny punk with slicked-back hair and a gold chain.

"Call for an ambulance and police," Janusz shouted over the music.

The man nodded while the circle of spectators stared at the knife lodged in Iman's lifeless body. None of their faces betrayed the slightest emotion. They were either shocked or high, perhaps both. Janusz scanned the crowd in search of a suspect. The place was packed wall to wall, a perfect location for a cluster fuck. He pushed his way through the crowd once more. The vibrations of the music shook his body with each beat. The air was thick with a cool mist that fell from above. Janusz opened another button on his shirt and took several deep breaths. The sweat poured down his arms. He could not be sure if it was the music, the number of people packed like sardines, or the lack of air-conditioning. He desperately gasped for air before locking eyes with a man across the room. The bearded man had bushy brows and wore a dark suit.

That had to be Iman's killer. Janusz quickened his pace, shoving dancers aside to close in on his target. When Janusz was within ten feet, the bearded man turned right. Janusz's eyes moved instinctively in the same direction. A second man, with similar attire, stared intently at him. Without warning, the second man raised an arm over the crowd. His right fist clutched a micro Uzi submachine gun, pointing straight at Janusz's head. Janusz grabbed two women standing next to him and pushed them to the floor. As soon as they hit the floor, the rattle of the Uzi pierced through the air. It was only a one-second burst but seemed much longer.

Pandemonium broke out as the bullets flew. Janusz remained crouched, approaching stealthily like a lion wading through the tall savannah grass. Bare legs and jeans scattered all around as the sea of bodies parted in front of him. A pair of black trousers appeared through the thicket. Instantly, Janusz pulled the SIG P365 compact pistol from his waist. He racked the slide to chamber a round. Bystanders continued to block his view. After another burst of fire from the Uzi, his line of sight was clear. He pulled twice on the trigger. Two nine-millimeter bullets tore through the target's left and right kneecaps, and he collapsed on the hardwood. One more shot to the head for good measure.

Janusz proceeded to crawl along the floor in search of his next target. Several patrons stepped over him while retreating toward the exit. When Janusz spotted the second pair of black trousers, the shit hit the fan. The fusillade of bullets prompted him to roll several times in evasive action. He came to a complete stop and raised his pistol. He aimed toward the center of the torso. Two bullets hit their mark. His target took several steps back, seemingly unfazed. It dawned on Janusz that the target was wearing Kevlar. He made the appropriate adjustment to his aim by focusing on the head. The first shot missed the mark. The second connected with the target's head. Blood sprayed out, hitting several panicked dancers. Janusz made a beeline for the exit. He needed to disappear before the police arrived on the scene. He ran down the stairwell toward the street. Panicked patrons pushed one another out of the way. Janusz walked toward the curb to find his bearings.

The wail of the sirens was audible in the distance. From behind, a man shouted, "*Allahu Akbar*" for the second time that night. Janusz turned in the direction of the battle cry, his pistol ready to fire. A roundhouse kick connected with Janusz's right hand. The force of the kick threw the SIG several feet into the air away from him. The attacker straightened himself and pulled out a knife. The handle was exactly the same as the one lodged in Iman's back. Janusz prepared for the advancing strike. His opponent thrust several times in quick succession. Janusz deftly avoided the blows, moving side to side with the grace of a dancer. His opponent was impatient. The man held Janusz's left arm and jabbed the knife. Janusz grabbed the knife-wielding arm by the wrist, using it to swing his opponent around.

Standing behind him, Janusz forced the man to stab himself in the neck. The gushing blood spatter was from a direct cut on the left carotid artery. His opponent went limp instantly as Janusz flung him toward the ground, narrowly avoiding the blood spray. Bystanders were too busy running to pay attention. For several seconds, Janusz watched the pool of blood accumulate around the body of the assassin. He melted into the scattering crowd to make his getaway. There was little time to leave the country.

23. RESEARCH CENTER FOR EMERGING AND REEMERGING INFECTIOUS DISEASE, AKANLU, IRAN

October 11

Dr. Ahvazi was busy reviewing the RCERID's budget. The phone on his desk would not stop ringing.

"Hello," he said with irritation in his voice.

"To digeh che marge te?" *What the hell is wrong with you?*

"Sorry, Haj Kalantari, didn't realize it was you."

"What happened during your last experiment?" General Kalantari asked with a raised voice.

"*Ehhem*, I'm afraid there was nothing we could do. We took every precaution possible while following your instructions. We lost another technician," Dr. Ahvazi reported to the QF chief.

"May Allah bless you with more wisdom. That's three people in as many weeks. At this rate, you'll run out of personnel before this project is done."

"I appreciate your concern. Don't worry about us, we're on budget and on schedule."

"Reporters buzzing around Vali-Asr Hospital are asking questions. Local citizens want to know what kind of disease has closed off the top floor."

"That's why you're the chief of the QF, and I'm just a lowly servant out here in a provincial village. I'm sure you'll figure it out," Dr. Ahvazi said facetiously.

"Never mind. I have more bad news. Iman Vakili is dead."

"Say what, *khhhh*?" Dr. Ahvazi replied in disbelief. His blood pressure was starting to rise.

"May Allah bless your hearing too. I just got off the phone with MOIS. There was a shoot-out at a club in Geneva. They had to kill Iman," General Kalantari explained.

"My hearing is just fine. Why did the MOIS kill my deputy? I needed this man for the Marburg treatment effort."

"It gets better. Losing another man is the least of your problems. He was working for the Americans. Iman helped the infidels kill Yahya in Geneva. Looks like you handled all the details just like you promised me."

"I had no way of knowing that—"

General Kalantari finished his sentence. "Your assistant was a traitor to the regime and the supreme leader."

Dr. Ahvazi fell silent. A million thoughts bombarded him. How could this have happened again?

General Kalantari was shouting now. "I figured you'd be speechless. Now listen to me carefully. I'm sending over two counterintelligence experts to reinvestigate your staff. The American who recruited Iman killed three MOIS officers. It won't be long before our entire delegation is thrown out of Switzerland."

"Yes, sir, I understand."

"May Allah also bless me with patience to deal with you. I can't afford another fuck-up, and neither can you. Are we clear?"

"Yes, sir, I couldn't agree more, *ghoolp*. My men and I are at your disposal," Dr. Ahvazi said while weighing his options. The punishment for treason in Islamic Iran was death. Anyone whose organization had two traitors in it would surely not remain in his position for long.

"Very good. Keep working on the virus, and forget about the cure. We'll let the Americans worry about containing the outbreak. Do not deviate from my orders again." General Kalantari let the vague threat hang in the air.

"I understand, sir," Dr. Ahvazi replied in despair.

There was a knock on the door. An assistant popped his head in. He was holding a stack of papers. Dr. Ahvazi motioned for him to take a seat as he remained on the call. Finally, after another minute of verbalizing his consent with a series of "yes" replies, Dr. Ahvazi hung up.

"What was that all about?" the assistant asked.

"Bureaucratic bullshit, *Achuu*. What do you have for me?"

"The blood sample results from the chimps are ready."

"And?"

"Complete failure. They all came back negative, except the one Mohsen sprayed in anger."

"That doesn't count, the idiot sprayed that one too long."

"I'm aware."

"You mean to tell me not one of the other eleven fucking apes is infected with Marburg?"

"Afraid not, here's the data." The assistant dropped the stack of papers on Dr. Ahvazi's desk.

"Ironically, our own fucking ape, the idiot Mohsen, is lying in the hospital with a Marburg infection. His mere presence there is giving me a migraine."

Dr. Ahvazi read the results silently, occasionally writing his own notes along the margins. "We need to take this show on the road. Start gathering our equipment and personnel for a road trip. I think Haj Kalantari's source provided faulty data."

"Where are we going?"

"Haj Kalantari will let us know when everything is ready. In the meantime, I want to take a closer look at these figures."

"Sir, I think we should use a different solution this time."

"I agree, *khhhh*. We'll also change the temperature at which the solution is stored. I was never comfortable with the numbers provided in the notes from America."

His assistant was barely out the door when the phone rang.

Damn it, what now?

"Good day, Dr. Ahvazi. It's Akbar Shadi, the deputy assistant to the minister of health," came the reply over the phone.

"Yes, yes, of course, how can I help you?"

"It's come to my attention that some of your staff have recently been fired without explanation. Two of your technicians are at Vali-Asr Hospital, reportedly with a deadly infectious disease. There is increasing pressure on the health minister for answers."

"*Ehhem*, of course. We've had an uptick of Crimean-Congo fever lately. RCERID is tasked with researching a vaccine, and the work is quite dangerous. Unfortunately, there is always the possibility that our own staff becomes infected—"

"There are rumors that one of your men has that German virus ... It's at the tip of my tongue. Oh yes, Marburg. Are you conducting research on the Marburg virus without the health minister's knowledge?"

"Marburg is not German. It occurs primarily in Africa, near the border between Uganda and Kenya, to be precise. But these are all rumors. No one at the RCERID is working with—" He was cut off once more.

"Dear Dr. Ahvazi, thank you for the lesson in epidemiology. However, the health minister does not intend to lose his job over whatever kind of unauthorized game you're playing at the RCERID. I'm coming down to your lab with a team in a few days for an inspection. I'll send you an email with the exact date."

"But, sir, there's no need—"

"No buts, my decision is not open to negotiation. I want to see for myself what you're up to. Consider this a courtesy call."

The deputy assistant to the health minister hung up as Dr. Ahvazi pondered his next move. He was not about to take a dive for someone else's pet project. There had to be a better way to deal with Akbar Shadi.

24. UNIT 81 SAFE HOUSE, MCLEAN, VIRGINIA

October 12

A gentle breeze blew against her face as she rocked back and forth on the porch. After a hectic move to the US, she finally had a moment to relax. The picturesque house on Buchanan Street was everything she had imagined about America. The grass was freshly cut, and the bushes were neatly trimmed. A quaint brick pathway went over the lawn toward the street. A wooden picket fence surrounded the property, painted white to complement the rest of the house. Three wooden chairs faced Buchanan Street, part of a set that included the swing on which Marjan sat. A basket of purple flowers hung delicately on each side of the stairwell, giving off a pleasant aroma reminiscent of Tehran. Marjan stopped swaying to take a sip of the lemonade. If only Roozbeh had taken her advice.

She had warned him many times about the dangers of opposing the regime. The problem with Roozbeh, similar to every man she had known, was that he never listened. With the children safely enrolled at school, she finally had the time to plan her next move. The Americans had offered her a job as an analyst with High Risk Capital. It was a front for an organization they called Unit 81.

It was all too good to be true, but it had come at a high cost. She had no choice but to move forward. It was the least she could do for herself and the children. She looked up at the shiny black sedan that parked in front of her house. A middle-aged man with blond hair and a subtle paunch stepped out. Another man several centimeters shorter than the first, with dark hair, stepped out of the passenger's side. The second man was fit, and more handsome than the first. They were both wearing a suit and tie.

"Ms. Navabi? We're with Unit 81. We just want to check on you, see if you need anything."

The men closed the white picket fence behind them. They approached the stairwell with friendly smiles.

"Please call me Marjan," she replied while taking turns to shake their hands.

"My name is Bill. This is my colleague, Jim. Do you have a few minutes?"

"Oh dear, certainly. Would you like to come inside?"

"That won't be necessary. Out here on the porch is fine if you don't mind?"

"Of course not. Just a moment now." Marjan excused herself to go inside. A few minutes later, she emerged with two glasses and a fresh pitcher of lemonade. After pouring their drinks, she took a seat facing them on the swing.

"Thank you, this is wonderful," Bill said, wiping his mouth.

"I'm glad you like it. I got the recipe from that nice lady who works with you, Heta, Hita, not sure how you pronounce it."

"Heather."

"Heater, yes, thank you."

"Marjan, we're wondering if you can help us learn more about your deceased husband's employment in Iran. Specifically, his work at the RCERID in Akanlu."

"I'm happy to help in any way, but Roozbeh did not discuss work with me."

"Before we get to that, what did *you* do for work in Iran?"

"I stayed home with the children." She paused for a few seconds before feeling the urge to explain.

"Don't get me wrong. I have a degree in English from Islamic Azad University. But Roozbeh made enough money to support us. It was best for me to stay with the kids."

"So you've never worked for the Iranian government or military?"

"No, of course not. The way they treat women and dissidents is just dreadful."

"And your husband? How long was he working at RCERID?"

"Let me see, seven years."

"What did he do for the institute?"

"Research."

"On what?"

"Vaccines mostly. He conducted research on vaccines for the plague and tulamu something."

"Tularemia?"

"Oh yes, that one, and something with a Q."

"Q fever?"

"Yes, that's it."

"What about Crimean-Congo fever? Did you ever hear your husband mention working on that?"

"Let me think now. As a matter of fact, he did."

"Marjan, did your husband ever mention research on African tropical viruses?"

"Like what?"

"The Ebola virus, perhaps?"

"Oh dear, that's not a problem in Iran."

"How about a virus called Marburg? Did you ever hear him mention the word Marburg?"

"Is that a German disease?"

"Not exactly," Bill said with a smile. "It's a rare but deadly African virus similar to Ebola."

"No, he never said anything about that. Roozbeh did not like to talk about work when he came home. I tried to respect his wishes."

"Marjan, I want you to think very hard. You may have heard that the Iranian government also has a new biological weapon program. Can you think of a time when Roozbeh mentioned anything like that?"

"I discussed the same thing with the man you sent to Brazil.

John, that was his name. Like I told him, my husband was a pacifist. Like me, he was opposed to the Iranian regime."

"Very well. If you remember anything else, you know how to reach us. In the meantime, your background investigation is complete. You can start on Monday if you like."

"I'd like that very much. The work will help take my mind off the loss of Roozbeh."

"Excellent. You'll be safer in this house for the moment. We'll set up a bank account for you right away."

Marjan wiped the tears from her eyes before hugging both men. They were visibly moved.

"I'm so grateful for what America has done for us. Roozbeh would have been very happy too now."

Bill provided a few details about her first day on the job. He wrote down the address of Unit 81 before telling her the best time to get to work to avoid the dreaded northern Virginia traffic.

"What do you think, Jim, is she being truthful?"

"I've no reason to doubt her. Her answers match the information she provided Janusz. We've also run her through all the usual databases. She's clean."

"I happen to agree with you and Janusz. I feel so bad for those kids. They'll grow up without a father. I hope we're not pushing her to start too early. She needs time to heal."

"I think the work will be good for her. It'll help get her mind off the tragedy."

"I hope you're right, buddy. I sure hope you're right."

25. WHITE HOUSE SITUATION ROOM, WASHINGTON, DC

October 13

"Quiet please, quiet. This meeting will now come to order," the president shouted loud enough to drown out the whispers in the room.

"I need to cut this meeting short for a personal matter. We'll be out of here by zero eight thirty. What do you guys have for me?"

"Mr. President, we're taking heat from Congress about Russia. They want to know why you're not placing more sanctions on the Kremlin to curb their activities in Eastern Europe," Karl Sanders, the president's chief of staff, said. He was an affable man, a graduate of Harvard Law School, more concerned about his own political ambitions than anything else.

"Because that's not how you deal with the leader of a country that was a superpower not long ago. The Russians have myriad faults, but they also have an immense arsenal of nuclear weapons and a large dose of pride to top it off. Putting them in a corner only serves to strengthen their resolve, and that's not what I want. Anyone else?"

"But, Mr. President."

"Not now, Karl. I'm in a hurry. What's next on the agenda?" the president said to his national security team in the White House Situation Room. Beneath the Oval Office, the Situation Room was the nerve center monitoring global affairs for the

American president.

"Sir, the ROK has been begging to restore the joint military exercises. The South Koreans are concerned that the suspension is hurting the readiness of their troops if war breaks out," Air Force General Peter Beck, chairman of the Joint Chiefs, said.

"We've already been over this, Pete. This type of behavior is a reflexive reaction to preserve the status quo. It hasn't gotten us anywhere for over seventy years, and it isn't going to get us anywhere now. I'm in the middle of a deal that will finally put an end to the tensions on the Korean Peninsula. The exercises will remain suspended until I say otherwise."

"Mr. President, I agree with General Beck. Allies in the Pacific are questioning our resolve. The Japanese parliament is clamoring to increase its defense budget. They think we might abandon them. On top of that, opposition is building in Congress against your foreign policy. There are rumors that our defense budget proposal for the upcoming fiscal year might not win approval," said Ryan Irving, the secretary of defense.

"Ryan, I know you have political aspirations of your own. You can take any position you like regarding the Korean Peninsula when you run for office after my departure. My administration is not the place to showcase your bona fides to the Washington establishment. I'm short on time today, and I want to resolve pressing problems, so please only speak up if you have something to contribute."

"Mr. President, I was informed this morning by the chief of the Kurdish YPG intelligence service that the Iranian QF has taken up positions south of Idlib. YPG informants in the area are telling us the QF is planning an attack from this location. The YPG will not take further actions until they hear from us," David Schultz, Director of National Intelligence, said.

"Let's hit these sons of bitches, David. The Iranians just downed one of our surveillance drones flying over international waters in the Persian Gulf. I want to send a clear message to Supreme Leader Mashhadi that there will be a cost for attacking American assets. Let's drop a couple of JDAMs on the QF positions near Idlib," the president said.

"Sir, we can't do that. The press will frown upon a retaliation that costs Iranian lives for the takedown of an unmanned drone. Congress isn't going to be happy either. My fear is that they'll cut appropriations to our counterterrorism strike teams," Secretary Irving said once more.

"Mr. President, there's another problem. The Russians will be up in arms if we hit the Iranians under their noses. We need their cooperation in Syria," General Beck added.

Karl Sanders added his voice to the chorus. "Mr. President, I'd also like to caution against the use of force. The Europeans will not take kindly to an attack on Iranian forces. Many of your domestic opponents, including members of Congress, are going to have a field day calling you out in the media as a warmonger."

"So we can't retaliate against a hostile power that attacks us whenever they feel like it? What the hell has become of this country? Are we no longer a superpower?" The president slammed an open fist on the table. Several of the principals around the table and a few of their assistants sitting along the wall jumped up in their seats.

"Would someone like to tell me what the fuck we *can* do around here? Our assets are attacked in international waters, and we worry about ruffling the feathers of our opponents in Congress, the media, and the Europeans? We must not infringe on the sensibilities of allies in the Muslim world? What's become of this country? Shame on all of you. Political correctness has transformed you all into a bunch of pussies." The president said these words while looking around the room. Everyone tried his or her best to avoid eye contact with him.

Several young female staffers seated against the wall were at a loss for words. They'd never observed such a blatant display of politically incorrect behavior. Not in a public setting anyway. David Shultz was one of the few in the room who was laughing on the inside. His previous job, before he'd been picked by the president to lead the intelligence community, was as a member of the SSCI. During his tenure, David had become aware of a secret organization under the cover of a private equity firm.

Unit 81 operated outside the bureaucracy to defend American interests. David finally understood why the Unit was necessary. Although he did not show it on his face, he was satisfied with the president's outburst.

On his way out of the room, the president motioned for two individuals to follow him. "Pete and David, meet me in my office at sixteen hundred this afternoon. I think I know of a way to have our cake and eat it too," the president said with a grin.

26. UNIT 81 HEADQUARTERS, HERNDON, VIRGINIA

October 15

Marjan was escorted to the sixth-floor conference room, where a group was waiting for her. It was a meet and greet where she had the opportunity to learn about her new colleagues. Tony Volpe, Stan Roth, Bill Turner, and numerous others introduced themselves before describing what they did. A multicourse breakfast was served before Marjan was sent off with her new mentor.

"Thank you for the lemonade recipe. It's been such a hit with everyone who has come to visit," Marjan said.

"My pleasure, it was the least I can do. How are you holding up?" Heather asked.

"What?" Marjan asked for clarification.

"It's an expression. It means how are you doing, given what's happened?"

"Oh dear, I've still got so much to learn about the culture."

"You're doing just fine."

"Thank you, I'm doing my best to hold up. It's been only two weeks, but it feels like two years. Since Roozbeh died, I migrated to America, moved into a new house, put the kids in a new school, and today I started a new job."

"Yes, I can only imagine how difficult it's been."

"In a way, it's been good. I've been so busy I haven't had time to think about the tragedy."

"And the children?"

"They have the worst of it. They miss their father and cry every day. If not for them, I don't know how I'd feel. I block everything out so I can be strong for them."

"I admire you very much. I don't know what I would do in your shoes. Anyway, we've set you up on the Iran account where your skills will be most useful."

"Who will I be working with?"

"No one at the moment. Our primary person is out in the field."

"Tell me the truth, Heather, am I working for the CIA now?"

"What we said in the presentation this morning is the truth. High Risk Capital is a private equity firm that functions as a front for Unit 81. We generate our own funds and spend it to combat imminent threats against the United States."

"And the US government doesn't have a problem with this?"

"We have an arrangement. Anyway, you could not work for the CIA if you're not a US citizen. It also takes them over a year to investigate and clear most people. We're much more efficient because we're a private organization."

"I had never heard of such a thing before in my life."

"And we like to keep it that way, which is why we asked you to sign all those nondisclosure forms. We ask that you don't tell anyone about us."

"Of course not, I wouldn't think of it. I just hope I can be helpful against the Iranian regime."

"Patience, my dear, we'll teach you everything you need to be successful. Plus, you'll be working with the best in the business. Janusz is just great."

"Who?"

"Oh, I thought you knew already. Your partner is Janusz Soltani. He was the man you met in Brazil. He is our resident Iran expert."

Marjan was silent for several seconds before her eyes lit up like a Christmas tree. "Oh, you mean John King?"

"Yes, that's his operational name. We're given different

names when we go on assignment."

"How is he doing?"

"As far as I know, he's still working on the case related to your husband. Since I don't know much about Iran, you're going to support Janusz out in the field."

"Has he found the men who killed Roozbeh?"

"You're going to help him do that," Heather said as she guided Marjan on the computer. As Information Technology, or IT, lead for the Unit, Heather set up Marjan's accounts and accesses to various files.

"That's a lot of responsibility. I hope I don't disappoint all of you."

"You'll do fine. These are the files Janusz is working on. This is where Janusz is located at the moment. It looks like he's on standby until further notice. Can you research these names for him?"

"It'll be an honor," Marjan said.

After setting up her accounts, Heather left Marjan alone to do her work. She spent the next several hours solving network-access-related problems around the office. When she returned, Marjan was clutching a card in her hand.

"What's that?" Heather asked as Marjan quickly turned.

"Oh dear, it's a business card. I think I need to speak with a therapist about all this. My neighbor gave me this card," Marjan said.

Heather changed the subject to give her space. "Well, a bunch of us are headed out for lunch. Do you care to join us?"

"I would love to, I'm starving," Marjan said.

27. OLIVE FARM, SOUTHERN IDLIB, SYRIA

October 16

The smoke clung to the air like soot on a chimney. The Iranians, Kalashnikovs slung over their shoulders, all wore masks over their faces. The captured jihadist rebels were not so lucky. They sat on the ground as the masked QF operatives inspected the scene.

"*Pasho, pasho,*" the QF operative shouted like Darth Vader in full battle gear. *Get up, get up.* The captured prisoners represented the breadth of the Muslim world. From Chechnya in Russia to Java in Indonesia, they came to reestablish the modern caliphate, a new world order for Sunni Islam. They also came to fight the Shia. None of them could speak Farsi. They were forced to their feet by the gyrations of the Kalashnikovs, guiding them in the proper direction. The jihadist prisoners were escorted several hundred meters away to a small clearing. The air was cleaner, away from the rubble and debris of the smoldering buildings.

"*Neega Kon, een che vazeshe. Een reeshe ya pashm Kos?*" the QF operative taunted as he slapped a jihadi in the face. *Look at this. Is this a beard or pussy hair?* The ISIS fighter kept his mouth shut, weathering the abuse as best he could. The QF operative moved down the line, continuing his inspection of the prisoners. He suddenly stood face-to-face with a broad-shouldered man whose arms resembled the branches of an oak tree. His face was covered with soot, while his eyes shone like obsidian glass. The prisoner stared at the QF operative with palpable hatred.

"*To digeh be chi nigah mikoni?*" the QF operative asked. *What are you looking at?*

"*Az to Khoshesh meeyad,*" his QF comrade roared, bursting into laughter. *He likes you.* Without warning, another QF operative struck the prisoner with the butt of his rifle. The blow landed on the victim's groin. The jihadist bent over and fell to the floor. The QF operative raised his rifle once more before freezing in midstride.

"That's enough. Leave him be. I told you this group is off-limits," General Kalantari said as the QF operative lowered his weapon. A few minutes later, a man in a white lab coat walked up and promptly removed his mask.

General Kalantari pointed at him before speaking. "This man is here on a special assignment. He only answers to me. You're to obey every single one of his orders or else, as Allah is my witness, you'll live to regret it. I hope that's clear," the general shouted as his men nodded. His guest proceeded to walk in front of him.

"Please choose twenty of the healthiest individuals from this group. Take them to our field headquarters south of Idlib. Do not mistreat them in any way, and make sure they get something to eat, *ghoolp*. They'll be examined by a medical doctor shortly," the guest explained.

A QF operative on the scene motioned for his subordinates to start the process of selection. He then walked over to General Kalantari. "Sir, what should we do with the others?"

"Shoot them and scatter their bodies in the rubble of the smoldering buildings. I don't want any witnesses. Make sure to detonate the buildings and destroy all traces of the bodies. I don't want any evidence either."

The QF operative nodded and walked away. He seemed eager to grab one man in particular. It did not take long to find him, the man with the obsidian eyes.

"What's your name?" he asked in Arabic.

"Tariq, Tariq al-Manbiji," the barrel-chested man replied.

"You're Syrian?"

"Very observant. I'm the last member of my family to survive the slaughter in Manbij. The Russian air raids killed my wife and son."

"Well, Tariq, today is your lucky day."

"Huh!" The man sneered.

"You're one of the few who is going to survive this battle. Most of your brothers will not live to see tomorrow. You, on the other hand, have a nice lunch and shower waiting for you."

Tariq stared at the unlucky souls escorted toward the rubble. The ragtag army of volunteers from across the Sunni Muslim world hung their heads low. Their eyes were already dead. They knew what was waiting for them.

"We'll see about that," Tariq said.

"Bring them out one by one. Make sure their eyes are covered," Omid ordered.

"Should we give them a mild sedative to make them more co-operative?" the QF operative asked.

"Negative, we have clear instructions not to give them any medication that could contaminate their blood. Have they all received a physical?"

"Yes, we had them checked out by our doctors. Their blood was drawn and run through your machines. This must be important work if you've dragged this equipment all the way from Iran," the QF operative said.

"Never mind that. What were the results?" Omid asked.

"Everyone checks out fine based on the screening criteria you gave us. A few of them had high cholesterol and high blood sugar. That's about it," his QF assistant replied.

"Cholesterol and diabetes will be the least of the problems for this group. Okay, bring them out," Omid said before walking over to his boss. "Dr. Ahvazi, when do you want to start the experiment?"

"Right away, Omid, and by that I mean today," Dr. Ahvazi said.

"Very well."

One by one the jihadi prisoners were marched out into the open field. Each man came out of the tent blindfolded with his hands shackled behind his back.

"Are you going to kill us?" one of the prisoners asked.

"Shut up and do as you're told," came the reply from a QF operative. The man shifted his focus toward Omid.

"What about the other ten? You want them brought out now?"

"No, absolutely not. Dr. Ahvazi specifically requested only half the group for the first experiment. The other ten will be brought out this evening, during a second round. We must test during both day and night conditions."

In the open fields south of Idlib, there stood numerous orchards where olive trees grew abundantly. Olive growing was the lifeblood of the local economy. The owner of the orchard where they stood had been an ally of the jihadist rebels killed by the QF during battle. His land included huge tracts of open fields. In between the fields were vast rows of olive trees. All the land belonged to the QF now. Without water and proper care, the precious trees on this farm would soon be dead.

"Take these ten and divide them into two groups of five. Tie each man to a tree, in a straight line. The first group goes to the northern edge of the orchard; the second, to the southern edge," Omid told the QF operative.

"Do we keep the blindfolds?" the QF operative asked.

"Yes, and remember, one man to one tree, in a straight line," Omid said before calling Dr. Ahvazi. "Sir, are you sure you want to do this out in the open? We have no control over environmental conditions. Plus, the sun is not good for—"

"I know about the effects of the sun on our agent, dear Omid.

This is exactly what I want, *khhhh*. To test the way our QF brothers might deploy the virus in the real world. Let's get moving. I don't expect these men to bite as hard as the chimps," Dr. Ahvazi said.

Omid accompanied the QF operatives walking the prisoners. The man with the obsidian eyes was blindfolded. The prisoner was taken to the northern edge of the orchard. The QF operatives tied him to an olive tree.

"Why are you doing this? Why don't you just kill us already?" the prisoner protested in Arabic.

"No one is going to kill you. Just stand still for a few minutes, and it'll be over before you can count to ten," the QF translator replied.

"What will?"

"I guess we'll both find out together," the QF translator said jokingly. They moved on to the other prisoners. When it was over, there were five men in orange jumpsuits tied to five olive trees on both the northern and southern edge of the orchard. It was a strange scene, not that different from an ISIS video. A QF operative then turned back to Omid.

"We're ready."

"Very well. Clear the area, back to your barracks," Omid said.

"What do you mean? We have to stand here and observe. What if one of the prisoners escapes?" the QF operative objected.

Omid called Dr. Ahvazi on the radio. There was an awkward silence for several minutes. Finally, the radio came to life once again. This time it was General Kalantari barking orders.

"All QF personnel, clear the area around the orchard and report back to your barracks at once. The only people who'll remain outside will be the men in the biohazard suits."

Ten minutes later, General Kalantari faced Dr. Ahvazi. They were standing underneath the afternoon sun, a hundred meters from the tree line. "Are you sure we'll be okay at this distance?"

"Relax. There's no wind, and the virus does not normally spread through the air. Use your binoculars. This should be an interesting show, *ghoolp*."

Both men brought their binoculars up. Dr. Ahvazi gave the orders through the radio to commence. Within thirty seconds, two men appeared outside. Omid and another technician from the RCERID, Sohrab, each wore a yellow biohazard suit, blue gloves, and a white headcovering. Tight-fitting plastic goggles covered their eyes. A mask covered their mouth with two external air filters. Duct tape was used to seal the blue gloves to the suit. The same process was repeated at the point where the suit came in contact with their combat boots. Omid held an aerosol canister in his right hand, ready to begin. He seemed unaffected by the tragedy that befell Mohsen during the last experiment in the RCERID.

"On my command. *Ya'Ali amir al-mu'minin, Ya'Ali amir al-mu'minin*," General Kalantari said. *Ali, commander of the faithful.*

Upon hearing this phrase, Omid moved toward the first prisoner in the row. He stepped on the white chalk line indicating he was exactly sixty centimeters away from the target. His right hand pointed the canister directly toward the face. He mouthed a three-word phrase slowly in English as he sprayed.

"Trick or treat."

It took exactly two seconds to verbalize the phrase. That's how long his index finger remained on the valve. There was no wind; otherwise, the calculations from the lab would've been thrown off. The subject's eyes were covered. He sneezed twice and wiggled his nose. Omid remained in place to make sure the target breathed in the Marburg-filled mist of blood. Omid moved down the line, repeating the same action until all the prisoners had consumed exactly two seconds' worth of blood spray. When Omid was done, he moved down to the southern edge of the orchard with his assistant. The phrase "trick or treat" was used once again, this time to count off one second. The solution in this canister contained twice the concentration of the virus. Fearing that it might not be possible to spray someone in the face for two seconds, Dr. Ahvazi wanted to see results of exposure at one second.

When he finished spraying the last man, Omid cleaned the prisoner's face like all the others. This was to prevent the subjects from realizing they had been sprayed with blood, a realization that could lead to panic. Now it was time to wait. The first symptoms were expected in eight days. In the meantime, the prisoners would be cared for with ample food and rest. There was no need to transport them to prison. They would stay at the nearby farmhouse belonging to the deceased owner of the property. The only thing not allowed was to escape. There was no telling what kind of havoc an uncontrolled Marburg outbreak could cause in the Syrian countryside. A direct order was issued by General Kalantari to hunt down and kill any Marburg-exposed prisoner who escaped. Dr. Ahvazi flew back to Tehran with General Kalantari that evening. His meeting the following day could spell disaster for the RCERID.

28. SUPREME COUNCIL FOR NATIONAL SECURITY MEETING ROOM, TEHRAN, IRAN

October 17

The oval table in the center of the room had a teacup and plate in front of every chair. Small bottles of water sat next to each teacup. An eighty-inch Samsung LED TV hung on the wall behind the oval table for slide shows. This was the main meeting room of the Iranian Supreme Council for National Security, known as the SCNS. Similar in function to the American National Security Council, the SCNS was the main national security decision-making body in Iran. The statutory members of this body included representatives from all branches of the Iranian government. Among these were the Iranian president, head of the Judiciary, and speaker of the Iranian Parliament, in addition to the high-ranking officers of the Iranian military and intelligence community.

Ordinarily, the SCNS secretary, appointed to his position by Supreme Leader Mashhadi, ran the meetings. The SCNS building itself was located on Azerbaijan Street, overlooking Supreme Leader Mashhadi's compound on one side. When the double doors opened, only four men entered the room, however. Another odd detail about this meeting was its timing. The clock on the wall indicated that it was ten past one in the morning. The participants had gone to great lengths to keep this meeting secret. Once all four men were seated, General Kalantari was the first to speak.

"*Besmillah Rahman-e Rahim*, pardon me if I sound a bit tired. I just returned from Syria. I'll start by thanking Supreme Leader Mashhadi for attending at this late hour. My thanks also to you, Minister Ansari and Ayatollah Kazemi."

"Very well, Vahid. I'd like to get back to bed before the sun comes up," Supreme Leader Mashhadi said, stifling a yawn. The eighty-two-year-old cleric rarely stayed up past ten and was cranky. The chief of the QF continued without missing a beat.

"I called this meeting to inform all of you that I've finalized the target. A small town in California by the name of Pine Valley has been chosen as ground zero. Since the effects of this virus are the work of the devil, the operation will be referred to by the code phrase *Amaliat-e Entegham-e Sheitan*." *Operation Devil's Vengeance.*

"Okay, Vahid, now that you have your fancy code phrase, can you hurry up and get to the point?"

The QF chief tried hard not to let Supreme Leader Mashhadi's interruptions get the best of him. The old man had grown impatient over the years.

"As I was saying, Pine Valley is a small town in California with a population of one thousand five hundred, quite isolated from nearby urban centers. Once the initial outbreak spreads, the American CDC should be able to contain it. If they quarantine Pine Valley in time, the only people who'll die will be its unfortunate inhabitants."

"And you think the Americans will accept this without retaliation?" The words were spoken by Ali Ansari, the chief of the MOIS.

"That's beside the point. This operation is meant to be payback for their interference in our missile program. They killed our top missile engineers. We'll kill about a thousand people in a small town of little consequence. I think that's fair."

"This operation is suicidal for the regime. The Americans will surely retaliate," the MOIS chief reiterated.

"Only if they know who did it. My assault team will fly

the virus to Mexico City using a diplomatic pouch. From there, they'll drive north to a safe house in Tijuana. They'll cross into the US on foot."

"What happens on the other side of the border?" the MOIS chief asked.

"A Hezbollah cell will leave a vehicle with supplies and weapons for their drive to Pine Valley. When they finish their assignment, they'll drive back the same way to the safe house in Tijuana. They'll be back in Tehran before anyone knows what happened."

"Do you think the Americans are stupid? This virus is tropical. It does not grow on the trees in California," Ayatollah Kazemi, head of the Khorasan Foundation, said with a chuckle.

"That's a problem for them to struggle with. Perhaps an African tourist on vacation traveled to this town. Or perhaps an American who had recently traveled to Africa drove through. The point is, it'll be almost impossible for them to pin this on us as long as my assault team can get in and out as planned."

"What if they don't?" Ali Ansari asked.

"What if the sun does not come up tomorrow? What if my brother was my sister? We can't base the regime's security policies on fears and a series of what-ifs."

"What is your method of attack?" Supreme Leader Mashhadi wanted to know.

"Praise be to Allah, Dr. Ahvazi says the best way to do this is with a spray. The virus lives longer in a blood solution. We plan to have several canisters filled with blood—"

"Blood? How do you expect to spray people with blood and not have them call the police immediately?" the MOIS chief asked.

"The Americans have a holiday called Halloween. It is similar to our own *Ghashogh Zani* tradition on the evening of *Chaharshanbeh Suri*. The Americans wear costumes, knocking door to door for food. Our research indicates that many of the costumes deal with scary monsters and killers. It is the perfect opportunity for my assault team to dress up and spray people with the blood. American companies even manufacture cans of fake blood spray. Our special equipment group will produce an exact replica for the tainted blood solution."

"What about your men? Won't they become infected during this ritual?" The supreme leader asked.

"That's the beauty of Halloween. My men can dress up as health workers, allowing them to wear real biohazard suits that no one will question."

"This leaves a very small window to carry out the attack," the supreme leader said.

"Indeed, about three to four hours on the evening of Halloween."

"What day is Halloween celebrated this year?" the supreme leader asked.

"The Americans celebrate Halloween every year on October 31."

"October 31, why, that's only—" the supreme leader said.

"Exactly two weeks away."

"Is the mixture ready?"

"Dr. Ahvazi assures me it will be shortly. We're awaiting test results from our latest experiment."

"What about a vaccine or cure?" Ali Ansari asked.

"There is none in the world at the moment. I've asked Dr. Ahvazi and his team to work on one," General Kalantari said.

"We're going to release this thing without a cure?" Ali Ansari asked.

"If African countries such as Uganda can contain Marburg outbreaks and prevent its spread to the whole world, surely the Americans will not have a problem doing the same," General Kalantari replied.

"Very well, Haj Kalantari. You have my full blessing to proceed with the attack on this infidel holiday of Halloween. Ayatollah Kazemi will provide all the funding you need for this operation from the proceeds of his foundation. I'm sure he won't mind, now that his investments have topped twenty billion," the supreme leader declared before Ayatollah Kazemi could raise an objection. "Not a single dollar from Operation Devil's Vengeance should appear on the official budget," he said as he stood up to leave. With the funding issues out of the way, it was time to eliminate the pest who had killed Yahya.

29. RESEARCH CENTER FOR EMERGING AND REEMERGING INFECTIOUS DISEASES, AKANLU, IRAN

October 17

D r. Ahvazi jiggled the knob several times. No matter how hard he tried, the door to his office would not open. After two kicks and a slew of obscenities, he remembered the keyless entry system. The QF had installed a biometric lock on all doors before his trip to Syria. He placed his index finger on the scanner. Before entering, he shouted down the hall for service.

"Will someone bring me a pot of tea, *khhhh*? Make it extra black."

After arranging his caffeine fix, Dr. Ahvazi perched himself on the sofa. The QF helicopter had delivered him straight from Imam Khomeini Airport the prior evening. There had been little opportunity to sleep in Idlib, and fatigue had crept up on the RCERID director. He was grateful for the opportunity to rest as he elevated his feet on the other end of the sofa. Sleep got the best of him seconds later. He woke to the dreadful ringing that ripped through his ears. He stared at the office phone with intense hatred before hurling a cushion and shouting obscenities. The phone fell off the desk as he stared at the ceiling.

"Dr. Ahvazi, can you hear me?"

"What?" Dr. Ahvazi replied to the assistant who had just entered his office.

"Your tea is ready."

"What the hell took you so long, *ghoolp*?"

"You sent everyone to Syria. Farshad and I are the only ones here, besides the guards."

"Very well, put the tea down and leave."

The assistant placed the teapot and glass on his desk. Dr. Ahvazi was not done with the man.

"On second thought, bring me some dates. I seem to have lost my energy."

The assistant nodded before turning to grab the phone off the floor on his way out. Dr. Ahvazi spun in his chair several times before burying his head in his hands. Just when he thought things could not get worse, his phone rang once again. He stared at it for several seconds before picking up.

"What is it?"

"Sir, Akbar Shadi and his delegation are here. They just pulled in through the gate."

"Who's here?"

"Akbar Shadi, the deputy assistant to the minister of health."

"Fffffuck! I'd forgotten all about that. Try to stall them in the lobby for a few minutes. I need to wash my face in order to wake up."

Dr. Ahvazi blew on his tea to cool it down. He needed caffeine more than anything else at the moment. After emptying the glass, he made his way to a small sink. As he stared at the mirror on the wall, he barely recognized himself. His eyelids were droopy, and his complexion was pale. He managed to throw some cold water on his face before three knocks in rapid succession grabbed his attention. The RCERID director wiped his face and walked across the room to open the door. His assistant and a few strangers were standing outside.

"Javad Ahvazi, a pleasure to see you again," Akbar Shadi said with a shit-eating grin.

"You're too kind. The pleasure is all mine."

"I hope I didn't arrive at a bad time. I'm on a tight schedule. If you don't mind, I'd like to get the inspection out of the way so I can examine your books."

"Absolutely. Let's walk over to the labs. It shouldn't take more than an hour. Excuse me for just one second."

Dr. Ahvazi proceeded to walk over to his assistant, whispering in his ear, "Go to the black vault in the archive room. On the third shelf, I've saved a presentation for these men on a thumb drive. Prepare the conference room before we return."

"Yes, sir," the assistant replied.

A few minutes later, Dr. Ahvazi walked over with the group to the labs. After forty-five minutes, they reemerged outside.

"I hope you're satisfied, Akbar. If you don't mind, we can go back to our conference room. I've prepared a presentation about the types of experiments we carry out here at the RCERID."

"Before we go back to your conference room, where is everybody?"

"I've sent my personnel out on field assignments to our various provinces, *khhhh*. Can't afford to have everyone here when there are infectious outbreaks around the country," Dr. Ahvazi declared, trying his best to keep a straight face.

"How about a tour of that building over there?" Akbar Shadi asked, pointing at the drab building at the far end of the facility. It was the location of the hot chamber. "Why is there tape around the perimeter?"

"*Ehhem*, those buildings are currently being renovated. Perhaps another time."

"We're used to walking around buildings under renovation. Surely there are no harmful pathogens around?"

"Of course not. I'll make the necessary arrangements, *ghoolp*." After calling Farshad to remove the tapes, Dr. Ahvazi walked into the hot chamber with his guests. Akbar Shadi and his men were each handed a mask before entering. The deputy assistant health minister studied his surroundings, taking great care not to touch anything. His entourage followed his lead.

"What kind of testing takes place in here?" Akbar Shadi asked.

"The same tests that I showed you in the other rooms. There is nothing special about this lab," Dr. Ahvazi explained.

"What are these metal posts doing here? And where is the equipment for this lab?"

"As I explained, this lab and the one next door are undergoing renovation, *ghoolp*. We've ordered a new set of equipment for this room."

"I'm sure you've kept the receipts of the purchase orders?"

"The orders were placed with companies abroad."

"Not a problem, we have employees at the ministry who speak all the main European languages. We also have a few who speak Mandarin, Japanese, Tagalog, and Vietnamese," Akbar Shadi said with another one of his detestable grins.

"I see. I'll have my assistant locate those records and send them to you without delay," Dr. Ahvazi said, trying hard to hide his disdain for Akbar Shadi.

"What about the metal posts?"

Dr. Ahvazi needed time to think. He had not anticipated the question. He casually walked the room in search of his answer. "*Ehhem*, the metal posts are for a new type of experiment one of our scientists has come up with. I forget exactly how he explained it. It's a new method of—"

"Not to worry, make sure to send me a full report of his experimental design along with the other documents," Akbar Shadi said with the utmost seriousness this time. "Now let's get back upstairs for your presentation."

Ten minutes later, they were all seated in a small conference room located next to Dr. Ahvazi's office. The RCERID director turned off the lights in preparation for his slide show. As soon as he started talking, Akbar Shadi cut him off.

"It's come to my attention that one of the scientists under your supervision recently defected to Brazil. Interestingly, he gave a press conference claiming the Iranian government is producing a new biological weapon."

"The man was a disgruntled employee. I fired him for incompetence, and he was angry. The press conference was given as revenge against the RCERID and the Iranian government," Dr. Ahvazi replied without hesitation.

"I find it strange that his allegation was made just before two other members of your staff were quarantined at Vali-Asr Hospital. Rumor has it that both men are infected with a deadly pathogen. Since Roozbeh Navabi is no longer with us, I'll have to arrange a talk with the bedridden fellows in Tehran. Are they also faking their illness after you declared them incompetent?"

Dr. Ahvazi's blood boiled as his face flushed. He sensed smoke emanating from his ears. After losing two scientists and two technicians on the Marburg project, he was at his wit's end. Who would blame him for picking up the blue pen, mere centimeters from his wrist, to stab Akbar Shadi in the eye?

"Now, now. It's not becoming of a man in your position to be so petty. You can talk to my bedridden subordinates whenever you like. I'm sure you won't hear anything different than what I've told you so far."

The tension in the room prompted the other participants to shift uneasily in their seats. After an awkward silence, Dr. Ahvazi finished his presentation without further interruption. When the lights came on, Akbar Shadi thanked his host, declaring his intention to return to Tehran immediately. On his way out the door, he faced his host one last time.

"Don't forget. You owe me some receipts, purchase orders, and an experimental design report."

"*Kose Nanat khhhh ehhem khhhh,*" Dr. Ahvazi mumbled. *Your mother's pussy.*

"What's that?"

"Have a safe trip."

"Thank you."

Dr. Ahvazi stormed to his office in anger. He locked the door before calling General Kalantari.

"*Ya'Allah,* did you miss me already? We spoke only a few hours ago."

"I don't have time for bullshit. Akbar Shadi was here today. I just wrapped up a meeting from hell. They're asking questions that could cost both of us dearly," Dr. Ahvazi explained in a panicked voice.

"Oh yes, I forgot he was visiting you today."

"You knew about this? Why didn't you put a stop to it?"

"I can't just stop a high-ranking health ministry official from inspecting one of his own facilities. Besides, I figured you'd be able to handle it."

"For your information, Akbar Shadi is planning to shut down the RCERID. You know what that means, your precious Marburg program will not see the light of day."

There was silence on the other end.

"Hello, Haj Kalantari?"

"Yeah, I'm still here. Are you sure about this? He told you he wants to shut down the RCERID?"

"Those were his exact words. He said the rumors of the RCERID's involvement with biological weapons were an embarrassment to the minister of health and may cost him his job. Therefore, he had no choice but to shut us down."

"Well, we'll just see if we can change his mind."

"What are you going to do? Haj Kalantari, *ghoolp*? You still there?"

30. LES CÔTES-DE-CORPS, FRANCE

October 18

The sun forced his eyelids open. Outside the window, the snowcapped peaks were a charming contrast to the leafy valley below. Nestled in the French Alps, the town of Les Côtes-de-Corps was barely a two-hour drive south of Geneva. She had driven nervously after the shoot-out in Studio Twenty. Janusz had slept while Kim navigated the winding roads to the safe house with the help of GPS. Halfway between Lyon and Marseilles, it was the perfect location to lie low. They had spent the past eight days hiking, reading, eating, and resting. They occasionally drove to the town of Corps for food.

Janusz was growing restless by the day, but there was no sense in pushing forward without fresh intelligence on Dr. Ahvazi's next move. The fiasco at Studio Twenty had come as a surprise. The Iranians always seemed one step ahead. What else did they know about his efforts to stop them? He had used proper tradecraft yet failed to protect another source. It was eating him alive.

Janusz peered at the valley below after walking out to get fresh air. The blue waters from the nearby Lac du Sautet were partially visible. The high-pitched whistle of the Alpine chough, an indigenous bird, shifted his focus to the calming sounds of nature. The icy crispness of the air rejuvenated his senses. Strolling down the pebbled path, he heard the distinct sounds of another pair of feet from behind. Turning abruptly, Janusz pointed the pistol at her face.

"Easy, boy, this is no time to shoot your load prematurely," Kim said half in jest.

"Jesus, Kim, I thought you were sleeping."

"I was. You have a phone call. It's Tony."

"Lovely, what does he want?"

"You can ask him yourself," she said, handing over the phone.

"Tony, shouldn't you be sleeping?"

"I'm in no mood for jokes. We have too much going on."

"Sorry, how can I help?"

"Michele Camus, chief of DGSE, called CIA Director Kellerman five hours ago. French intelligence intercepted a call between the CEO of ProtoVax, a pharmaceutical located in Lyon, and a man who identified himself as a representative of the Iranian Pasteur Institute. The Iranian offered to make a fifty-million-euro investment in ProtoVax in exchange for a twenty percent stake. He agreed to meet them in Lyon four days from now. You won't have far to travel from where you're standing."

"Let me guess, ProtoVax is developing a cure for Marburg?"

"Not just developing. They're approved for human trials. We believe ProtoVax doesn't expect to make money on the Marburg treatment. The media exposure surrounding a cure for the world's deadliest virus is what they're really after. The cash infusion from Iran could help speed up the timeline of bringing this drug to market."

"Do the executives at ProtoVax have a clue about Iran's motives?"

"They don't care; money is all that counts. DGSE, on the other hand, knows where this is headed. That's why they contacted the CIA to propose a joint operation."

"So nice of them."

"Listen up, they want to work with the US government to recruit the man who is headed to Lyon. The CIA immediately briefed the SSCI. That's how I heard about it, a call from Senator Donald Patrick."

"Who are the Iranians sending?"

"We don't know yet."

"Come again?"

"The man on the phone used a voice synthesizer and a fake name we've never heard before. When ProtoVax offered to pick him up at the airport, he declined."

"What's the CIA going to do?"

"They're waiting for the French to take the lead. Once DGSE figures out the identity of the Iranian, they'll call back."

"By then it'll be too late. I'm sure he's not sticking around for dinner. What's our plan?"

"You're our plan. You need to get this guy before DGSE does. Time is not on our side here."

"Great plan, how am I going to do that?"

"That's entirely up to you. I'm sure you'll come up with something."

"Thanks, Tony."

"You bet. Don't worry, we got your back!" Tony said before hanging up.

"What was that all about?" Kim asked.

"French Intel informed the CIA that a representative of the Iranian Pasteur Institute is coming to Lyon. The Iranian wants to collaborate with ProtoVax, a French pharmaceutical on the verge of a breakthrough with Marburg."

"Who's coming?"

"DGSE and CIA don't know, which means neither do we."

"When are they coming?"

"October 22."

"Well, at least they're coming to France. Lyon is not that far."

"We don't exactly know who we're searching for."

"Neither do the French, which gives us an advantage."

"How do you figure?"

"Because they don't have Reza," she said with a wide grin.

"Reza?"

"He is head of the Lyon Islamic Chamber of Commerce. It's a Shia-run outfit established by Reza's family after they arrived from Iran. The family is involved with exports and imports."

"Where exactly are you headed with this biography?"

"Given his family connections, the MOIS picked him to run both their overt and covert operations in France under the cover of the chamber. The point of this biography, dear Janusz, is that if Iran is sending someone to Lyon, Reza will be the first to know."

"And why will Reza tell you what he knows?"

"Long story. I met him before my first job with the FBI. I was at a club in Lyon many moons ago. He has a thing for blondes. The rest is history."

"That still doesn't mean he'd help us out on this thing."

"No, I don't think you understand. When I say he has a thing for blondes, I mean a deep-seated fetish. From the beginning, he played the role of the submissive. He wants to be humiliated by a blond woman. At the time, I thought it was cool to have my own sex slave."

"Yeah, no shit."

"It wasn't until after I joined the bureau that I recognized the advantage of the relationship. I never formally recruited him to work for the US government. I give him orders and he obeys."

"So if I understand this correctly, the MOIS's top asset in France is your personal bitch?"

"Such is the power of the vagina. Surprisingly, the more I put him at risk, the more of a thrill he gets out of it."

"What a sick bastard he is," Janusz commented sarcastically.

"It's not that bad. I kind of enjoy wielding my powers over him. You're the first person in the world I've mentioned this to, so please keep your mouth shut."

"Don't worry. I kind of wish I didn't know this side of you. Now I'm apprehensive about becoming your next victim, I mean slave."

"You're quite safe. I never mix business and pleasure."

"We'd better get to Lyon and figure things out before our man arrives from Iran."

"Right behind you."

◆ ◆ ◆

The drive to Lyon took just under three hours. When they arrived, Kim dropped Janusz off in front of a bus stop by the river. She then made a right turn onto Rue d'Ypres, a narrow backstreet. She drove up the winding street toward the cemetery on the Croix Rousse. The street had high walls with a chain-link fence on top. Near the summit of Rue d'Ypres, she turned left into a secluded parking lot. There were five cars parked there. One end of the lot was empty. She parked the car under a tree before calling Reza with instructions on how to find her. When their business was complete an hour later, Kim drove down Rue d'Ypres, where Janusz was waiting for her by the same bus stop.

"What now?" Janusz asked, entering the vehicle.

"Now we grab lunch."

"And then?"

"And then we wait."

"Wait for what?"

"Our next appointment at the Golden Head Park nearby."

"How did the meeting go?"

"He got into the car, excited to see me as usual. I shoved his face in my boobs, which got him even more juiced up. I asked him if an important visitor was expected from Tehran in the days ahead. He said that there was. I ordered him to bring me the details of this man's visit as soon as possible. He's meeting me on a secluded bench in the Golden Head Park at four this afternoon. Don't worry. He'll deliver the details we need."

"He doesn't even ask why?" Janusz was curious to know.

"Like I said, he enjoys the risk."

"You realize the Iranians may kill this poor bastard one day?"

"That's why I try not to use him unless absolutely necessary. At the moment, I don't see any other way to attack this problem, do you?"

She was right. After lunch, they headed to the Golden Head Park. Janusz stayed hidden while Kim met her contact at four. At four-thirty, she emerged with an envelope in her hand.

"Here you go. I bet neither the DGSE nor the CIA has this information."

"Only because they don't have you, Kim," Janusz said while opening the envelope. There was a travel itinerary inside. "Holy fuck!"

"I knew you'd be happy," Kim said.

"I don't believe it. Our mystery man is Dr. Ahvazi. Here's what I'm thinking. We'll grab this bastard and take him back to the safe house."

"It's your call. What if he doesn't cooperate?"

"There are ways, my dear Kim. There are many ways."

"That's what I'm afraid of. Your reputation in this arena precedes you."

"Says the woman who uses a personal sex slave for information," he said.

Kim fell silent as they walked toward the car. *Which technique will make Dr. Ahvazi sing like a canary?* Janusz thought.

31. OLIVE FARM, SOUTHERN IDLIB, SYRIA

October 21

"Sohrab, get the tranquilizer. Quick!" Omid screamed.

"You son of a whore, fuck your mother!" the patient cursed.

"I'm choking, khhhhhhh, help me," Omid cried, trying to break the grip of the powerful man.

Sohrab rushed toward the bed holding the syringe. Without hesitation, Sohrab plunged the syringe into the IV bag feeding the patient. Seconds later, the patient slackened his grip on Omid's neck.

Sohrab pulled his colleague back to safety.

"What's wrong with him? Has he lost his mind?" Omid asked.

"It's the virus. It transforms people into raving lunatics. This one here had the shiniest obsidian eyes. Now look at him," Sohrab said as Omid massaged his own neck.

"I have to check your suit. If it's punctured, there's a high probability you're infected," Sohrab warned. They were both wearing their yellow biohazard suits with white headcovering.

"Okay, but I'm updating Dr. Ahvazi on what's happening here as soon as you're done."

Omid sprinted to the makeshift decontamination room. His suit was sprayed with disinfectant before he was able to strip and take a shower to cleanse his body of the pathogens. Sohrab

checked the suit for small punctures as Omid waited frantically for the news. Moments later, Omid was relieved that his
suit had not been punctured. After grabbing a bite to eat, Omid
made his way to the communication center. The guard waved
him through upon checking his badge. The room was filled with
electronic equipment, including tall computer servers, a cluster
of multicolored cables, and monitors. A uniformed QF captain
finally acknowledged him.

"I need to speak with Dr. Ahvazi at once."

"Regarding what?"

"I'm Omid Reyshahri, his personal assistant from the
RCERID. I don't have to answer your questions. Where is he?"

"The QF is responsible for all security matters on this base.
You have no choice but to deal with me if you want to reach Dr.
Ahvazi."

"I'm in charge of administrative affairs for Operation Devil's
Vengeance in his absence, you fool. Now get him on the line!"

"Shhhh, keep your voice down. Dr. Ahvazi is on a special
mission abroad. We don't talk about Devil's Vengeance over the
phone. I'll arrange for him to contact you when he returns. Now
go back to your barracks."

After the futile attempt to contact Dr. Ahvazi, Omid headed
to the cafeteria, where Sohrab was munching on pastries. Omid
suddenly remembered the cell phone the general had given him
when he arrived.

"Any luck reaching him?" Sohrab asked.

"No, Dr. Ahvazi is no longer in Iran. We'll have to observe the
patients ourselves and relay the test results when he returns."

"I'm warning you. It's not pretty in those rooms. The patients are all falling apart. They look like aliens."

Omid and Sohrab went through the routine one more time.
After donning several layers, they zipped up their suits before
wearing their masks.

"Let's start with Tariq, the one who *had* the obsidian eyes,"
Sohrab said.

As they approached Tariq's room, neither man was too eager

to walk back in. Omid pushed the door wide-open. Tariq was out cold after being injected with the tranquilizer.

"What the hell is going on with him?" Omid asked.

"I was here yesterday. He's been bleeding profusely through his anus. It's not just any old kind of blood either."

"What do you mean?"

"The blood coming out of his ass is black, like tar. You've never seen anything like it before."

"Intestinal lining?"

"Precisely, the virus destroys the intestines, causing the lining to flake off. Unfortunately, the intestines come out of the anus through the blood. Check out his skin."

Omid examined the patient's chest. It was covered with blood-filled blisters. As they stood in silence, Sohrab pointed toward something Omid was not expecting to see. Tariq's nipples were bleeding. That was not the worst of it. Tariq was also bleeding from the sides of his mouth while his eyes produced blood-filled tears. He resembled a monster out of a horror film.

"How the hell did all this happen?" Omid asked.

"I've been reviewing the literature. Marburg pulverizes collagen. As you would imagine, the skin dies and then liquefies. This causes drops of blood to ooze out of every pore in the body. It's as if the virus was put on earth to destroy the human race. Marburg is eager to infect any human that tries to ease the pain of the dying."

"He looks like a ghoul now."

"I'm surprised he's still alive. Take a gander at this." Sohrab pointed to the monitor next to the bed. The computer readouts indicated Tariq had a fever of forty-one degrees centigrade. His blood pressure was seventy over forty.

Sohrab continued. "That's just one of his myriad problems. Marburg destroyed his major organs. His last urine test indicated his kidneys are no longer functioning. There is something very creepy about this virus, Omid. It sends shivers down my body."

"What do you mean?"

"I mean it's not just the code name of this project. The virus is the work of the devil himself. It's evil."

"You're just tired, Sohrab. Don't let your imagination get the best of you."

"Am I? Check this out." Sohrab walked cautiously toward Tariq. He was hesitant to touch the body as if expecting it to attack all of a sudden. Sohrab placed his gloved hand over Tariq's face as he gently opened the eyes. Omid shuffled backward in fear and held on to a wall to keep from falling.

"I don't need to see any more. Close them, close them," Omid said in shock. Tariq's brilliant obsidian eyes had disappeared. Marburg had destroyed the eyeballs, leaving them filled with blood.

"Worst of all is this," Sohrab said as he pulled the sheet completely off Tariq to reveal his lower body. "His testicles have putrefied. The virus has a special love for the male reproductive organs. It represents the destruction of mankind. His balls are swollen. They turned black as you see here."

"That's enough, I can't take any more. I'm going to my room to get started on our report. I'll enter the data on a spreadsheet. I want to make charts and graphs of the test results for Dr. Ahvazi," Omid said.

"Does anyone back at the RCERID know what's happening here? Perhaps we should send an email with pictures to the others?" Sohrab said.

"There's no one left at the RCERID except security. The entire team is scattered on this base with us."

"I'll email Dr. Ahvazi."

"You can't. QF security won't allow it. They're afraid of American snooping. No communication of any kind with the outside world except by courier!"

"We need to put our data on a thumb drive and send it to the RCERID to be archived. All our findings are stored on this base at the moment. You know what this could mean if something goes wrong," Sohrab said.

"I'll take care of it right after my smoke break," Omid said, walking toward the decontamination room.

After a shower and change of clothes, Omid stood outside in the cool evening air sending a text with his new phone. He then placed a cigarette in his mouth and struck the lighter with his thumb. Seconds later, he was puffing smoke into the night air. It was all he could do to keep calm after the macabre scene in the examination room. Omid stared up at the moon visible from behind the clouds. For the first time he could remember, he was uneasy about their experiments and its implications. At the very least, he was going to send their data to a safe place for storage. A spark in the night sky caught his eye. Seconds later, the cigarette fell out of his mouth. As the object got closer, he ran for cover. The fireball blinded him instantly.

32. QODS FORCE HEADQUARTERS, QASR-E FIRUZEH DISTRICT, TEHRAN, IRAN

October 22

He grabbed his cell phone off the table. To his surprise, there was an unread message from the previous evening. Through his glasses, he read the short text on the encrypted cell phone:

The eggs have hatched, and the chicks are out. Incubation was faster than expected.

He read the message several times to make sure there was no mistake. It had to be accurate. His personal spy on the inside would not have sent it otherwise. He had to act fast to make the deadline for Halloween. There was no telling if Dr. Ahvazi would return in time.

Looking out the window of his office, he stared at the barren hills of Dowshan Tappeh in the distance. A bit closer, Hamas foot soldiers trained on the dusty range. Their minds filled with rage and their hearts filled with hate, they released their anger at the mock targets that dotted the landscape. Surrounded by walls, the entire compound was shielded from the prying eyes of Tehran residents. The QF chief gazed at a few pictures on an end table next to the window. Most of them were snapshots of fellow soldiers who had died during the bloody war against Iraq. Friends that were luckier than himself, rewarded by martyrdom on the battlefield against the enemy.

One picture stood out from the rest. It was a picture of him surrounded by old friends. All of them killed years ago on the front. It brought tears to his eyes every time he stared at their faces. If only they had access to better weapons back then. If only they'd been able to build their own weapons. If only they'd had Marburg back then, Saddam Hussein would never have dared to attack their country. General Kalantari was determined more than ever to push forward. He picked up the receiver from his desk and made the call. Twenty minutes later, his special unit assault team commander entered.

"*Besmillah*, the moment of truth is here. I just received word from Syria that our latest tests are a success. You're to take a chopper down to the RCERID immediately and extract the package for America," General Kalantari said. Although he could not be sure, the reaction on the commander's face was not what he expected.

"What's the matter? Did you see a ghost? You'll do fine, just go there and bring the package. Remember, you're a soldier of Allah."

"Of course, sir," the commander said. "I thought Dr. Ahvazi and his men were all out of the country."

"They are, but the security and maintenance staff are still there. You're to request access to a building known as lab five. A scientist from the Pasteur Institute here in Tehran will accompany you."

"Does he know what to do?"

"There is not much to do. Dr. Ahvazi left a quantity of the mixture before going on his mission. Everything your companion needs will be at the lab. Our special equipment group downstairs will provide the aerosol canisters for your mission. The canisters are already painted for the Halloween festival. The microbiologist from Pasteur will fill the canisters at the RCERID and explain safe handling instructions. Any questions?"

"No, sir."

General Kalantari felt the need to reassure him again. "Just remember, a mission such as this is a win-win no matter what happens. If you carry it out successfully, the supreme leader himself will recognize you as a hero. If you're killed for some reason, you'll be revered as a martyr of Islam. May Allah give you strength!"

"Thank you, sir," the commander said with a determined look on his face. "I'll deliver the dagger to America's heart."

33. ISLAMIC CHAMBER OF COMMERCE, LYON, FRANCE

October 22

Located in a nondescript stone facade building, the Islamic Chamber of Commerce did not draw much attention. Rue Franklin was a one-way street, with vehicular traffic moving away from the Rhone River. The buildings on this street were at least a hundred years old. Building number 17 was the sixth one from the intersection with Quai Perrache. Janusz passed by a long row of bicycles parked along the side of the street. A group of buttoned-up prep school students emerged from a nearby building, converging on the cobblestoned street without warning. As their numbers grew, they blocked his line of sight to building number 17. The well-dressed high school students minded their own business, although a few glared at Janusz suspiciously. Maybe they were worried he was an undercover policeman.

Not long after, they were engrossed in conversation among themselves, boys and girls engaged in the ageless art of flirtation. He headed over to the group to avoid detection by possible countersurveillance teams. An attractive young brunette began eye-flirting with him. He smiled. She seemed momentarily surprised when he approached and spoke in English. Several of the boys gave him the evil eye, jealous of the intruder who had moved in on their action. None of them dared to interrupt.

"How long are you staying in Lyon? A group of us are going

to a club tonight. Perhaps you'd like to join us?" the beautiful brunette asked with a strong French accent.

"I'm actually here on business and—" As Janusz said these words, a man emerged from number 17 and began walking in his direction. Janusz was silent as his eyes followed the man. Reza had provided a description of Dr. Ahvazi to Kim the day before. The man matched that perfectly. The target was lost in thought as he passed by Janusz on the other side of the street. He walked toward Quai Perrache.

"Please continue, you're here on business and?" The brunette picked up where Janusz left off.

"I'm sorry to be rude, but I have to leave," Janusz said once his target was down the street. Janusz followed in the same direction.

"What? At least give me your number so I can text you," she shouted after him.

When Janusz reached the corner of Quai Perrache, the man had crossed the street. Janusz ran after him in haste, narrowly avoiding a collision with oncoming traffic. The street was divided by a tree-lined median, full of parked cars. At the moment, his target was about to enter a Renault hatchback parked on the median. It was too late to grab him. Janusz locked eyes with Kim, standing several meters away. She immediately headed toward the target. As Janusz crossed the street, there was a gentle tap on his shoulder. He turned to see who it was.

"*Monsieur, nous devons vous parler,*" one of two men said, flashing a badge.

"Sorry, I don't speak French. I'm from Australia," Janusz said innocently.

"We need to speak with you. I'm Claude, and this is my partner, Arnaud. We're with the General Directorate for Internal Security."

Janusz froze in place, not certain what they wanted.

"Can we have a word with you, sir?" Claude demanded.

"By all means, how can I help you gentlemen?"

"Not here, please follow me," Claude said, and pointed to

an unmarked car on the other side of the street. Janusz took a furtive glance around. There were too many vehicles and pedestrians to make a clean getaway at the moment.

"Very well."

The three men walked quietly toward the corner of Rue Gailleton and Quai Perrache. They crossed the street, where Claude came to a halt next to a four-door white Peugeot sedan. Claude pressed a remote from inside his pant pocket, opening the doors.

Claude gestured to the open backseat door. "Monsieur," he said as Janusz entered. From the other side of the vehicle, Arnauld entered the backseat. At the same moment, Claude walked around the vehicle and entered the car from the front passenger's side. They were now both facing Janusz.

"What is this about?" Janusz asked.

"Sir, can I see your passport?" Claude said.

"Certainly." Janusz handed over an Australian passport.

"Mr. Ian Phillips?" Claude said while leafing through the blue passport with the kangaroo and emu emblem on the cover.

"Yes, that's me."

"How long have you been in France?"

"Four days."

"This stamp shows you were in Zurich."

"Yes, I had business in Zurich before my arrival in France."

"Where have you been staying in France?"

"My company owns a chalet near the town of Corps. I was there till this morning."

"You staying by yourself? Can anyone vouch for you?"

"I'm staying with a female friend."

"What brings you to Lyon today?"

"Shopping. We're running out of food. We also wanted to buy some gifts for friends. Now can you please explain what's going on?"

"Have you also traveled to Geneva recently?"

"Geneva, no. Why?"

"You sure you've not passed through Geneva? Perhaps for an evening, to go dancing?"

"No, I have not. Where are you headed with this line of questioning?"

Claude turned to Arnaud. After a slight pause, Claude broke in once again. "Are you watching the news, Monsieur Phillips?"

"No, I have no interest in the news. I'm here on vacation."

"Well, if you'd watched the news, you would know about the shooting at Studio Twenty in Geneva. Three men were killed and several others injured. We're working closely with the Swiss authorities. Of course, given the proximity of Geneva to Lyon, it's only natural that the suspect may try to hide in this city."

"That's terrible! Was it the Chechen mob?"

Both Frenchmen stared at him silently.

"Perhaps the Albanians?" Janusz suggested without hesitation.

"We don't know yet. The Swiss are still trying to put the pieces together. Which brings us back to you," Arnauld replied suggestively.

"Yes, I'm late for an appointment with my friend, who is probably worried by now. Please get to the point."

"The only clue we have from the Swiss is this," Claude said. He unfolded a computer printout that was hidden in his coat pocket. It was a picture of a man holding a pistol.

"Who is this?" Janusz asked.

"We thought you could tell us?" Claude said

"How so?" Janusz stared at both Frenchmen inquisitively.

"The image was sent by the Swiss this morning. This man is their prime suspect," Claude said, pointing at the picture. "Arnauld and I are in Lyon on a separate matter, however. We need to locate an individual who has traveled here on business. It just so happens that our suspect was supposed to come down the same street where we spotted you. When I recognized your face from this photo, I was certain it could not be a coincidence." The French were apparently just as close to Dr. Ahvazi as he was. They would grab him soon, if they had not already done so.

"So you're telling me you're here for someone else, yet you grabbed me instead because I resemble the man in this photo?"

Janusz replied in anger.

"Something like that. We've got people around the city searching for the other man. Since we've not spotted him yet, we thought it might be good to check in on our other suspect. I just have this feeling that you're somehow connected with all this."

"I can assure you that I'm not the man in your photo. For one thing, his nose is thick, and mine is not. For another, his eyebrows are bushier than mine. I also don't own a pistol, and I have not been to Geneva in years."

"So you say. We need to corroborate your story to be sure. I don't believe in coincidences."

"This is ridiculous. You can't just detain me because I resemble a man in a picture," Janusz said.

"The man in the photo is wanted for a triple murder. We need an hour of your time at the station to take some pictures. The computers will take care of the rest. If there is no match, you're free to leave."

"I don't have time for these games. I'm not the man in the photo. I demand to be released or taken to the Australian consulate at once."

The Frenchmen seemed unsure of themselves now. They obviously did not want a diplomatic incident. On the other hand, they would be foolish to let the Geneva suspect slip through their fingers. Janusz was certain the facial-recognition software would match him to the surveillance photo.

When Claude took out his cell phone, Janusz acted without hesitation. A quick jab with his right elbow smashed Arnaud's head against the backseat window. Claude dropped his phone to reach for something in his coat pocket. Before he could do so, Janusz wrapped his right arm around his neck from the backseat, locking it in with his left hand. Janusz squeezed with all his might, choking the Frenchmen's neck tightly. Claude flailed around, gasping for air. No need to worry, the windows were tinted from the outside. Janusz took his time squeezing Claud's neck until the Frenchman passed out. In the backseat, Arnaud was moving again. Janusz punched him in the face once more before exiting the vehicle.

He closed the door behind him and ran toward Rue Gailleton, divided in half by a small park. Janusz passed several concrete benches placed in front of the waterspouts. He took out his cell phone to contact Kim.

"Where the hell are you, Janusz?"

"No time to explain. Forget about our suspect for now. I'm headed down Rue Gailleton away from the river. The French police are after me. Use the tracker on my phone to meet me in the back alley," he said before checking his tail. Someone was running at full speed toward him. Unfortunately, Arnaud had recovered much faster than expected. Janusz slid the phone in his pocket before taking off. He ran past the memorial at the end of the Rue Gailleton toward Rue de Fleurieu. It was another street with a high cobblestone wall on one side. The other side of the street was lined with shops. Arnaud was closing in rapidly.

"Stop, stop," Arnaud shouted. It would not be long before a uniformed policeman would appear. An outdoor café was several meters ahead, small tables and green chairs on the sidewalk. Janusz crossed the street to avoid a collision. Two women seated outside stared at him running by. A narrow alley to his left emptied into an intersection where three streets converged. Janusz ducked into the alley under a restaurant sign.

He gasped for air. Within seconds, the approaching footsteps of Arnaud reached his ears. Janusz clenched his fist. As soon as Arnaud emerged in the alley, Janusz struck with a right cross. The shot instantly connected with Arnaud's jaw and dropped him to the ground. Arnaud landed with a loud thud and was out cold. Janusz shrugged at the onlookers as he quickly left the scene. Several patrons came out of the restaurant to check on Arnaud, who would probably not be able to talk for a while. In front of Janusz was Rue de la Charite and the Tissue Museum. He veered left, trying hard not to draw attention to himself. He passed a bakery on his left in search of Kim. He continued past several stores, keeping an eye on the next intersection. Any minute now, Kim would emerge to rescue him. Straight ahead was Rue des Ramparts. He breathed a sigh of relief when he spotted the vehicle.

Before Janusz took his next step, he felt a sharp object in his back.

"Ah-ah, no sudden moves, please. Face forward and keep walking."

The voice sounded familiar.

"You fucking Australian, you almost killed me. Keep walking."

Janusz wondered whether Claude would shoot him in the back.

"I have a perfectly good explanation," Janusz said.

"Shut up," Claude yelled.

A boisterous group of men turned the corner in front of them. They had to be North Africans. He waited until they were several meters in front.

"Hey, you fucking Arabs," Janusz said in broken French.

"What are you doing, you idiot? I told you to shut up," Claude said nervously.

"Yes, I'm talking to you cunts," Janusz continued.

The four men gathered around them.

"You have something to say?" one of them shouted as he stood face-to-face with Janusz.

"My friend here says Arabs should stay in North Africa," Janusz said as he pointed to Claude. The group turned to face the Frenchman.

"Well, perhaps he wants to tell us himself," one of the North Africans said.

Claude froze in place. Janusz suddenly struck him in the face. The Frenchman shouted out in pain as he hunched over. The Arabs stared in confusion. Janusz grabbed Claude's head, bringing it toward his knee. The strike knocked him unconscious for the second time. The Arabs were stunned.

"He's a police officer, better run," Janusz said as he ran toward Rue des Ramparts. Kim was still waiting in the car. He opened the door to jump in next to her.

"What the hell happened?" Kim asked.

"I don't want to talk about it. Where is our suspect?"

"On the way to the meeting."

"Let's get on with it before we lose him."

"Not to worry. When I saw you leaving with those men, I placed a tracking device on his vehicle before he drove off."

"Lovely girl, we don't have time to waste. Those guys were DGSI, and they're also looking for Dr. Ahvazi. We need to get to him before they do."

"Roger that," Kim said.

"Where are you going now?" Janusz asked.

"Following the tracking device, of course," she said as she made her way across Gallieni Bridge toward Avenue Leclerc.

34. WHITE HOUSE SITUATION ROOM, WASHINGTON, DC

October 22

"Excellent work, gentlemen! You can all pat yourselves on the back."

"Thank you, Mr. President. The best part is no one can pin this on us," DNI David Schultz declared proudly.

"What's the damage assessment on this, Pete?" the president asked.

"A predator overflight an hour ago indicated the QF camp south of Idlib was completely annihilated. The Russians demolished the adjacent olive farm as well. It was a temporary QF headquarters," General Beck replied.

"Any numbers on casualties?" the president asked.

"Our satellite indicates there were no survivors. The Russians confirmed our observation. The NSA sent a transcript of the Russian reports from Idlib."

"Do they know what's happened?"

"You mean the deception operation, Mr. President?"

"Not that, David. Do the Russians know they've attacked the Iranian QF?"

"Yes, sir. That was about an hour ago. General Zelnikov sent a Spetznaz team to get a ground visual on the damages," the DNI replied.

The president flashed a smile at those seated around the table. The only other person in the room besides himself, David

Shultz, and Peter Beck was the national security adviser, Paul Upman. Outside of this small group, the president did not trust anyone. As an outsider to Washington, President Robert Adkins was constantly under attack by the establishment. To make matters worse, his administration had been subject to damaging leaks, the kind that had never been seen before in Washington. The president opened his briefcase to pull out a long red box, tied at the top with a black bow. After removing the wrapping, he placed the box of chocolates in the middle of the table.

"Gentlemen, I'd been saving these for a special occasion. President Devereaux of France gifted them to me during our last summit in Paris. It's the first time since my inauguration that I feel we've done something worthwhile without interference from the politically correct police. Help yourselves."

"I'd hate to rain on this parade, but you forgot one thing, Mr. President." It was the national security adviser who spoke. Paul Upman folded his hands, glancing around the table.

"What's that, Paul?"

"Congress! The success of this SOCOM deception operation is something the Armed Services Committee will want to hear about."

President Adkins took a moment to consider Paul's warning as he put another piece of chocolate in his mouth. He washed that down with a sip of coffee.

"Fuck 'em!"

"What do you mean, sir?"

"You heard what I said, Paul, fuck 'em. We're not going to tell those assholes anything because the second we do, it'll be on every TV set, website, and newspaper around the world. This town has become a partisan sieve. My opponents will leak this to the press just to get even with me. That means the Russians will know what we did."

"Not necessarily. This whole thing came to fruition because we learned the Russians had broken the encryption of ISIS leadership and were monitoring their conversations. At that point, we transmitted a fake conversation between the ISIS leader and his deputy stating that ISIS was planning an immediate attack on Russian forces from the olive farm in Southern Idlib," Paul said.

"Yeah, so what's your point?" the president asked with palpable irritation.

"The point is the Russians can only be certain they were duped if they learn that ISIS never planned that attack. But the Russians can't do that, sir."

"Why not?"

"Because I authorized General Beck to destroy the ISIS leadership complex right after our fake transmission. The Russians will suspect some sort of foul play, but they'll never be able to put their finger on it."

"What so we tell the Armed Services Committee?"

"Simple, we tell them the clandestine operation used ISIS communication channels as a prelude to a decapitation strike. We leave the Russian angle out of the briefing. This way, the press leak will indicate that our operation was setting up ISIS for elimination. As long as the Russians don't know they were the target, the rest is manageable," the national security adviser declared.

The president took a moment to let the words sink in. "Paul, that's brilliant, just brilliant." The president popped two more chocolates in his mouth. He picked a champagne truffle and a raspberry ganache, his favorites.

"I'm starting to enjoy this way of doing business, gentlemen. We get things done without interference from our enemies in both Congress and the press. The Iranians will also think twice before causing trouble outside their borders," the president said while wondering how the Iranian regime would respond to this incident.

35. PROTOVAX HEADQUARTERS, LYON, FRANCE

October 22

They waited under the shade on Rue Jean Grolier. To the left was an abandoned lot with overgrown weeds and bushes. Across the street was a modern three-story building with Swedish architectural designs. The outside of the building had rectangular windows with colored glass in shades of green, white, and black. Horizontal metal railings, resembling a steel cage, covered the exterior of the second and third floors. Metal gates sheltered the interior courtyard of the facility. The headquarters of ProtoVax, located in the industrial section of Lyon, resembled a fortress. Security cameras adorned the outer edge of the building like coconuts hanging from a tree.

Inside their vehicle, Janusz and Kim talked facing each other to avoid raising the suspicions of the frequent security patrols cruising the street. Between them, the GPS tracker showed their target to be inside the compound. There was little to do but wait patiently for him to come out.

"Jesus, I wish you'd brought some snacks," Janusz said, agitated after his skirmish earlier in the day.

"I wasn't expecting you to get picked up by the French."

"I didn't get picked up, I was briefly detained."

"You should've been watching your six. What if they'd been assassins?"

"It was your job to watch my six. You're the one responsible for the delay. If —"

The GPS tracker came to life unexpectedly. The target was on the move.

"Let's not lose sight of him now," Janusz said as he fired up the engine.

"That's fine by me," Kim replied, visibly annoyed.

Janusz made a U-turn on Rue Jean Grolier and waited. The meeting had ended rather quickly. Perhaps the French were no longer interested in a joint venture. It was odd, though, the ProtoVax website was littered with elicitations for foreign investors. The Iranians probably lowballed as they usually did in negotiations. When the target's vehicle was on Boulevard Jules Carteret, Janusz was not far behind. He kept enough distance to not spook the target.

"You're going to lose him, hurry up," Kim complained.

"That's what the GPS tracker is for, Kim. Would you like me to leave you here on the side of the road while I follow him by myself?" Janusz said, annoyed. She turned away in silence. With Kim's warning in mind, Janusz stepped on the gas. He panicked briefly when he could not see the vehicle. It had come to a stop.

"All right, he's stopped moving," Janusz said to his partner. She was in no mood to respond. He stepped on the gas, weaving around several cars to reach Avenue Tony Garnier. On his right was a Total Gas Station, a subsidiary of Total SA, the largest energy company in France. Janusz glanced around frantically.

"Do you see him anywhere, Kim? Do you see his vehicle?"

"Yes, there he is, parked next to pump number eight."

"He's not in the car. Probably inside the minimart."

Janusz parked across from the minimart. He handed the GPS tracker to Kim and asked her to follow.

"And where are you going?"

"Don't worry about me. You need a little time to get over whatever it is that's bothering you. Just follow the target vehicle."

"I'm sorry, Janusz. It was a close call this morning. I just—"

"No need to explain. Follow the vehicle wherever it goes.

Chances are, I'll be in it," he said without explanation.

Several minutes later, the target returned with a bottle of water. He was so distracted that he did not bother to look inside his car before entering. As soon as he sat behind the wheel, the SIG P226 pistol was pointed in his face.

"*Salam*, Dr. Ahvazi," Janusz said in Farsi, trying to confirm the man's identity.

"*Salam*, who are you?" Dr. Ahvazi replied.

"Keep your mouth shut and drive. If you make a noise or a move without my permission, I'll send you on a one-way trip to hell."

Dr. Ahvazi drove off without further protest. Down highway A43 to the A48 and on to highway N85 for another hundred and sixty kilometers. After two and a half hours, they finally arrived at the chalet in Les Cotes-de-Corps. To his credit, Dr. Ahvazi had not made a single move in protest. He turned into the driveway on Janusz's command. Five minutes later, Kim arrived behind them. Janusz walked up to her while keeping an eye on Dr. Ahvazi.

"I was sure we lost you, dear Kim," Janusz said playfully to gauge her mood.

"Not to worry, I'm feeling much better now. I just needed to clear my head."

"Perfect time for you to drive down to Corps and get us some food. I need a little time alone with our guest," he said before pushing Dr. Ahvazi up the stairwell toward the chalet.

The door to the cabin opened with a creak. It had not been oiled in ages. Janusz motioned for the Iranian to enter in front of him. As soon as Dr. Ahvazi stepped inside, it happened. Janusz struck him in the back of the neck with the butt of his pistol. The force of the blow was just enough to launch him inside, head-first. Dr. Ahvazi landed on his face with a large thud.

"That was for Roozbeh Navabi and Iman Vakili. They were killed to protect your precious program. I hold you personally responsible," Janusz said.

Dr. Ahvazi did not reply. He rose on one knee, wiping himself off as he massaged his neck. He was bleeding from the mouth. Janusz grabbed him by the collar and threw him into a rocking chair next to the fireplace. Dr. Ahvazi sat facing his captor.

"Who are you, and what's this all about, *khhhh*?" Dr. Ahvazi asked.

"Spare me the nonsense. You know damn well what this is about. I need answers, and I need them quick."

"*Ehhem*, answers for what?"

Janusz was in no mood to play games. He struck the Iranian across the face with the back of his hand. The sound of the impact ricocheted around the room. "Does that focus your mind, or do you need another explanation?"

"Are you an American, *ghoolp*? Your Farsi is so polished," Dr. Ahvazi said without missing a beat.

As Janusz clenched his fist, it dawned on him that the Iranian was trying to get under his skin. He needed this man alive. "How lovely of you to ask. My father is Iranian, you see, and I've been perfecting my skills for my job."

"Oh, really, what is it that you do?"

"That's not important. What's important for you to keep in mind is that we're far away from civilization, allowing me to play all sorts of interesting games with you. Are you still interested in what I do?"

Dr. Ahvazi sat quietly.

"Let's start over again. What are you doing here in France?" Janusz said.

"You seem to know the answer already."

"Yes, but I want to hear it from you."

"I'm in France on a business trip. *Achuu.*"

"Are you sick?"

"No, why?"

"Never mind, continue."

"As the head of RCERID in Iran, I want to enter a joint venture with the French to manufacture viral treatments. Specifically, a cure for the Crimean-Congo fever, a disease that is ravaging my country," the Iranian said as if reciting a scripted line.

"Tell me about Iran's biological weapons program," Janusz said.

"What biological weapons program? The RCERID is concerned purely with the elimination of infectious diseases."

"Didn't Roozbeh and Iman work for you?"

"Am I supposed to know who they are? Besides, there are many people who work at the RCERID. I don't know them all."

"Perhaps not," Janusz said, slightly amused. "Are you familiar with the Marburg virus?"

"Yes, in the same family as Ebola. Deadly African virus that kills over ninety percent of infected victims."

"Why does the Iranian regime seek to weaponize this bug?"

"*Ehhem*, you must know something that I don't. We have no use for such things."

"Yes, just like you have no use for nuclear weapons or intercontinental missiles. Yet I helped to kill the top engineers in your country's missile program over a year ago."

The wheels turned in Dr. Ahvazi's head as he rolled his eyes. Janusz had the right man.

"You know, in my line of work, I'm responsible for the lives of assets. Informants as you probably like to call them. I'm sure there are things in your profession that you take seriously. The Hippocratic oath, perhaps? Well, maybe not in your case," Janusz declared.

He walked across the room to a cabinet by the window. From one of the drawers, he pulled out a metal object before walking back toward Dr. Ahvazi.

"Do you know what this is?" Janusz asked calmly, holding the object in his hand. Dr. Ahvazi's eyes opened wide as he breathed faster.

"Wha ... Wha ... what's that?" Dr. Ahvazi said with a sudden stutter. Janusz tied him to the rocking chair before grabbing his pants. He unzipped and pulled them down along with his boxers.

"That, my dear Dr. Ahvazi, is a nutcracker. It's most often used to crack such delicacies as walnuts and chestnuts. I, on the other hand, plan to crack a different kind of nut with this one."

The Iranian gasped, squirming in his seat. His pupils dilated as his stutter grew more pronounced. "You … you … you don't really mean that?"

"Oh, I most certainly do. I stood over Roozbeh's dead body in the morgue, and I watched Iman stabbed to death in front of me. Do you think I'm going to wince at the sight of cracking these measly nuts?" Janusz said, pointing at Dr. Ahvazi's testicles. At that moment, a gust of air rushed in. Kim stood in the doorway holding a bag in one hand. Her mouth was ajar as she dropped the groceries on the foyer.

"What the hell is going on?" she cried out.

"Come in and shut the door, please," Janusz said. She just stood there motionless. Janusz had to walk over to bring her inside. He guided her to the kitchen to explain the situation. Several minutes later, he reemerged, standing in front of Dr. Ahvazi.

"Sorry for the delay. My partner will prepare our meal while I finish with you. Now, where were we?" Janusz asked.

"What kind of sick people are you? This is against the Geneva convention. I know even the US government does not allow this kind of thing."

"Very true, but I never said what I did or who I worked for. I also don't give a shit about the Geneva convention when the lives of innocent Americans are on the line. Now let's see how long it'll take me to crack your nuts," Janusz said while picking up the nutcracker.

"Okay, I'll talk. The QF came to me with an order to make a Marburg weapon. General Kalantari, he's the one you want. He's running this show. He gives me orders and I follow."

"What about Roozbeh and Iman? Did you order their execution?"

"Of course not. They were two of my best men. I tried to save them. I always gave them great evaluations to help with their promotions. It was General Kalantari. He said they were both working for the Americans. It was out of my hands."

"The weapon, is it ready?"

"No, I refused to build it without a treatment. That's why I'm here. I told General Kalantari I'm going to France to get help with the cure," Dr. Ahvazi replied.

"Who is the target? Who are you sick bastards planning to infect with the virus?" Janusz shouted at him.

"How am I supposed to know?"

"You're lying," Janusz shouted once more.

"No, you have to believe me. I'm not lying. The QF runs the program. They don't provide details. I'm just supposed to present a working weapon. Once it's ready, the QF takes delivery and that's that. I don't know anything about intended targets, nor do I want to know."

Janusz placed the nutcracker underneath the Iranian's scrotum as the man screamed out for help. "You're going to help me get this information from General Kalantari or else."

Kim ran into the living room from the kitchen. She yelled for him to stop. "John, I can't let you do this. It's unacceptable."

"Just watch me. This bastard is responsible for the death of one asset and a defector. I'll make him pay."

"This is not how it's done," she yelled again. Dr. Ahvazi jumped in to interrupt them.

"Okay, okay, I'll help you," Dr. Ahvazi said, addressing Janusz. "On one condition."

"What's that?" Janusz asked.

"I want to visit Monte Carlo. We're not allowed to gamble in Iran. I've always dreamed of going to the casinos in Monte Carlo. I can help you get the information you need from General Kalantari. I just want to go to Monte Carlo for a day. I also want ten thousand euros to play with."

Janusz took a few minutes to ponder the request. "That won't be a problem. We'll leave the day after tomorrow. Let things settle down a bit. I'll give you exactly ten thousand euros, but I'll be standing over your shoulder the whole time. Even when you're in the bathroom."

"Fine," the Iranian replied.

"You know something? It's funny how the annoying sounds you make suddenly stopped amid all the excitement just now."

Dr. Ahvazi turned his face as Janusz walked away.

Once inside the kitchen, Janusz and Kim laughed as quietly as possible before hugging each other.

"I told you it would work. All he needed to know was that one of us was reasonable," Janusz said.

"I'm just glad you didn't have to crack his nuts. I really didn't want to clean up all that blood."

"I wasn't going to. We need him alive. I'm sorry about this morning."

"Me too. What happens when you get to Monte Carlo? There are a lot of people looking for you."

"It's worth the risk to get his help. Besides, with the disguise I'm planning, my own mother won't recognize me."

36. SEQUOIA RESTAURANT, WASHINGTON, DC

October 22

"**A**nother glass of champagne?"

"No, thank you, Brad, I've had quite enough," Jennifer said with a giggle.

"You ready to order the main course?"

"Quite ready. Whatcha recommend?" she asked.

"Oh, I think a beautiful lady like yourself can make up her own mind," Brad Paisley said without hesitation. After several rounds of champagne, she was in a friendly mood.

"Brad, I'd forgotten how fun it is to hang out with you. Why haven't we done this sooner?"

"Oh, I don't know. After graduation, I joined the dirty world of politics, while you went off to fight the bad guys. Then you got married, and I stayed single. We had different ambitions. You probably didn't want to be seen with me."

"You're the lead partner of DC's top political consulting firm. You've done quite well for yourself, dontcha agree?" Jennifer said.

"As have you, I think. Can't be sure, since you were never able to tell me what it was you did in service to our country," he said playfully.

"Most of it was bullshit. My first assignment abroad was as a desk jockey in one of our African embassies. My boss was not particularly fond of women. Very old school. He retired soon after."

"I'm sure you had your fair share of excitement."

"I didn't do it for the excitement. I did it because I believed in something, call it youthful naïveté."

"I'm curious now. You must have done something during your time with the government that's worthy of a novel or perhaps a short story?" he said before sipping on his champagne.

She stared at him, desperate to say something. It took a few minutes before she figured it out.

She leaned forward. "Since you're so curious, I was on assignment once, doesn't matter where."

Brad's champagne glass was frozen half tilted toward his mouth.

"The man we were after was one of the financiers of the 9/11 bombings. We'd chased him halfway around da world to some forsaken small desert town. I was at a command post twenty miles away while four of my teammates were on the ground. The villagers spotted them as soon as they arrived. The team called for backup before the firefight. They just had a bad feeling."

Jennifer was squeezing her spoon. Her eyes were distant, and her voice was hushed. "You'd figure that any fool would send all available assets to support them, eh? You'd be wrong. Management did not want to send additional assets for fear of provoking the locals. The request had to go up da chain for approval. Not just one, but three different people had to review and consent. Unfortunately, da real world does not stop to accommodate a bureaucracy. A firefight broke out ten minutes later. Over thirty insurgents had surrounded them. Without telling anyone, I picked up an M-4 and jumped into a jeep."

She paused briefly to think.

"What were you going to do?"

"I don't know. But I couldn't sit by and let them die."

"You went by yourself?"

"Yes. I did not make it to the village in time. The insurgents were gone, while my teammates' lifeless bodies were left on the street like dogs. I picked them up one by one and threw them in the jeep. Boy, they were heavy! Something inside me couldn't leave without them. On my way out of town, I saw the backup team in armored Humvees. They were an hour too late."

"Wow, you must have been devastated."

"Yes, but also disappointed. I can deal with death. We all knew what we were getting into. What I can't stand is betrayal. Those men would be alive today if the bureaucrats had been more aggressive. If they had not covered their own ass with needless red tape," she said, staring at him intently.

"That's when I quit. The realization that our government has become so risk-averse was too much. Our leaders don't have the spine to support the very people who put their lives on the line. I was disillusioned for a long time."

"I'm sorry you had to endure that, Jennifer. I think I understand you better now. You should apply your passion from another angle. At a much higher level," Brad said emphatically. She knew what he was hinting at. The man sitting across the table from her in the expensive Brioni suit had just been hired to run the presidential campaign of Senator Donald Patrick. The long-time chair of the SSCI had recently set his sights on the highest office in the land. Brad had agreed to advise the campaign for a hefty sum.

"Your talents are wasted in the bureaucracy. You need to work directly with the policymakers. I can make that happen if you allow me to."

Sitting inside the dining hall of Sequoia Restaurant in Georgetown, with a view of the Potomac River, she felt open to new possibilities. "And you know this from direct experience? You feel like you've had a positive impact on da direction of our country through your work?"

"Me? No. But I had other ambitions. I was always interested in power and money. But you don't have to follow my footsteps. I can connect you to the right people. You can finally have a say in the direction of the country. I'm sure you'll make things better."

"You're just saying that to be nice, and you're drunk."

"I may be a tad drunk, but I meant everything I said. It's a shame for someone as beautiful and talented as you to be jaded at such a young age."

"Well, I'm not that young, but whatcha have in mind?"

"I'm organizing a fund-raiser for Senator Patrick on the twenty-fourth at the Mayflower."

"It's not at your house?"

"Hell no! I don't want all those drunk politicians on my property. Let the hotel worry about all that. I'll introduce you to Senator Patrick and a few others."

"I'd like that. What time should I be there?"

"Why don't you stop by my house first? We'll take an Uber to the Mayflower together."

"Brad, I'm married. I'll meetcha at the hotel."

"Suit yourself."

"We should order. I'm getting hungry," Jennifer said.

"As you wish. Where the hell is that waiter anyway?" he said with a hand raised. They continued in this manner for the rest of the afternoon. For some strange reason, she wondered what Janusz was up to at that exact moment.

37. SALEHI RESIDENCE, HAMADAN, IRAN

October 23

Mrs. Salehi poured a second glass of scalding tea immediately after the first. It was the best she could do to stay warm. The unfortunate turn in the weather forced her to choose between warmth and nutrition. The boiling water came straight from a simmering kettle on the stove. The steam from the piping liquid warmed the tips of her fingers as she watched the tea fill up her glass. Wearing two layers of socks with her slippers, she walked across the kitchen for more biscuits. There would be nothing else to eat before dinner. She made up her mind, right there and then, to only eat half a loaf of bread for supper so the kids could get more meat in their stew. She sat behind the kitchen table across from the fridge. It was the perfect angle to stare at the birds outside her window.

Mrs. Salehi took a bite of her biscuit before sipping on the tea. Her thoughts drifted uncontrollably to Mohsen, lying there alone in his hospital bed, far from home. Only God could save him now. She wanted to see him more often, but the price of airplane tickets was prohibitive. Mohsen had taught her how to drive their car, the Iranian-made Samand, but the rising price of gasoline meant she had to conserve the precious fuel for the most essential tasks. Activities such as driving the kids to school, grocery shopping, and trips to the doctor devoured her fuel budget. According to the hospital, Mohsen's condition was deteriorating rapidly. No one, not even that lecherous Dr. Nader, was willing to give her a straight answer about his prognosis. Earlier in the day, Dr. Nader had called to inform her about a new blood transfusion for Mohsen, his second this week. Mohsen was continually hemorrhaging blood, and the hospital refused to tell her why. By the grace of God, she vowed to find out what was wrong with him. She made up her mind to drive to Tehran with the kids the next day.

After finishing her tea, she threw the last biscuit on the table as nausea overwhelmed her stomach. She placed her hand over a stack of papers growing taller by the day. This month's water bill was on top. The expense had never been a problem, but that was before Mohsen was out of work. Underneath the water bill was another reminder about the rent. She had warned Mohsen about the dangers of renting in a fancy building, but he never listened. She was out of ideas on how to replace his salary. Like most Iranians, she was not able to afford necessities through honest work on her own. Time would only tell if she could make it through this. Time and God.

She grabbed another document from the pile. It was her fifth time reading this particular letter from the Ministry of Health.

Dear Mrs. Zohreh Salehi,

After careful review of your case, I must inform you that the Ministry of Health will not be able to compensate you for your husband's injury. Mr. Salehi had been extensively trained and given specific guidance on proper safety procedures in the laboratory. He had a long history of not following instructions provided by the lab director, Dr. Javad Ahvazi, who wrote me a personal letter about this case. In the latest instance, Mohsen was briefed on proper safety procedures for an experiment, which he subsequently did not abide by. Given his unwillingness to follow instructions, the Ministry of Health is not liable for his injuries. I regret to inform you of this decision. Mohsen's expenses at the hospital will continue to be paid by his health insurance, but your request for his salary will be denied. His pension will also not be paid out. He had not worked long enough to meet the required threshold.

Sincerely,
The Honorable Akbar Shadi
Deputy Assistant to the Minister of Health

After reading the letter, she could take no more. She needed to shop for groceries before picking up the kids. The drive around town would help clear her mind. Driving toward Azadi Bazaar, she recalled an article in *Shargh Daily*, a reformist newspaper. The article explained how Iranian women, some single, others divorced, were flocking to the Emirati city of Dubai for money. Most of these women were either uneducated or runaways from abusive families. The Gulf Arabs had a particular fondness for Iranian women. The women ended up as prostitutes in various brothels, catering to the demand for Iranian flesh. The lucky ones became mistresses to emirs who took better care of them. Most likely, they would be abused, their passports taken away, and forced into sex slavery.

With two young kids to feed, she gave serious thought to her own prospects in Dubai. The children could stay with her parents. At least she wouldn't have to worry about food and shelter for herself as her sponsor would provide those. She burst into tears at the desperate turn of events. Mrs. Salehi parked on a side street before entering the meandering streets of the bazaar. The narrow alleys were packed with shoppers. She stopped at a spice vendor. The shop owner had bags full of spices in all the colors of the rainbow, from purple sumac to golden saffron.

"Come, come, dear lady. You've never seen spices like this. I picked out this batch of sumac myself on my last trip to Kerman."

"How much?"

"Why is a beautiful lady like you worried about the cost? I'm sure your husband will pay any price to bring these effervescent spices to your kitchen."

"How about that one?"

"That, dear lady, is the finest saffron you'll find in the world. My own son goes out to the saffron farms every week to get them for this store."

"How much?"

"Again with the how much?"

"God is my witness, I don't have much this month."

"I'll give you a terrific price, the kind of price you won't see anywhere else in this bazaar. One gram for two hundred and ten thousand tomans, what do you say?"

She only had a total of two hundred fifty thousand tomans in her purse. It was either the saffron or another half kilo of meat at the butcher's. Saffron gave an excellent flavor to the rice, but the children needed the protein to grow.

"I'm sorry, sir, that's too much now. With the grace of God, I may return next month. Thank you for your time."

"My dear lady, I keep telling you not to worry about the price. Come back, come back. I'll make you a deal you can't refuse."

"I'm sorry, I must leave," she said before walking out the store. The shop owner was still pleading as she turned the corner.

Down the narrow streets of the bazaar, past the candy and textile shops, Mrs. Salehi was planning her next move. The Khorasan Foundation had its headquarters near the hospital. She could plead her case for money. If they refused, she was determined to resort to more drastic measures.

38. VALI-ASR HOSPITAL, TEHRAN, IRAN

October 24

An ominous feeling grabbed hold of Mrs. Salehi as she entered the waiting room. Perhaps it was the gray skies gathering outside. Perhaps it was the glum expression on the faces she encountered in the lobby. Or perhaps it was the nauseating odor from the cafeteria, permeating every square centimeter of the hospital. Whatever it was, she felt sick to her stomach, and she was not certain why. She waited with the children in the designated room. It was strangely empty. Even the other lady was gone now. But what if—

"Oh, hey, there you are. I was wondering if you'd turn up. I'm so sorry I didn't get a chance to introduce myself last time. I'm Nargess, Peyman's wife."

"Yes, I remember you. I'm Zohreh Salehi. I thought maybe ..." She paused for a second. "... maybe something bad happened to him. Please forgive me for such thoughts," Mrs. Salehi said.

"That's not necessary, I've wondered the same thing. I must apologize for being so abrupt when we first met. It's just that they don't give us any answers. I've been staying with my sister's family. Without Peyman, we could've lost the house. There was no way for me to pay the bills."

"Heaven only knows I'm in the same predicament. I've been trying to figure our finances for the past few days," Mrs. Salehi said.

"We got the news this morning. Peyman never caught it and is finally being released. I don't know what took so long, but they allowed me to see him only twice since he checked in."

"I'm happy for you. I've not seen Mohsen once. That sleazy doctor wouldn't even allow me near his room," Mrs. Salehi said.

"Oh, you mean Dr. Nader. Such a dreadful man. He has zero empathy for the families but a wandering eye for the ladies. Besides flirting with me, he's lied about everything, and I mean everything."

"What type of virus was your husband infected with?"

"They wouldn't say, lying bastards. Dr. Nader said he infected himself in the lab by not taking proper precautions. I find that hard to believe. Peyman is quite fastidious."

"I'm tired of this. I'm going to give that Dr. Nader a piece of my mind right after I visit Mohsen."

"Please do. He should still be on the top floor," Nargess said.

They hugged each other, and Mrs. Salehi told her kids to stay in the waiting room while she went to visit their father.

When she emerged from the elevator, she was stricken by the eerie silence. It was a great contrast from the floors below. The lights were dimmed, perhaps to trick potential visitors into thinking the floor was abandoned. She searched the halls for his room. The IRGC sentries were nowhere to be found. A fluorescent light flickered on and off in the distance. With no one in sight to ask directions, Mrs. Salehi made her way down the dimly lit corridor. The cold air on this floor sent a chill down her spine as she walked from door to door. No one had ever bothered to tell her which one Mohsen was in. Most of the rooms were locked. Others were oddly empty with the lights out. She reached the end of the hall with no luck. She walked back to the elevators to reorient herself.

Then it hit her, a flashback to the last time she was here. Dr. Nader had stopped her somewhere nearby. There were several more hallways. She picked the one most familiar. She walked slowly at first. Each step was taken with great care not to alarm the guards who might be lurking in the shadows and empty rooms. Placing one foot in front of the other, she marched forward in the hope of seeing Mohsen's face once more.

Down the corridor, underneath a door, was a sliver of light. Since the other rooms were all dark, her choice was clear. She approached with her right arm extended. The hairs stood on the back of her neck as she grabbed the door. Mrs. Salehi thought about the cavalier attitude with which Peyman's wife was treated. She turned the knob in anger. A gush of wind pushed against the door. It weighed a ton. Mrs. Salehi used all her might until it cracked open. The room was blinding compared to the hallway, sending a jolting pain through her eyes. Electronic equipment covered in plastic littered every square centimeter. There was an abundance of plastic everywhere. Plastic curtains that came down to the floor cordoned off an entire section of the room. It was difficult to see the other side. She put her hand out while keeping her eyes closed. When she felt her hand clutching the plastic, she pulled it aside in one motion.

As she opened her eyes, she was immediately taken aback. In front of her was a plastic cocoon. Inside was a futuristic bed surrounded by instruments. Several computer monitors displayed information in English. As she stepped closer to the cocoon, it was clearly audible. The distinctive *beep, beep* of the heart-monitoring machine. She had been hooked up to one of those at the hospital in Hamadan while giving birth to her son and daughter. Oddly enough, her nerves were more on edge now than the day they were born. The voice in her head told her to run out the room to the elevators and down to the lobby. She chose to ignore the voice. It was a decision she would live to regret. As she got closer, a figure emerged inside the clear plastic cocoon.

She needed to be more daring. Mrs. Salehi took a few more steps. Did she really want to know? She could never forgive herself for not trying. She dared to walk all the way up, only centimeters from the mangled figure behind the plastic. Perhaps

Mohsen was not infected, according to what Peyman's wife had said in the waiting room below. Mrs. Salehi was probably in the wrong room. She turned to walk out. But she had to know for sure. A one-hundred-eighty-degree turn and several steps later, she stood over the ghastly figure once more. What was it exactly? A man? A beast? An alien, perhaps? She put her face right up against the plastic. The figure inside was completely bald, unlike Mohsen, who had a thick head of hair.

This could only be the work of the devil. There was blood oozing out of the left arm at the point where an IV needle had been inserted. Mrs. Salehi was not sure how she had missed it at first. It was as plain as the miserable creature in front of her. The sheets covering the man were soaked in blood. She wanted to call a nurse for a sheet change. No matter how hard she tried, she could not turn away. The man, it was definitely a man, was not wearing a shirt. Drool rolled down his chin. It was not just any kind of drool. It was black blood, something one expected to see coming out of the mouth of a demon. Suddenly, *beep, beep, beep.* The heart-monitoring machine picked up its pace in rapid succession. There was movement inside the cocoon. The figure shivered as if he was freezing. That's when she finally spotted it. The little star-shaped mark above his left elbow. It was usually covered with hair. But here it was now, exposed, because this poor man no longer had hair. It wasn't just any man. This was Mohsen Salehi, her husband of thirteen years. Lucky number thirteen. His birthmark was staring right at her.

She shuffled back, trying hard to breathe. Mohsen suddenly opened his mouth. He was convulsing now while the machine *beeped* rapidly. Without warning, Mohsen vomited. A gush of liquid tar came out like lava from a volcano. Most of it landed on the sheets, but some made it onto the plastic cocoon. Mrs. Salehi had never seen anything like it. What could it be, that substance which resembled crude oil more than anything else? When Mohsen finally cleared his mouth of the black sludge, he turned to face her. She froze, unable to speak even though she was desperate to shout for help.

"You bitch, I'm going to kill you," Mohsen screamed.

The voice was harsher now, with little emotion, but it was definitely him.

"Mohsen, is that you? What have they done to you? Oh, dear God, what have they done?" Mrs. Salehi cried as she fell to the floor.

"You fucking whore, I'm going to tear you apart." Mohsen lunged at her, trying hard to peel back the plastic surrounding him. The straps and the IV needle held him back. Blood oozed out from his veins as the IV popped out. Mrs. Salehi pedaled back on the floor toward the nearest wall. The plastic curtain flew open as several people rushed into the room. They were all wearing white spacesuits. One of them, wearing a mask, held a rifle that was pointed right at Mohsen. Three others ran toward the bed. They opened the cocoon to hold Mohsen down while injecting him with something. A fifth suited man emerged to pick her up from the floor.

"Mrs. Salehi, what are you doing here? Who gave you permission to enter this room?"

"Dr. Nader? Is that you? What have you done to my husband, you bastard? God will not be able to save you from my wrath. What have you done to my husband?" She kept repeating the same words over and over again.

"Mrs. Salehi, this is not your husband. This is the room of a very sick man. Now please come with me."

"God only knows you're lying to me, Dr. Nader. My poor husband, what have you done to him?"

"Guards, help me," Dr. Nader cried out as two more space-suited figures emerged to grab her arms and legs. They carried her away as she stared at the cocoon one last time. The man inside was still convulsing while spewing black tar once again.

"I saw his birthmark. It's him, I know it's him. You're lying to me," Mrs. Salehi said as they dragged her out into the hallway. God was her witness, she was not going to let the government get away with this.

39. MONTE CARLO, MONACO

October 24

There it was, the principality of Monaco, the world's second smallest country. With a population of nearly forty thousand, it was also the world's richest country per capita. Similar to Washington, DC, Monaco was divided into the four quarters of Monaco City, La Condamine, Fontvieille, and Monte Carlo. It was in Monte Carlo that the famous casinos were located. After five hours of driving, Janusz and Dr. Ahvazi entered Monaco, driving down the Exotic Garden Boulevard. The hills overlooking the Mediterranean were reminiscent of Malibu, California. The rocky cliffs provided a stark contrast to the blue waters below.

"Wow, we're finally here. *Khhhh*, this is how I dreamed it would be," Dr. Ahvazi said.

"Take it from me, dreams can be deceiving. We have a place like this in America called Las Vegas. There are many whose dreams have turned into a nightmare after only a day there."

Dr. Ahvazi ignored the comment, sticking his head out the window.

"Be careful, now, I don't want you to lose your head. At least not before you help me get to General Kalantari," Janusz said in jest.

"Don't worry about me," Dr. Ahvazi said flippantly. "I'm hungry. When can we eat?"

"According to the GPS, we'll arrive at the Hôtel de Paris Monte-Carlo in fifteen minutes. We'll eat as soon as I turn the car over to the valet so we can get on with our business."

"*Ehhem*, since you're paying for lunch, I'll wait as long as you like."

Janusz continued into Boulevard Princess Charlotte. This street, like all the others, was wedged narrowly in between a series of high-rises. Once they arrived, Janusz handed the keys to the valet.

"You're paying for all my expenses, right?" Dr. Ahvazi asked once more.

"Spare me the drama. I told you my people will take care of everything. Just don't get carried away."

After checking in through the elegant lobby, they took an elevator to their rooms. Overlooking the sea, Janusz's elegant suite had a small balcony for dining with a view. Within minutes, Dr. Ahvazi was knocking on the door.

"You ready to eat, *khhhh*?" Dr. Ahvazi wanted to know as Janusz contemplated punching him.

"How about Le Grille? It's on the eighth floor with great views of the Mediterranean, *ghoolp*?"

"Sounds lovely, do I have your permission to get dressed now?" Janusz said.

At Le Grille, they waited another thirty minutes for a table on the terrace. Janusz was on edge, not certain why Dr. Ahvazi was eager to visit Monte Carlo. In his pant pocket, he carried a .22, just in case. Once seated, Dr. Ahvazi grabbed a baguette as soon as the basket was placed in front of him.

"You realize, of course, that gambling is not allowed in Islam. Your colleagues back home will not be pleased," Janusz said to lighten the mood.

"I don't care what they think. I've spent the last twenty years of my life locked away in a lab. I think I'm entitled to some fun, *khhhh*."

"Dubai is nearby. I'm sure you've played there before."

"It's not the same. Does a hamburger taste like an Iranian kabob? They're both made of ground beef."

"I see your point."

"If you want to know the truth, the main reason is James Bond. I've watched all his movies in Iran. Always wanted to gamble in the casinos of Monte Carlo like he did."

"Ah yes. It's the same the world over. No matter how much people hate America, they love her movies. Don't tell me, you also like pretty girls to stand beside you at the craps table?"

"I don't hate America. I hate its government. And yes, it would be great if you could arrange some girls for us as well."

Janusz had neither the patience nor the inclination to explain why in a democracy a government represents its people. By default, if Dr. Ahvazi hated the American government, he also hated the people who voted for its politicians.

"I'll see what I can do about the women."

They drank to good fortune, enjoying the sunset over the water. From there it was back down to their rooms, where Janusz napped while Dr. Ahvazi made his way to the spa for an hour-long massage. When he woke up, Janusz made arrangements to visit the hotel boutique with Dr. Ahvazi. They bought matching 007-style tuxedos. After a shower and shave, Janusz searched his phone for the number provided by a bellhop. He called Monaco's top escort agency to arrange for their dates. As instructed, Janusz requested one blonde and one brunette for the Iranian scientist. He also arranged a companion for himself. At that point, both men proceeded to the lobby to wait for the ladies. It was quite a show when the girls arrived. All three were drop-dead gorgeous. For the price he was paying, Janusz was not surprised. Their tight outfits and the scent of their perfumes turned every head in the lobby.

"What do you want to play first?" Janusz asked.

"*Ehhem*, I'm in the mood for roulette."

Dr. Ahvazi walked over to exchange Janusz's money for chips. They then headed to the tables, where Dr. Ahvazi placed several bets, each in the amount of a hundred euros. The Iranian scientist surprised even Janusz with his ability to lose fifteen hundred euros in less than ten minutes.

"You better slow down, buddy," Janusz warned as Dr. Ahvazi

ignored him. From there it was on to the craps tables. An hour later, Dr. Ahvazi had lost another four thousand euros.

"Wow, this is great. Let's move over to the card games," Dr. Ahvazi said.

"Don't you think you need a break? You've lost quite a bit."

"Yes, but America is paying, *khhhh*. My assistance does not come cheap."

"Well, either way, I'm going to have to put a limit on your losses before you do too much damage. Why don't you have a drink? I'll go look for the girls. I think you scared them away."

Janusz was only too happy to get a break from the Iranian scientist. Dr. Ahvazi was like the kid in a candy store, eager to get a taste of everything in sight.

Next to the craps table, the girls talked among themselves.

"Excuse me, ladies," Janusz said. "I paid good money for your services this evening. How about joining my friend and me once more?"

"Oh, we like you, but he's sooo boooring. He did not say a word to us all night. Does he speak English?" one of the girls asked with a Russian accent.

"Just a little. He is a businessman from Iran. How about this? I'll see if I can prod him to be more friendly if you come back?"

The girls nodded reluctantly and gathered around Dr. Ahvazi. He was back at the craps table. After losing several more rounds, he turned to kiss the three girls while motioning for Janusz to have a roll.

"Come on, my friend. I'm tired, and it's your turn now."

"No, thank you. I don't like to gamble."

"Come on, *khhhh*, just once."

Janusz continued to shake his head until the girls started to egg him on.

"Don't worry, it won't kill you," the blond escort said.

Dr. Ahvazi asked the waiter to bring shots from the bar.

"Well, at least take a drink with me, *ghoolp*. Tonight's not the night to be a good Muslim," Dr. Ahvazi said in jest.

Feeling the pressure, Janusz thought it best to play along. He threw back a shot of vodka while watching Dr. Ahvazi roll the dice.

"Come on, John, take another shot."

On they went, drinking in that fashion with the girls.

"How about a lucky roll, John, just for me?" Dr. Ahvazi said when Janusz was half drunk.

"Okay, but just once," Janusz said as he rolled the dice.

"Wow, a seven. You're a lucky man. How much did you win?" Dr. Ahvazi asked.

"A thousand euros," the croupier declared.

"You can't stop now, John. Let's have another roll," Dr. Ahvazi said.

Janusz was not sure if it was the alcohol or Dr. Ahvazi's infectious attitude. Either way, he continued to roll the dice. An hour later, he was up twenty thousand euros.

"Hey, let's take a break and celebrate," Dr. Ahvazi said, motioning for a waiter.

"Please get us another bottle of Grey Goose," the Iranian requested in English, to Janusz's surprise.

"That was pretty good. I see you've been practicing your English," Janusz said, slightly slurring his speech.

When the bottle arrived, he drank some more with Dr. Ahvazi and the girls.

"John, I think it's time to spin the wheel. What do you say?"

"Okay, but just once," Janusz replied.

As Janusz stood by the roulette table, Dr. Ahvazi handed him another drink. Things were moving rapidly and he lost track of time.

"Come on, spin it again, *khhhh*," Dr. Ahvazi said enthusiastically.

Amazingly, his winning streak continued. At midnight, he was up half a million euros. The pile of chips had grown into a small hill in front of him. Dr. Ahvazi was now his personal cheerleader.

"You've made so much money. There is enough here for both of us to enjoy a wild shopping spree in Monte Carlo." Dr. Ahvazi took three yellow thousand-euro chips from the pile, handing each to one of the escorts. Then he tipped their waiter with a hundred-euro chip for carrying their drinks.

"You've become quite the big spender, Doctor. I'll have to keep my eye on you," Janusz said under the influence of alcohol.

"Hey, it's not my money, although I'm getting a cut of your prize if you want my cooperation."

"We'll talk about that later. For now, I need to get back to this game."

"That's what I've been waiting to hear. How about another drink?" Dr. Ahvazi ordered more vodkas as Janusz's lucky hand continued.

"Wow, this is crazy. I think I'll call it quits," Janusz finally declared at one in the morning.

"*Ehhem,* what are you talking about? You're just getting warmed up."

Dr. Ahvazi volunteered Janusz for a new game. The stakes kept getting higher and higher. Finally, it happened. With a pot of over a million euros, Dr. Ahvazi encouraged Janusz to risk everything at the roulette table.

"Come on, you can do it."

The girls were just as enthusiastic. With the number of chips Dr. Ahvazi was throwing their way, they would have said anything he asked them to. Acting on impulse, Janusz bet it all. The mood around the table turned tense. Several Russians were seated across the table. They glared at Janusz, then at Dr. Ahvazi, back to Janusz again. A Saudi sheikh also sitting at their table threw in his pot for the next spin. When the ball landed, Janusz came up empty.

"I guess I'm finally out of luck," Janusz said, ready to walk back upstairs. Dr. Ahvazi grabbed his elbow as the floor manager walked up to them.

"Not so fast. We have lawyers in America. How much are your house and assets worth?" the floor manager asked in perfect English.

"What do you mean?"

"Don't worry, we can help you stay in the game," the manager said as Janusz thought it over.

"I have half a million dollars' equity in my house. My car is worth another sixty grand, plus the half million in my retirement account. But this is crazy, I can't believe you're actually—"

"Fantastic, that's over a million dollars. I can have our lawyers draw up the paperwork for you. You can use your assets as collateral to get your winnings back. That is, if you think you can win?" the manager taunted.

"Of course I can win," Janusz boasted without thinking. "Okay, bring the attorney."

Within minutes, the documents were drawn up, signed, and notarized.

"What an honor, *khhhh*. I think this is the most exciting night of my life," Dr. Ahvazi said.

"Yeah, mine too, except now my entire life is on the line," Janusz said.

Dr. Ahvazi patted him on the back. "I'm not worried. You can do this."

The numbers were called out as the faces grew stiff. The five men around the table all glanced at each other before the croupier closed off the bets.

Then it happened. The ball landed. Paralyzed by and unexplained feeling, he was not sure what hit him. His head suddenly throbbed before spinning round and round. All he could see now was Jennifer's disappointed face. He scanned the room without luck. Where the hell was Dr. Ahvazi? Where were the girls? Was it all a dream? Janusz got up to search for them. The only thing he accomplished by this effort was to throw up on a poor Arab fellow standing next to him. Two attendants from the hotel next door were called to take him to his room. On the bed, he cried out her name in horror. "Jennifer, what have I done?"

40. MAYFLOWER HOTEL, WASHINGTON, DC

October 24

Jennifer stood in the corner of the ballroom staring at the buffet line. The people passing her constituted the apex of Washington's political class. She'd already spotted Senator Donald Patrick and his top staff aide, Jason Osborne. Supreme Court Justice Joel Katz, who'd had a rough confirmation hearing after his appointment by President Adkins, was walking arm in arm with a girl half his age. Ryan Irving, the secretary of defense, was making the rounds among the crowd as if running for office. Jennifer had a sudden urge to leave. There was enough pomp and arrogance in the room to inflate a hot air balloon, perhaps one of those old German zeppelins. It seemed that Brad, her companion for the evening, was a different man. He was not the character she had lunched with at the Sequoia days earlier. Perhaps he too was infected by the sycophancy in the air. Whatever it was, Brad was much sleazier this evening.

There was a tap on her shoulder.

"There you are, Jennifer. I thought you decided not to come," Brad said.

"Sorry, I tried to get food and realized I'd lost my appetite."

"Very odd. Allow me to introduce Karl Sanders, the president's chief of staff," Brad said.

"How'd ya do, Mr. Sanders?" Jennifer said.

"Please call me Karl. It's a pleasure to meet you. Brad here was telling me that you're interested in a political career."

She turned to Brad with inquisitive eyes. He spoke before she could object.

"Jennifer has served our country as a CIA officer. She's disillusioned with the bureaucracy but still eager to keep our country safe from the bad guys," Brad declared as if speaking for a political advertisement.

"Perhaps a stint on the National Security Council would be in order. We have an opening for a director of Near Eastern Affairs, I believe."

Jennifer stared at both Brad and Karl. The two men were having a conversation in which she was merely a spectator. She bit her lip to stay quiet before changing her mind. "So, how aboot those Iranians? They just downed one of our UAVs and are spreading their tentacles in Syria. Is the NSC prepared to turn up da heat on the tyrannical theocracy in Tehran?"

Brad's jaw lowered slightly as he shifted his weight from side to side.

"It's not that simple, Jennifer. Iran is one of our most intractable problems. We've been encouraging President Adkins to take a more nuanced approach, one emphasizing carrots over sticks," Karl said.

"In other words, we're exhibiting weakness to a regime that only understands strength?"

"Well, the problem is our allies. We must take their interests into account. The Europeans have numerous business interests in Iran," Karl said, trying to shift blame.

"I thought the job of the NSC was to safeguard America's national security."

"Well, let's save this discussion for a later time," Brad said. "Excuse us, Karl. I want to introduce Jennifer to Senator Scarsdale."

"It was a pleasure meeting you, Jennifer," Karl said, shaking her hand.

I can't say the same for you, Jennifer thought. She turned toward a waiter carrying a tray of chocolate truffles. The conversation with the president's chief of staff had left a bad taste in her mouth. As soon as she took a bite, Brad's voice pierced her eardrum once more.

"Jennifer, this is Senator Scarsdale, chair of the Armed Services Committee."

"Pleasure to meetcha, Senator," Jennifer said with a forced smile.

"Likewise, Brad's been singing your praises to me. I can't say that I blame him either," Senator Scarsdale said as he eyed her up and down.

Not wanting to make a scene, Jennifer attempted a conversation. "President Adkins is turning up the heat on our adversaries in his last year in office. It's about time we start putting our foot down after years of apologetic administrations."

"President Adkins is a menace. He doesn't understand the first thing about foreign policy. We need someone in the White House who is willing to work with allies, not someone who antagonizes them."

"Agreed. Someone who doesn't bully," Jennifer shot back without hesitation.

"Precisely."

"Or start unnecessary wars."

"You got it."

"And yet you and da other senators oppose the president's initiative to pull our troops out of harm's way in the Middle East. How is that not a contradiction?" Jennifer was in a combative mood. The hypocrisy of Washington insiders was one of the reasons she'd left government service. The other was the duplicity of officials who worked in the federal bureaucracy.

Brad shifted his weight once again. He turned his face from side to side as if searching for someone. It was obvious that Brad was not the kind of man to take a stand on any position other than for his career.

"Well, this president is all over the place. He has no experience, and he's always saying offensive things."

"So the job of the president is to be nice and make everyone feel good?"

"You know, I love a woman with strong convictions. How in the hell did the CIA let you get away?"

"Whatcha mean by that, Senator?"

"I mean really, who in their right mind wouldn't betray their country for you?"

"That's very flattering, Senator, but I'd like to think the CIA hired me for my ability to think on my feet, not my appearance."

"Of course, young lady, that goes without saying. But no one in their right mind will fail to appreciate your other assets."

"As a matter of fact, my first boss at the agency did not like my assets, as you put it. He sidelined me to a desk job precisely because he was intimidated by my beauty."

"Damn shame, damn shame. Brad mentioned you're his guest for the evening. A few staffers on the Armed Services Committee and I are having an after party upstairs. We'd love for you to join us. I'll introduce you to everyone."

"I'm sure ya would, Senator. Perhaps another night," Jennifer said curtly. She quickly made her way over to the snack table. Her face was hot, and her breathing had quickened. She took a glance around the room. When she was sure no one was watching, she grabbed a metal fork from the buffet table and bent it in half. She then dropped the mangled fork on a table and was about to leave when she turned to acknowledge another tap on the shoulder.

"Are you Jennifer Soltani?"

"Yes, I am."

"Such a pleasure to finally meet you."

Jennifer rolled her eyes at the prospect of another lecherous senator hitting on her.

"I'm Donald Patrick, a fan of your husband. I've only met him once, but he's a legend on the Intelligence Committee."

The compliment about her husband brought a genuine smile to her face. "Oh, hello, Senator Patrick. Pleasure to meet you too."

"Brad told me you'd be here tonight. I wanted to talk to you in private, since he's not aware of the work of your husband."

"That's very thoughtful. I appreciate it."

"I trust my colleagues here tried to chat you up about a career on the policy side. Brad has a lot of influence in this town. He's been talking you up. From what I know about your husband, I wouldn't recommend it."

"Why not, Senator?"

"Because unlike a lot of people in this room, you folks have integrity. Your husband has helped this country in more ways than anyone in this room, except you and me, can imagine. I wouldn't want the world of Washington politics to corrupt the two of you. This is a dirty game. I've made my deal with the devil."

"That's refreshing to hear, sir. Why are you running for the White House, if I may ask?"

"You're the only one asking that question who is going to get a straight answer from me tonight. We need someone to continue the work of President Adkins. Unfortunately, he was not able to implement his policies due to unprecedented opposition. I believe President Adkins has taken us in the right direction, and someone needs to pick up the baton when he leaves office."

"You think the establishment will let you implement your program?" Jennifer asked.

"Someone has to try. Take this room for instance. Do you think Secretary Irving or Karl Sanders would compel our NATO allies to pay their fair share or put pressure on Iran? All these people care about is not offending anyone so they can get re-elected."

"Senator Patrick, I want you to know that my husband and I will fully support you during your campaign. I'm so glad I ran into you tonight."

"Why is that?"

"Because I would've left this place feeling jaded and angry."

Senator Patrick laughed as he shook her hand. She was surprised by what he said before walking away. "Watch out, behind you."

Jennifer turned to see Brad staring at her. "Oh, hi, Brad. I think I'll call it a night. I'm quite tired."

"Come, now, the night's still young. I was about to introduce you to Secretary Irving. Plus, Senator Scarsdale is throwing an after party in his suite upstairs."

"I know. He already invited me."

"That's great."

"Perhaps another time."

"Well, in that case, I'll fetch us an Uber back to Georgetown," Brad said, and placed his arm gently around her shoulder.

She stared at the extended arm with her cold blue eyes. The arm was immediately withdrawn. "Brad, why would I go to Georgetown when my house is in Arlington?"

"The Uber was for us. I thought we'd go back to my place and get a nightcap."

"You know I have a husband?"

"Jennifer, you have this all wrong. I just wanted to continue our conversation at my place over drinks. I can drive you back to Arlington whenever you like," he said with a fake grin.

"Brad dear, I'm not a drunk college girl for one thing. Second, there are plenty of bimbos here for you to take back to your Georgetown pad. Third, Janusz is an old-school motherfucker. Trust me when I say you don't ever want him to hear that you tried to fuck his wife." Her words wiped the shitty grin off his face as quickly as the spring rain wiped the pollen off the trees in Washington. He was finally at a loss for words.

"Thanks again for the invitation, Brad. I'll be leaving now by myself. Enjoy da rest of your evening." She walked past him toward the lobby. She was comforted by the thought that her own husband could always be relied upon to do the right thing.

41. HÔTEL DE PARIS MONTE-CARLO, MONACO

October 25

Wow, what the fuck happened last night? Janusz thought as he massaged his head. He moved the pillow under his neck before grabbing the watch on the nightstand. It was forty-five minutes past nine in the morning, and his head was spinning. Memories from an undergraduate keg party came to mind. Am I in college? He scanned the room. It was too nice to be a college dorm. He sat upright on the bed, studying his surroundings. He was wearing a tux without a bow tie. His shirt was open at the collar. He wore dress socks, no shoes. Janusz mustered enough strength to get out of bed. He wondered if a sledgehammer had slammed him on the head. Peering out the window did nothing to jog his memory. Pulling the curtains back only served to heighten the pain. He turned his head for the safety of the shade like a vampire. The floodgate of memories suddenly flew open. The shoot-out in Geneva, the fight with DGSI, the nutcracker in the chalet, and the drive to Monte Carlo, it was all a blur.

Monte Carlo, fuck, Dr. Ahvazi!

Janusz ran to wash his face with cold water in the bathroom. After that, he opened the minifridge for bottled water. Where the hell was Dr. Ahvazi? Maybe the Iranian scientist was back at the hotel spa. Or maybe he was taking a swim in the fancy indoor pool. The man was a menace.

How much did that idiot Ahvazi lose at the tables last night? I'm too fucking tired to care!

Janusz moaned as he grabbed the bathroom doorknob once more. A sharp stabbing pain emanated from his stomach. It was the pain from another flash of memory.

Fuck Dr. Ahvazi! How much did I lose last night?

Janusz stumbled back into the room. He perched himself on the velvet chair as his head spun uncontrollably from the thought.

I lost it all! Goddamn it, I lost it all!

He threw his head down in despair. The stabbing stomach pain turned into nausea. He ran into the bathroom, opened the faucet, and placed his face in the sink. He wondered now if he'd been poisoned. The churning in his stomach caused him to vomit three times before gaining full command of his body. The rush of cold water against his face was amazing. His stomach had not expelled much. It was his body that was in full rebellion.

How could you lose everything? How the fuck could you lose everything, you stupid bastard?

Janusz fell back on the velvet chair. The full weight of his actions finally dawned on him. He had signed away his life at the roulette table the night before. He stopped thinking about Dr. Ahvazi. It was fair to say that he no longer cared about the Iranian scientist, at least not at the moment. Certain things are more important to a man than even the security of his country. First among those is the security of his family. Janusz had violated the most sacred rule. How could this have happened? He had quit gambling months ago. More importantly, he'd promised his wife that he was through.

There was a knock at the door. He tried to ignore it, but it did not stop.

"Go away. I don't need room service."

The knock continued.

Maybe it was Dr. Ahvazi. He did not care.

"Go away!"

"*Daro Vaz Kon,*" the voice came back. *Open the door.* It

was definitely not Dr. Ahvazi. Janusz stumbled to the door. He opened it and stared at the grinning man standing in front of him. The man was half a foot shorter with thinning hair. He wore rimmed glasses, and there was a tinge of devilishness in his eyes as if he'd done something he was not supposed to do.

"Are you going to just stand there and stare like an imbecile, or are you going to let me in?" the man asked. Having never met the man before, Janusz was at a loss for words. How did this Iranian know him? How did he know what room he was in? Why was he even here, and why was he so rude? With his head still spinning and his mind still wrapped around his losses at the roulette table, Janusz no longer cared. He opened the door wide for the man to enter.

"*Befarma, Ghorban,*" Janusz said, feeling deflated. *Welcome, sir.*

The Iranian glanced around. "Quite a nice room you have here."

"You're too kind," Janusz said.

The Iranian nodded and stood by the window. After several minutes of staring out into the blue waters of the Mediterranean, he walked over to the minibar, helping himself to a bottle of Perrier. Janusz had a belated epiphany about his guest.

"Have you come to speak to me about Dr. Ahvazi?" Janusz asked.

"We'll get to him in a second, Mr. Impatient. I'm more interested in you at the moment."

His tone and choice of words indicated the Iranian felt in control. That stirred up an immense feeling of resentment in Janusz.

"How can I help you?" Janusz said begrudgingly.

"I think you've got the situation backward. I'm the one who's here to help you." The Iranian sat and spread his arms on the back of the chair. He was evidently relishing his position, literally and figuratively.

"Do you know who I am?" the Iranian asked.

Janusz took a moment to think. As much as he racked his

brain, he could not recall this man. The only thing that was certain was his affiliation with Iranian intelligence, either MOIS or QF.

"Here's a hint. Does the name Morteza Karami mean anything to you?"

As soon as the words entered his ear, Janusz was transported to the rooftop in Brazil. His arms were holding someone upside down. He then opened his hands and let the man drop. *Morteza Karami, yes, of course!* Janusz's brow furrowed as he stared daggers at the intruder.

"I can tell from your face that you've heard my name before," Morteza said. "Perhaps it was Shahram Sabeti that mentioned me before you dropped him from the roof. Or perhaps it was Iman Vakili who blabbed before we were able to shut him up. Either way, it makes no difference now as long as we're properly introduced."

Janusz moved to sit on the sofa, keeping an intense gaze on the man. It was all too much to digest in one morning. His hangover from the previous evening, his losses at the casino, the disappearance of Dr. Ahvazi, and now this.

"Thanks for refreshing my memory. You're with MOIS," Janusz said.

"Correct. I'm normally head of operations for Europe as you've probably heard. Currently, I'm serving as the head of counterintelligence for our virus project, under the direction of General Kalantari. My latest duty is cleaning up every fucking mess you've made for us."

"That's strange. General Kalantari is the chief of the Qods Force. You are, after all, an MOIS officer, are you not?"

"We're not here to discuss my chain of command. You seem to have a big problem on your hands if I'm not mistaken?" Morteza said quickly, seemingly annoyed.

"And what is my problem, Mr. Karami?"

"If I recall correctly, you lost your life savings at the roulette table last night. And if that wasn't enough, the man you'd taken so much trouble to kidnap has disappeared. Does that capture your predicament adequately?"

It finally made sense to Janusz. He had been ensnared in an Iranian counterintelligence operation. They had dangled Dr. Ahvazi to draw him out into the open.

"What gave me away?" Janusz said. He was no longer trying to be evasive.

"We have our own sources and methods. If I gave away our secrets, the magic would not be as entertaining to watch. We had to pull a lot of strings to put on that show for you last night."

"I see. Let's get on with it. What do you want?"

"You're looking at this all wrong, John. May I call you John? Or is that a name you only use to issue warnings to Iraqi virologists at fancy cocktail parties?"

"If you say so."

"The way I see it, John, it's the MOIS that can do something for you. You lost over a million dollars while gambling last night, including your house, your car, and your retirement savings. We can make you whole once again if you're willing to work with us."

"You mean work *for* you?"

"Those are semantics, John, but take it any way you like."

"Spare me. Get to the point."

"Very well, since you insist, we'd like to turn you into a double agent. We'll give you the million dollars you need in exchange for feeding false information to your government and collecting information for us."

"Like what?"

"Specifically, to inform your government that Dr. Ahvazi told you the project to weaponize the Marburg virus was a hoax. Roozbeh Navabi, Iman Vakili, and Dr. Ahvazi were all sent out just to fool the American government into thinking Iran is developing a Marburg weapon when in reality it is not."

"The US government is not run by fools," Janusz said, trying to maintain a straight face. "They already know something important prompted you to kill Roozbeh and Iman while risking an international incident at the club in Geneva."

"Theatrics, dear John. Your government suspects that we don't value human life to the same extent as you. Perhaps the murders were the cost of doing business to make all this seem believable. If that's what you tell them, your people will believe it."

"And if I tell you to fuck yourself?"

"Then you'll have a lot to explain to your wife. Your problems with your government and with us will pale in comparison to what your wife will want to do to you. I know for a fact that the American legal system does not favor the males of our species."

As much as Janusz did not want to admit it, Morteza had a point. He also had the upper hand in this game. Janusz could not think of anything to regain the advantage at the moment. "I suppose you're right."

"Good, glad to see you're coming to your senses. I'll arrange for your payments, spread over several months, of course. In return, I expect to learn that America no longer suspects Iran has a Marburg weaponization program. I'll be your handler going forward."

Morteza's last sentence was a dagger in his heart. Janusz never expected to have a handler. For the first time in his life, someone was trying to turn him into a bitch. It was all he could do to not kill Morteza.

"How will you pay me?" Janusz asked.

"Cash. I'll arrange for cash payments to be delivered in a duffel bag. Two hundred and fifty thousand dollars over four meetings."

"I have to fly home now that Dr. Ahvazi is gone."

"Not to worry, we have assets in Washington for the payments. That's how we knew about Dr. Simmons's work."

"The murdered scientist in Virginia?" Janusz repeated to make sure.

"Same exact wretched buffoon. Dr. Simmons participated in a panel about African diseases at one of the think tanks in Washington. He could not help mentioning that the US Army had given him a large grant to research the potential of Marburg virus as a biological weapon. Dr. Simmons was not aware that the CEO of this think tank, who shall remain nameless, was working for us. The Alavi Foundation in New York has been financing the work of this particular think tank for years. The CEO has been quite reliable tipping us off on a variety of topics."

"Lovely, it appears you've learned how things work in Washington. Money."

"Like you, we maintain a network of assets around the world. Now, what do you have to say about my offer?"

"I need some time to think about it. I still have a headache from last night. I'll use the day to rest and get back to you by tomorrow."

"Very well. My hotel is not too far from here. I'll meet you for breakfast downstairs at eight tomorrow," Morteza said before making his way toward the door.

"Oh, and, John?"

"Yes?"

"Or should I call you Janusz Soltani?"

Janusz's lower jaw dropped as he felt his head spinning again.

"I do hope you're aware the Iranian nation appreciates your cooperation," Morteza said before walking out. Janusz felt the knife twisting in his heart as the world collapsed around him.

42. ZAHEDAN AIRPORT, ZAHEDAN, IRAN

October 25

"**W**hat's the status of the patients at Vali-Asr Hospital?" Akbar Shadi yelled as he ascended the stairs to board.

"Just one patient now, sir. His name is Mohsen Salehi. The other one was released with a clean bill of health," came the loud reply from his assistant, Hamid, speaking over the roar of the engine.

"And?"

"It appears that Mohsen Salehi is in critical condition. We're still not sure what he has."

"Why the hell not?"

"The QF won't let our people into his room. They've denied our repeated requests to visit him."

"We'll see about that. They must have forgotten that the Pasteur Institute and the RCERID belong to the Ministry of Health."

Akbar Shadi stood on top of the staircase. He reached for a handkerchief in his pant pocket. The unusual heat wave caused the sweat to pour down his forehead and over his nose. As he wiped his face, the deputy assistant health minister was grateful to be leaving Zahedan. The capital of the poverty-stricken Sistan va Baluchistan Province, Zahedan had some of the worst infrastructure in Iran. If that wasn't bad enough, the city was plagued by an incessant crime wave. It was a reflection of the porous border that enabled a constant stream of drug smugglers to enter from neighboring Pakistan. The region was considered Iran's "wild west." As he stepped inside, a lone mechanic descended from a staircase adjacent to the plane's rear engine. The mechanic, in his street clothes, stared at him before walking away. He felt goose bumps all over his body. He was not sure why.

"Sir, please take your seat. We need to get going if we're to make our next appointment," Hamid warned from behind.

"Actually, I want you to cancel our meeting at the ministry this afternoon. We're going straight to the hospital."

"You want to go straight to Vali-Asr Hospital from the airport? They're not expecting us, sir. That might not be a good idea."

"That's the whole point. If there is nothing to hide about that patient they got up there, then they won't mind our visit."

"What if this Mohsen Salehi really is infected with a deadly virus? Do you want to risk catching whatever he's got?"

"They won't let us near him if he is contagious, which means they'll have to come up with an excuse. Either way, I'll catch that lying Ahvazi in the act. I've wanted to crush that little bug for years. I finally have him right where I want him," the deputy assistant health minister said as he walked toward his seat.

Inside the cabin, the Ministry of Defense had redesigned this Russian Tupolev Tu-154 for high-ranking cabinet officials. It was the only one of its kind still in service. The Iranian government used it to carry VIPs around the country. The endless rows of passenger chairs had been pulled out to make room for plush leather seats. An attractive female crew member, with proper hijab, directed the passengers. Mango and watermelon juice was handed out as the crew made final preparations for takeoff.

"What's his deal anyway?" Hamid wanted to know.

"Who?"

"Javad Ahvazi."

"He's an egomaniac, the type that wants to take all credit for himself. We were classmates once at the University of Tehran," Akbar Shadi said.

"You never told me that, sir."

"It was the second year of our PhD program. A classmate of ours was conducting research on a type of genetically modified bacteria. It just so happened that this particular individual was also the top-ranked student in our class. He had the highest grade point average in the program. The man had a bright future ahead of him. Anyway, the poor fellow had borrowed the library's only edition of a biology journal, I forget which, to conduct his research. This was before the days of internet access in our universities. A couple of weeks before his research paper was due, there was a break-in at his dorm. The only thing that was taken was the journal."

"And you think it was the work of Javad Ahvazi?"

"Who else breaks into a college dorm room just to steal a biology journal? Without the journal, the poor fellow had to research another topic. It was too far into the semester for that, and he knew his grade point average would surely suffer. Being the perfectionist that he was, he could not handle the pressure. The night before his paper was due, the poor fellow committed suicide."

"My God! What a heartless act."

"We all suspected that devil Ahvazi, but we could never prove it. The university initiated an investigation, which never amounted to anything. I suspect that Ahvazi hired someone to do his dirty deed. Ironically, Ahvazi still came in second place that semester," Akbar Shadi said with satisfaction in his voice.

"Who came in first?"

The deputy assistant health minister grinned from ear to ear. "You're looking at him."

"No way, so this feud between the two of you goes way back. It's obvious that he can't stand you."

"I vowed revenge for our classmate all those years ago. Now I finally have a chance to crush this little cockroach."

"Well, then let's get to the hospital and catch this bastard with his pants down."

"Hamid?"

"Yes, sir?"

"Does it bother you that the Defense Ministry operates this plane for the whole government?"

"What makes you say that, sir? I know we have our differences with them, but at the end of the day, we're all on the same side."

"I suppose you're right. It's just that ..."

"Just that what?"

"It's just that, I thought I noticed something on our way inside the plane. It's probably nothing."

"This is a very expensive plane. I'm sure the Defense Ministry will not spare the cost to keep it safe."

The attractive stewardess came by once more to make sure they were wearing their seat belts before takeoff. At that moment, two uniformed IRGC marshals left the cabin before the hatch was closed.

Hamid turned to his boss. "Don't worry, sir. I think you're just nervous about our visit to the hospital. Everything will be fine."

Akbar Shadi opened a folder on his lap. He reviewed a series of questions for Mohsen Salehi, if the patient was still coherent. There was also a separate set of questions for the hospital crew. They would surely know what the QF had been up to in the infectious disease ward. The flight captain, a major in the Iranian Air Force, came on the speaker to discuss their itinerary. The deputy assistant health minister was relieved to learn that it was twenty degrees cooler in Tehran.

Several minutes after takeoff, the captain announced his approval to move about the cabin. Akbar Shadi turned to his right. Hamid was busy drafting a report on his behalf. It was a justification for why Dr. Ahvazi would be relieved from his position as director of RCERID. This was one of the many reasons Akbar loved having Hamid as an assistant. The man was always one step ahead. Akbar folded his hands on his lap, slowly closing his eyes as his head drooped.

The slopes of Dizin were covered in fresh snow. Akbar Shadi was skiing down Iran's most famous ski resort with two women. To his right was a buxom dark-haired beauty named Salumeh. To his left was another large-chested lady named Tahnaz. The women giggled as he grabbed their breasts while guiding them down the slope. At the bottom of the hill, they made their way to his cabin.

"Akbar, you're such a wonderful skier," one of the girls said before kissing him on the cheek. There were three glasses of cognac set out on a table. He grabbed one before sitting by the fireplace. The girls undressed in front of him. Once they were fully naked, he asked them to pick up the copy of the Quran on the bed. He then ordered the girls to read several of his favorite *ayat*, verses, as he sipped the cognac. He took particular pleasure in watching the women struggle with the Arabic passages while he stared at their jiggly breasts.

BOOOM. The loud explosion sent the deputy assistant health minister several centimeters into the air as he grabbed the armrests. He was upset at having such a pleasant dream interrupted unexpectedly. His disappointment rapidly dissipated in response to the captain's voice.

"Dear passengers, assistants, and crew, we're experiencing engine failure. Please fasten your seat belts and prepare for an emergency landing. I repeat, please fasten your seat belts and prepare for an emergency landing."

Akbar Shadi could not be sure if he was still dreaming. He turned toward Hamid, who was holding an armrest with one hand and a copy of the Quran with the other. Come to think of it, it was rather odd that the IRGC marshals had left the cabin before takeoff. The protocol was for them to remain on the flight in case of a hijacking.

"Hamid, call the office and ask my secretary to deliver the Ahvazi dossier to the public prosecutor."

"I can't hear you, sir. What are you saying?"

"Ask my secretary to deliver—"

BOOM. A second loud explosion shook the cabin. This time the plane was in a nosedive.

"Everyone on board, assume crash positions. We're going down, we're going down," the captain shouted in a panicked voice.

"Allahu Akbar," Hamid cried as they floated off their seats. Within seconds, the top of the plane came off. The wing sheared off before the plane fell apar—

43. OCEANOGRAPHIC MUSEUM, MONACO

October 25

The stone ledge under his arms felt cold. With his palms, he adjusted his stance against the rough barrier. The calm waters of the Mediterranean provided a stark contrast to his own life. Janusz fixated on a point out in the distance, purposefully breathing in and out. He glanced down several times, pushing his entire upper body over the edge. The collection of jagged boulders below was a wake-up call. It was not that long ago when he had chosen to serve his country instead of plunging into a lucrative Wall Street career like his classmates. The events of 9/11, coming seven years after the murder of his own brother, had crystallized his future. Fighting Islamists was the only thing that mattered for so long. But everything came at a price. After so many years on the road assuming fake identities, he had lost touch with what truly mattered.

Who was Janusz Soltani? What did Janusz Soltani do for fun? When the intelligence arm of the US government became so politically correct that it turned into a debating society, Janusz found another way to keep fighting. By joining Unit 81, he had only delayed the inevitable. While it was noble to avenge a dead brother, to protect a country, to defend a set of values, it was even nobler to be true to oneself. It was befitting that he found himself in this predicament. Those who didn't know themselves, those who had escaped their darkest demons by fighting external enemies, were bound to crash eventually. And this was the ultimate defeat. To be at the mercy of the regime he despised most. The one ideology more tyrannical than the others, Islamic extremism. Having spent an entire career fighting the executioners of Islamic Iran, the QF and the MOIS, he was now at their mercy.

He poked his head over the edge once more. Surely it was better to be dead than to surrender, or worse yet, to be a traitor. None of his choices were palatable. By accepting Morteza's offer, he would betray his country. By jumping over the edge, he would betray his brother. By going home empty-handed, he would betray his wife. Janusz felt completely powerless over his destiny. If he was already dead, he must have come straight to hell. The only thing that came to mind was the disappointment in Jennifer's eyes. There was no way he could face her again. It was time to say good-bye. He owed her that much. With a furrowed brow and a soul bereft of emotion, Janusz placed the cell phone against his ear.

"Janusz, wait till you hear this. You've no idea what I went through last night," she said with palpable enthusiasm in her voice. Her words barely registered with him.

"Jennifer, I love hearing your voice."

"So get this, remember my ex boyfriend Brad Paisely?"

"You've always been there for me."

"Anyway, he invited me to a big fund-raiser at the Mayflower. Everyone in DC was there, and I mean everyone. I met the president's chief of staff and the secretary of defense."

"Always made me forget my troubles."

"At the end of the night, he invites me back to his house in Georgetown, dontcha know? You believe the nerve of this guy? He knows I'm married."

"I'm sorry, Jennifer, I'm so sorry," Janusz said with sorrow in his voice. On the other end, Jennifer suddenly fell silent.

"Oh my God, Janusz, what happened? Are you hurt?"

"Why did you marry me? I'm serious now. Why did you marry me?"

"Janusz, whatever it is you may have done, we can talk about it. Please tell me what's wrong," she said in a panic.

"Come on, let's hear it. Why did you marry me, Jennifer?" he insisted.

She was silent for a long time before answering, "Because I love you."

"Why? Why do you love a son of a bitch like me?"

"Janusz, I don't want to lose you. I know something terrible has happened, so here it is. I love ya because of everything that makes you my life partner. I love ya because of your compassion, because of your sense of duty, because of your willingness to sacrifice for others. Above all, I love ya because of your integrity and your willingness to always do what's right, no matter how hard that may be."

"Jennifer, I've lost it all. Everything we own I lost. Can you still love me knowing that?"

"I don't know what you're talking about, but you're wrong, Janusz. You haven't lost it all, not as long as you have me. The rest doesn't matter."

"I lost our home, our car, our life savings while gambling in Monte Carlo. Am I still that man with integrity that you just described?" Her quickening breaths on the other end made him nervous. She was silent for a long time. Finally, she spoke up once again.

"Janusz, whatever you did, I know you did for a reason. I'm sure you'll get it all back. Just know that I love ya."

As soon as she finished saying those words, a jolt of energy pulsated from his head through his neck, to his arms, his torso, and all the way down to his feet. He could not remember feeling this lucid before. Jennifer had put things into perspective.

"I've gotta go, but you have no idea what your words mean to me. I'll call you as soon as I can. Oh, and, Jennifer?"

"Yes, Janusz?"

"I love you too."

As he took a moment to gather his thoughts, Janusz recalled a conversation with an Iranian asset not that long ago. The asset relayed minutes from a meeting of the Iranian Intelligence Coordination Council. One of the council's duties was the delineation of responsibility between various organs in the Iranian intelligence community. According to the asset, during this meeting, a fight broke out between the chiefs of the MOIS and the QF over resources for foreign intelligence operations. The MOIS chief was bitter over the growing budget of his rival while funding for his own organization was at an all-time low. Tomorrow was going to be a defining day.

44. HÔTEL DE PARIS MONTE-CARLO, MONACO

October 26

A cool breeze blew against his face as he stared at the ancient buildings perched on top of the rock in Monaco-Ville. The outdoor hotel restaurant, Omer, was a pleasant spot for breakfast. With its views of the yachts anchored in Port Hercule, Omer was an enjoyable location to discuss business. Janusz checked his watch before pouring cream in his coffee. At 7:50 in the morning, he was ten minutes early for the meeting with Morteza. After tossing and turning all night, Janusz wanted an early start. This was his first meeting where the adversary was trying to recruit him, or at least the first one he was aware of. Cornered, Janusz was more determined than ever to succeed. The only way it would work was to exude confidence. As long as Morteza believed Janusz was in charge, everything would go according to plan.

At five minutes to eight, Morteza walked the terrace in search of an open table. The Iranian moved with an air of arrogance until he spotted Janusz. He froze in place as he squinted to see more clearly. Finally, Morteza approached, a little less surefooted with each step.

"There you are. I wasn't expecting you so early," Morteza said.

"I've been here since seven. I find the morning air quite refreshing," Janusz said.

Morteza took a seat facing Janusz. "Unfortunately, I don't have a view like this in Tehran."

"You have the Caspian. Perhaps you can afford a villa up north with your next promotion," Janusz said sarcastically.

"I see you're in a good mood this morning. I take it you're accepting my offer?"

"I have nothing against you or the Iranian people. My problem is with the regime you serve. Never forget that I'm an American first. My loyalty will remain to the American Constitution." Janusz grabbed a pot. "Some coffee for you?"

Morteza pushed his mug forward, the wheels clearly turning in his head. "Sure."

"I took the initiative to order us bread, juice, eggs, and some fruit. I hope you don't mind?"

"Not at all. You have quite an appetite for a man who just lost everything in the world. But I'll play your game."

"I haven't lost everything, Morteza. I still have my integrity, which I'm sure you agree is a man's most valuable possession."

The Iranian stared, seemingly unsure of himself. The turn of events had caught him by surprise. Having come here to claim victory, he now seemed at a loss for words. The waiter arrived with a large tray, setting the table with an assortment of delicacies. Each man took a portion of the food, Janusz ate while Morteza studied him.

"Aren't you having any? This omelet is delicious," Janusz said. Morteza reluctantly took a bite from his plate as Janusz buttered a second slice of baguette.

"So, to what do we owe your strange zest for life this morning?" Morteza said with a mouthful of eggs.

"You've got this all wrong, Morteza. The way I see it, my zest for life is only natural, since I'm here to help you."

Morteza's eyes grew wide. He coughed to avoid choking on his food.

"There, there, drink some water. It'll help with the eggs," Janusz said.

Morteza grabbed the glass from his extended hand. Within

seconds, he had chugged the water and wiped his mouth. "What did you say?"

"You must be feeling better already. I said I'm excited because I'm here to help you and the MOIS."

"And how exactly are *you* in any position to help me or the MOIS?"

"Shhhh, keep your voice down. You don't want everyone to hear us, do you? God knows who could be sitting out here."

Morteza brought his face closer and spoke in a hushed tone. "How do *you* plan on helping the MOIS?"

"Well, since you're so eager for my help, here is my vision. MOIS becomes the premier intelligence agency in Iran, no longer cast aside while the QF takes credit for foreign operations. I also see a promotion for the man who makes all this happen," Janusz said with a poker face as Morteza stared.

Morteza suddenly chuckled. "Very good, you almost had me going, you wretched American."

"Remember the days when MOIS killed the dissident, Shapur Bakhtiar, in his apartment in Paris? How about that time your colleagues killed the Kurdish opposition leaders at the Mykonos Restaurant in Berlin? I bet you didn't have to share praise with the QF back then?" Janusz asked without skipping a beat.

"Okay, enough. Let's get back to business."

"We both know Supreme Leader Mashhadi only cares about loyalty and results," Janusz said, then took a sip of coffee. The dramatic pause was strategically placed to heighten the tension.

"The QF was given a leading role because MOIS could not be trusted after the 1999 student protests and the 2009 Green Revolution. What if General Kalantari fails in this monumental task the supreme leader has placed in front of him? What if he can't carry out a successful Marburg virus strike against the US? I'm sure the supreme leader would reconsider a leading role for MOIS in foreign operations, no?"

"And how exactly would the imbecile General Kalantari fail at this 'monumental task,' as you put it?"

Bingo! Janusz had turned the tables. "All you need to do is tell me where General Kalantari is going the next time he leaves Iran. I'll make arrangements to relieve him of his command while simultaneously ensuring that the Marburg attack is a complete failure. Nature will take its course from there."

"And you think I'm going to help you humiliate my country once again to save yours?"

"No, my dear Morteza, I *know* you're going to help promote yourself and your boss by humiliating a rival organization that has sidelined you. The best part of my offer is this. You don't have to use your own people, whom you can never trust with such a task. I'll do the dirty work."

"You're nuttier than I thought."

"All you have to do is present the facts to the MOIS chief, who'll then take it up with the supreme leader."

"How do you think you're going to get to General Kalantari? He travels with a heavy security detail."

"What difference does it make to you? If I fail, the QF will accomplish its mission, and you've got nothing to worry about. If I succeed, the QF will pay a price for its failure. Either way, the MOIS wins."

"What about me? I was sent here to recruit you."

Janusz tried hard to suppress a smile. "Consider it a minor setback. Anyway, you can blame it all on Dr. Ahvazi. Unless you've sent updates to Tehran about our meetings?"

"Not yet."

"Then you can help me get rid of Dr. Ahvazi to sell this story."

Morteza turned to gaze at the ancient buildings occupying the hilltop across Port Hercule on Monaco-Ville. The Iranian reached into his hip pocket and pulled out a pack of cigarettes. He placed one in his mouth and lit up. He took several deep puffs, then turned back toward Janusz. "I underestimated you for some reason. It seems that I was the imbecile."

"Well, I wouldn't put it that way."

"You may consider yourself an American, but Iranian duplicity runs through your veins," Morteza said. "You read me correctly. Headquarters will be thrilled to take advantage of this situation. I take it you won't publicize our cooperation?"

"Certainly not! My only interest is to neutralize the threat against America."

"And your losses at the casino?"

"No longer your problem," Janusz said.

Morteza pulled out a piece of paper from his coat pocket and scribbled a few words. When he was finished, he passed the note to Janusz under the table. "I wrote an email address with a password. I'll save a document containing the information you need in the draft folders by tonight. You let me know how I can help with Dr. Ahvazi. Our only chance is to eliminate that cretin before he gets back to Iran."

45. LA FEMME EXOTIQUE
GENTLEMEN'S CLUB, MONACO

October 27

One by one the girls sashayed across the room and came to a halt in front of his velvet couch. They were like the colors of the rainbow. The white ones came out first. They were all East Europeans, a blonde, two brunettes, and a redhead. Then came an Asian, either Chinese or Japanese, he could not be sure which. After that came a brown-skinned beauty, most likely an Indian. Finally, an African woman whose ebony skin and round bottom sent shivers from his head straight down to his scrotum. He was in the mood to be experimental. Why shouldn't he? He deserved this treat. After helping his country to trap the American, Dr. Ahvazi expected a substantial increase in pay. It was time to celebrate.

"I want one from both ends," Dr. Ahvazi said in English.

"Oh my, two for the gentleman?" the madame of the brothel exclaimed in a French accent.

"Yes, one vanilla and one chocolate, *khhhh*," the Iranian said as drool trickled down the sides of his mouth. "Send some champagne to our room as well."

"Would the gentleman like some food for himself and the ladies? We have a ham and cheese plate. I can ask them to hold the ham, if that is a problem," the madame said.

"No, no. Please send everything, the girls, the champagne, and the ham," Dr. Ahvazi said as he pinched the white girl with his right hand. A Russian, she introduced herself as Tatyana, playfully slapping his hand away. Within seconds, Tatyana and her Nigerian playmate, Adunni, were each holding one of Dr. Ahvazi's hands. They coquettishly walked him to a bedroom reserved for clients. As he entered through the door, Dr. Ahvazi stared while the girls slowly undressed him. Off went his shirt, belt, and pants. He was then pushed onto the bed while his two companions fondled each other. Tatyana and Adunni finally undressed, sending the Iranian into a frenzy. He was inspired to leave the bed for his pant pocket. The girls strenuously objected to his next move.

"Oh no, no, no. You cannot take a photo," Adunni said.

"This is for me, *ghoolp*, you are so beautiful," Dr. Ahvazi said.

"No, I have a family," Adunni said.

"Put the camera away, or we will leave," Tatyana said.

Disappointed, Dr. Ahvazi was about to drop his phone when it rang. Recognizing the caller, he had no choice but to answer. He chose to stay in the room, hoping neither of the girls would understand what he said.

"Hello?"

"Are you alone?"

"Yes, of course."

"Where are you?"

"Where am I?" Dr. Ahvazi repeated nervously.

"Yes, you imbecile, that's what I just asked you."

"I'm … I'm getting ready to leave on the afternoon train to Milan. I must get to Syria to check on the progress of my men in Idlib."

"Get ready to change your plans."

"Why?"

"You have to travel to Moscow at once."

"Moscow?"

"What's the matter? Did you develop a hearing problem at the casino? Yes, Moscow. The Devil's Vengeance program chief is in Moscow to discuss mutual collaboration with the Russians."

"Collaboration on what?" Dr. Ahvazi asked.

"Have you lost your mind, you moron? That's not something we discuss over the phone. All you need to know is that he's trying to solve the issue with the treatment."

"I thought the Russians refused to help us on that."

"I guess they changed their minds. You're to rent a hotel room and await instructions for a meeting with a man named Sergei Petrov."

"Petrov? He's their top microbiologist. He wants to meet *me?*"

"Hey, I'm just the messenger."

"Fine, what else?"

"You're to take two million dollars with you, in cash."

"What! Are you serious?"

"Don't argue with me."

"Where am I supposed to get that kind of money?"

"Your organization has a bank account in Zurich for emergency procurements. Have them wire the money to a bank in Monaco before you leave. Place the cash in two duffel bags. The Russians won't check your bags with your diplomatic passport."

"But—"

"Don't interrupt me."

"Sorry."

"You're to place the bags in an automated luggage locker at the Kievsky Railway Station on your way to the hotel. Bring the key and your passport to the meeting with Petrov."

"That money was supposed to pay for the salaries of my employees."

"Don't worry, you'll be reimbursed."

"Fine."

"Stop wasting time talking to me," Morteza said, and hung up. Dr. Ahvazi stood there naked, scratching his ass, hungry for the women on the bed. He did not want to leave.

"What's the matter?" Tatyana asked.

"I must go, *khhhh.*"

"Oh, that's too bad. You still owe each of us a thousand dollars for the session," Tatyana said calmly.

Dr. Ahvazi clenched his jaw as his blood boiled. He was losing more money than he cared to calculate. There was no way he would leave Moscow without getting Petrov's help for his project.

46. BEHESHT-E ZAHRA CEMETERY, TEHRAN, IRAN

October 29

The raindrops fell on her face, slowly merging with the tears on her cheeks. Before long, the clouds turned into a gray cluster that mirrored her heart. It was impossible to tell if the distant cries of crows were a figment of her imagination or a warning of more terrible news to come. Her reflection stared back somberly as she gazed at the granite footstone covering her husband. It was all a sham and she knew it. This fake grave site was the only thing the government had agreed to pay for. If only Mohsen had run away with Roozbeh Navabi, he would still be alive. Her children stood beside her in silent deference to a father they would never know again. God only knew what for. That was the hard part as she was never told the name of the virus that killed Mohsen. Mrs. Salehi bent over to gather several white flowers from her bouquet. One by one she laid them against the blackness of the granite.

Where would she go now? Who would help raise these children? Who would help put food on their table? Who would pay for their education? Those were the questions racing through her mind this dreadful morning. The entire period since Mohsen's infection had been a blur. It was a nightmare from which she could not wake up. She had lost the most important person in her life. Only God could help her now.

She opened the bottle of rosewater before sniffing it to

wake her senses. There was no use in waiting any longer. They weren't coming. Despite promises to the contrary, not a single person from the Ministry of Health, the Pasteur Institute, or the RCERID showed up. And why should they? Like her, they all knew his body was not buried here. They also probably knew that Mohsen's mangled corpse was so contagious it had to be cremated at the hospital. Despite years of faithful service to his country, her husband had been flushed down the toilet like an unwanted turd.

Mrs. Salehi knelt to get closer. From there she slowly poured the rosewater with her left hand as she "cleansed" the granite stone with the fragrant liquid.

The precipitation grew heavier, forcing her to perform this ritual over an empty grave in a hurry. She could take no more. As the bottle of rosewater lay empty next to the granite, she fell sobbing on his grave while her children watched. A moment later, the eldest began tugging on her shirt.

"Mommy, mommy?"

"What is it, dear?"

"You can't cry now."

"Why not?"

"Because the rain is picking up and we're going to get wet. Daddy wouldn't want us to get sick."

"I suppose you're right, baby. I suppose you're right," she whispered, blowing her nose into a handkerchief.

"Will Dad's friends be upset not to see us here when they visit him?"

"I don't think anyone is coming to visit him, dear."

"Why not?"

"Well, Papa is not really here."

"Where is he, then?"

How could she explain the cremation?

"He is in a better place. A much better place." Mrs. Salehi hoped that was true, but she knew better. Mohsen had been taken by the devil. Now she could think of nothing but the letter handed to her at the hospital. It was a slap in the face, one more instance of rubbing salt into her crushed soul. Her family had been sacrificed to keep a secret. The one-paragraph letter embossed with the emblem of the Iranian government was curiously unsigned. The only thing on the bottom was the seal of the Ministry of Health.

> *Dear Mrs. Zohreh Salehi,*
>
> *It is with the utmost regret that we inform you of your husband's death. Mohsen Salehi has passed away from an unknown complication. Since Mohsen had not followed the proper safety procedures at the lab, the Pasteur Institute is in no way liable for this tragedy. Therefore, no benefits will be paid out for this incident. Furthermore, since Mohsen had not accumulated enough time, or reached retirement age, the government cannot provide his retirement benefits to you now or at any time in the future. Peace be upon you.*
>
> *The Ministry of Health*

Mrs. Salehi stared one last time at the black granite before walking off. She had no choice but to survive, if not for herself, then for the children. She knew exactly who would help make things right.

47. BOSCO CAFÉ, KREMLIN, MOSCOW

October 29

D r. Ahvazi placed the empty coffee cup on the table, his third in the last half hour. He was not a coffee drinker by nature, but cigarette smoking was banned in this cafe. He studied the sludgy grinds that stuck to the white interior of his cup. He was hoping to predict his future by reading the shapes left behind like his mother used to do. He cursed himself for not picking up that skill. He was in desperate need to predict the upcoming meeting with Sergei Petrov, the legendary Russian military virus expert. The rumor was that Petrov had found a cure for Ebola, possibly Marburg too. Thus far, the Russians had rebuffed repeated requests for collaboration. The news of their willingness to share their secrets for two million dollars was too good to be true. Only a fortune-teller would know for sure, and there were none around when you needed one.

When the waiter approached, Dr. Ahvazi ordered another coffee. His hands were shaking, but he didn't care. Bosco Café had the best coffee in Moscow, or so he was told. It was now 1:35 p.m. and still no sign of Petrov. Perhaps he was making a mistake. Perhaps he should not have come at all. What choice did he have? The MOIS had ordered him here. He took the metallic lighter out of his pant pocket, the one with the QF insignia, opening and then closing the lid in rapid succession. It was interesting, the more he did it, the faster he got. *Ticktock,*

ticktock, ticktock. His thumb moved so quickly he was barely conscious of what he was doing. A thick-necked man in a leather coat stared coldly from the next table. Dr. Ahvazi quickly turned to place the lighter in his coat pocket, hanging behind his chair. When he turned back a man was sitting at his table. Dr. Ahvazi jumped up.

"There you are. You're late," Dr. Ahvazi said in Russian. He had learned the language while conducting viral research in Moscow years ago. The man stared without responding.

"Are you Petrov?" Dr. Ahvazi asked.

"No."

"Who are you, then?"

"My name is Aslan. I'll take you to him. You ready?"

I was ready half an hour ago, Dr. Ahvazi thought as he studied the man carefully. He was too dark to be Russian. His nose was quite prominent. He was clean-shaven with an athletic build.

"*Ehhem*, where are we going?"

"Zaryad'ye Park, down the street."

Dr. Ahvazi studied Aslan's eyes intently. His face gave nothing away. The Iranian scientist gathered his windbreaker before following Aslan out the door. From the café, they stepped directly onto Red Square, across from Lenin's Tomb. There were tourists walking out and about but not that many. It was, after all, the middle of a workday. The gargantuan square was remarkable in its grandeur, the backdrop of countless Soviet military parades he had watched as a child on the television. Back then, these Russians competed with America for global supremacy. Now they were a Mafia state, dependent on the export of oil and gas for survival just like his own country.

They passed another landmark, Saint Basil's Cathedral. His thoughts drifted to the impending attack on the Americans. This gambit with Petrov had to work. *What if the whole thing is a ruse?* The Russians were always strapped for money. They were also expert manipulators. If the Americans could not contain Marburg, humanity would pay the price. It would only take one tainted visitor to infect the entire population of his own country. He had to convince Petrov. They turned past Saint Basil's to enter Zaryad'ye Park.

"Quite scenic here, but why couldn't we meet in an office? It's much more private," Dr. Ahvazi said.

"The office meeting will come tomorrow. Right now Petrov just wants to see you."

"How much longer?"

Aslan raised a pointed finger. "Just a little farther." They finally arrived in a wooded area where the leaves had turned yellow. A pebbled trail led into the woods.

Dr. Ahvazi stopped dead in his tracks. "He is in there?" There were people around, but this part of the park was more secluded. He was ready to leave. "There is no one here."

"You don't expect him to talk in front of the whole world, do you? He doesn't want anyone to take pictures of the meeting. Please go," Aslan said, shoving the Iranian to move ahead of him. The sound of their footsteps on the pebbles was distinct. They walked past a wooden bench as the signs of civilization quickly disappeared. Dr. Ahvazi turned his head once more.

"Keep going, just a bit farther," Aslan said reassuringly.

"Where? I don't see him."

"Keep going." Several more steps and the sound of his own feet was the only noise that remained.

"Aslan, where are you, *ghoolp*?" Dr. Ahvazi wanted to know as he turned in every direction. He was definitely alone now. He walked farther ahead in search of Petrov. Out of nowhere came a cry he had heard countless times back home.

"*Allahu Akbar.*"

"Aslan?" Dr. Ahvazi cried before a sharp pain pierced his stomach. His windbreaker was immediately drenched in blood. The strikes came out of nowhere as if his assailant was invisible. Suddenly, someone grabbed his forehead from behind and raised it toward the sky. The cold steel of the blade cut through his neck as he gasped for air. "*Kkhhhh.*"

Aslan took his locker key and passport before he passed out.

48. TIJUANA, MEXICO

October 29

They turned onto a dirt road with run-down houses and graffiti. From Durango Street, they entered 7MA Road and drove up a hill. They were on the eastern edge of Tijuana, a decrepit neighborhood thousands of kilometers from home. More importantly, they were one kilometer away from the Great Satan, their mortal enemy. The assault team commander was too excited to be tired. Years ago, when he'd volunteered for the QF, it had only been a dream to defeat the evil Americans. Here he was now, a lethal warrior of Islam about to take the fight to the enemy for the second time. Near the top of the hill stood the safe house. The embassy in Mexico City had rented this location. Its owners received a handsome sum to stay away for a week.

They parked the SUV in the driveway, and all five men disembarked to stretch. After the forty-hour drive from Mexico City, the opportunity to stand was appreciated. The next twenty four hours were reserved for rest before the arduous trek into the heart of the enemy.

"Can someone open the trunk? I need to get our bags," one of the men yelled in his native language.

"Shhh, keep your voice down, idiot. No vun here has heard Farsi before. Ve vill speak English vhen ve're outside," his commander admonished. They gathered their bags before entering the house. Everyone took turns in the shower. The commander cooked a dinner of eggs and toast, which they ate heartily. After a restful sleep, they spent the next day mostly exercising their muscles. They avoided walking the streets for fear of being spotted as foreigners. Inside the house, the men prayed, read passages from the Quran, and watched movies on their mini tablets. At sunset, they sat around the living room table for a final briefing on the upcoming mission.

"Okay, listen up. You've been handpicked for Operation Devil's Vengeance because you're the best of the best. But don't let that fact go to your head. This'll be our most difficult mission to date."

"Piece of cake! We lived in America for four months before we killed Simmons and his wife. With Allah's blessing, we'll be back here in two days."

"Did I give you permission to speak?" the commander shouted. "You're the same idiot who couldn't wait a day for his tea. Because of you, we had to drink that Lipton shit at Simmons's house."

They sat quietly as the commander spoke again.

"We have a two-kilometer hike in front of us, all of it uphill. The terrain is extremely rocky, and we'll be carrying heavy packs. We'll be completely dependent on our goggles for vision. There are snakes and other creatures all around," he said as the men stared. "Here's the kicker. You can't use your firearms for any reason. Anything you kill you must do so with a knife. American border patrol agents may be sitting in their cars on top of those hills. This won't be easy."

"Where are we meeting our contacts?" one of the men asked.

"We're not. The Hezbollah brothers from San Diego will leave a fueled vehicle for us on a dirt road across the border. We're leaving at midnight. We need to reach our objective by 2:00 a.m. Any longer and the Americans will find our car."

"What if we get stopped in California?" another man asked.

"That's the best part. The state of California is in open rebellion against the federal government. If we get stopped, we show our IDs and keep moving. Once we're inside their borders, we'll be safe. They consider it impolite to target illegals from Mexico.

The worst that happens, we ask for an immigration lawyer," the commander said with a hearty laugh.

"The Americans are so strange. How the hell does the federal government allow a province to get away with such foolishness?"

"That's not our concern. The more the Americans fight among themselves, the better it is for us. Our main objective is to make it up the hill into America. From there, it's only eighty-four kilometers to Pine Valley. We'll make a stop along the way and wait for our hotel to open."

Half an hour before midnight, they gathered their equipment once more. Each man carried a serrated combat knife along with a Colt .45 semi-automatic pistol for protection. They put on custom-made thermal camouflage suits over their clothing, making them invisible to the border patrol's thermal cameras. At exactly midnight, they walked out from the back of the house onto a dirt road. They huddled together one last time as the commander prayed for their success.

"*Besmillah Rahman Rahim*, I hereby commence Operation Devil's Vengeance." *In the name of God, the merciful.* "*Ya Hossein, Ya Hossein, Ya Hossein.*"

From the dirt road, they walked down into a dry rocky ravine. They had rehearsed this mission over a dozen times, hiking twice the distance in the rocky terrain of the Alborz Mountains north of Tehran. Their military boots had extra padding to prevent ankle twists and sprains. Up the hill, they went methodically, with Allah in their hearts and victory in their minds. They moved in a straight line, each man falling five meters behind the one in front. The commander was the point man for the group. Halfway up the hill, a sudden vibration grabbed their attention. The commander put his hand in the air as they all came to a stop. Within seconds, they dropped to the ground as the border patrol helicopter flew overhead. They waited in silence. The commander grew more confident by the minute as they pushed on.

"Sir, what's that?" one of the men down the line shouted. Someone else threw a rock at him for breaking protocol.

"But I hear a wolf."

"Shut up. We'll kill it if it comes close," another man said. The commander ordered them forward. His thoughts took him away to a memory in a park with his wife and two boys. Ice cream on a scorching Tehran summer day. With each step, his throat grew dry. He desperately needed a drink. Between the hike, the gear, and the camouflage suit, he could feel the beads of sweat forming over his lips. What made it all tolerable was the cold desert breeze that periodically blew over them.

"Not much longer," the commander whispered as he quickened his pace. He took another step before stopping dead in his tracks. The hissing grabbed his attention before he saw anything. A sporadic rattle near his feet was not to be taken lightly. Among the most dangerous creatures in this region was the rattlesnake. Ordinarily, snakes have a thermal vision that enables them to see in the dark. However, his men were as invisible to the snakes as they were to the American helicopters. Was that a good or bad thing? He could not be sure. The sight of their commander, frozen in place, prompted the men to do the same.

"What's going on up there?" came a voice from the back.

"One more word out of you and I'll personally put a bullet in your head. I don't care if the Americans hear us or not," one of the others said in reply. The commander diligently searched the ground around his feet. He placed his right hand on the holster of his Colt but thought better of it. He moved the same hand farther down his leg where the combat knife was securely fastened. Once it was unsheathed, its sharp edges came into view through his goggles. The rattling sound was gone. In its place was a deafening silence that could only mean one thing. As he shifted his stance to turn sideways, the commander felt a tug on his pants. Within seconds, something was moving up his left leg. It was all he could do to stay still. Any sudden move could spell disaster for the mission and his life. Through the goggles, the reptile was slithering up slowly toward his waist. He made his move as soon as he spotted the head. With one motion, his left hand grabbed the rattlesnake around the mouth, squeezing it with all his might. The snake tightened its grip around his leg to prevent itself from being pulled off.

"Help, come quickly," he called out to the man behind as quietly as he could.

"What is it, sir?"

"My left leg. Use your hands to unwrap the snake."

His subordinate went to work unwinding the snake while the commander kept a grip around its mouth.

"Okay, now stretch him out and place him on the ground."

Once they had the snake uncoiled against the rocks, the commander brought his knife forward. In one strike, he decapitated the twitching reptile. Holding the severed head in his hand, he turned to address the men who were huddled around him now.

"This is a symbol of vhat ve'll do to the Americans. I'm bringing this head vith us for good luck. Forward march," he ordered.

With ten minutes to spare before two in the morning, they reached the hilltop on the American side. The assault team continued its trek in the darkness.

"I don't see a trail, do you?" one of the men cried out.

"There it is, over there," the commander replied.

"Oh yes, I see it now."

The assault team converged in unison around the KIA Sorrento. Its doors were unlocked, the keys inside. The men removed their camouflage, stored their gear, and piled in. Before long, the GPS guided them to the Otay Mountain Truck Trail. It was time to make the Americans pay.

49. VNUKOVO INTERNATIONAL AIRPORT, MOSCOW, RUSSIA

October 31

The Gulfstream landed in Vnukovo International Airport late in the morning. A Mercedes S600 was already waiting at 11:30. The doors of the private plane opened as Janusz stepped out. It was his first trip to Moscow in quite a while. His contact and friend, Federal Protective Service, or FSO, Colonel Roman Tomchenko, approached with open arms. The men hugged on the tarmac before speaking Russian, a language Janusz had mastered as a child.

"*Priviet*, Roman! Good to see you, my friend," Janusz said with genuine enthusiasm.

"Janusz, it's been a while. I've made the arrangements you requested."

"Lovely, I trust the first installment of funds has already been paid out?"

"Yes, we're good," Roman replied, reaching into a briefcase. "This is your FSO ID card. We used the picture you sent. Your identity is Colonel Ivan Vasiliev of the FSO. General Kalantari is staying at the Ritz-Carlton Moscow."

"Do you have the key?"

"Oh yes, here is one key and one passport from a dead Iranian scientist."

"Have they found the body?"

"Not to worry, no one will ever find his body," Roman said.

"What are my primary threats?" Janusz asked, eager to get going.

"There is a twelve-man FSO security team whenever he's at the hotel. You need to get in and out quickly. I suggest you leave the plane running after you refuel."

"Any Iranians with him?"

"Just one, his personal QF bodyguard, Majid, the only other person in his suite."

"What else?"

"He's been in town for the past three days, and is leaving tonight. This afternoon he's meeting with the defense minister and secretary of the National Security Council at 3:30 p.m. He takes lunch in his hotel room at 1:00 p.m. and rests for an hour before his afternoon appointments. Your only chance is to hit him between one and three this afternoon. General Kalantari is on the eleventh floor. Most of the FSO men are positioned one floor below his. Oh, and there are two FSO guards stationed outside his suite."

"What about the woman?"

"She's waiting in the Mercedes. Her name is Natalia Kalinskaya. The best escort in Moscow and happens to be on our payroll. Don't be shy to ask for favors if you like." Roman chuckled.

"She's not for me, Roman."

"I know, just busting your balls. You should get going now."

Janusz was halfway toward the car when Roman shouted, "One more thing."

Janusz stopped. "What's that?"

"If you fuck up and General Kalantari gets a chance to hit his panic alarm, you'll have less than five minutes before the entire block is flooded with FSO men. Our deal was to get you close. Beyond that, you're on your own. By the way, please make an effort not to kill any of my colleagues."

"I'll try to remember that," Janusz said as he sat behind the wheel of the Mercedes. Natalia was seated behind him. He turned briefly to explain their itinerary. "*Priviet*, we need to make a quick stop at Kievsky Railway Station for an important pickup. I need you to run in and get two bags from the lockers. If they ask for ID, show them this passport and explain that you're making a pickup for your husband. Do not open the bags, just come straight back to me. From there, we're headed to the Ritz."

Natalia smiled. "Whatever you say."

An hour and a half later, after Natalia's successful pickup, they arrived at the hotel. It was 1:00 pm. Janusz tipped the valet five hundred dollars to park the car in the front driveway on Tverskaya Street. As Janusz helped Natalia out of the vehicle, he was confident the plan would succeed. She had auburn hair flowing in waves below her shoulders, and bright blue eyes on a flawlessly made up face. A tight-fitting dress accentuated every part of her curvaceous body. She wore stiletto heels, and her fingernails, painted bright red, clutched her red purse. In short, she resembled his wife, a perfect ten. She grabbed his arm as they walked through the revolving door into the marble-floored lobby.

"Not bad," Natalia said.

"Yes, it's a step up from Motel 6 in America."

"What?"

"Nothing, let's go."

Janusz took a second to familiarize himself with the lobby. On either side of the front entrance stood a floor lamp made of decorative brass in the shape of a winged lion around the base. To his right was a white marble staircase spiraling to the second-floor balcony lounge. The seating area directly in front of the revolving door was decorated with embroidered red velvet sofas. A black Steinway piano was placed between them. Janusz counted five large men in suits walking the lobby. He suspected them as FSO.

"Let's get on with it," Janusz said before guiding her to a bank of elevators behind the seating area. As they stood there waiting, a refrigerator-sized man nearby shot a baleful glance toward him. Janusz ignored the Russian, staring forward as the elevator doors opened. Once inside, he turned to his companion.

"Natalia."

"*Da?*"

"Do you recall everything I told you in the car?"

"Yes."

"Good, once the general's guard comes outside, grab his hand and take him to the lounge. Just act confident and he won't mind the company. Now take my hand," Janusz demanded as the elevator doors opened once again.

"This is a restricted floor, authorized personnel only," the herculean FSO guard declared, blocking the doorway.

"I'm Ivan Vasiliev," Janusz said, flashing his badge.

"My apologies, Colonel. We're at your service," the FSO strongman said as he stepped aside.

"Very few are aware of my visit here. The Iranian general has made a special request, which is why I've brought Natalia with me," Janusz said.

"Let us know what you need."

"I need the two of you to disappear for a minute while I take the lady inside. The Iranian general is a modest man. He does not want anyone to witness his acceptance of this gift," Janusz said, gesturing toward Natalia.

"With all due respect, Colonel Vasiliev, we can't abandon our post. We have orders to—"

"Don't you think I know that? Do you think a man of my rank likes to perform such duties? The hotel manager has given me access to all rooms in this establishment. I'll open the conference room for the two of you to step inside temporarily."

"But—"

"After I deliver the girl, you can come back out before anyone notices."

"But, Colonel—"

"Don't interrupt me again—what's your name?"

"I'm Captain Gennady—"

"Unless you want your career in FSO to be a short one, you'll do as told. You're to speak to no one of my visit here today. My orders come straight from the top. By that, I mean the man who lives across the street." Janusz nodded in the direction of the presidential palace two kilometers down the road.

"Yes, Colonel," came the prompt reply as both FSO men stiffened their stance to show compliance. Janusz used a master key card from his pocket to open the conference room door. He stepped aside while the muscular FSO guards walked in. After locking the door, he turned to Natalia.

She smiled at him. "I'm not sure who you are, but you're damn good. Those two will be in big trouble before this day is over," she commented in jest.

"There'll be a lot of finger pointing, I'm sure. It's not like the days of Comrade Stalin. They'll keep their heads."

"What about their jobs?"

Janusz shrugged as he motioned her toward the master suite down the hall. He fell back for a second, allowing Natalia to walk in front of him. He quickly regretted this mistake as his loins came suddenly to life. Janusz grabbed her arm.

"Natalia, no man is safe around you. Perhaps you should walk behind me."

"Whatever you say," she said as they approached the suite. Janusz knocked while standing next to her. Seconds later, the door came ajar.

"Good afternoon, I'm Colonel Vasiliev—" Janusz said in Russian before being cut off.

"English, please," came the reply.

"Sorry, I'm Colonel Vasiliev with the FSO. I brought the girl General Kalantari requested," Janusz said, pointing at Natalia. The Iranian stared at the girl without acknowledging him. After a long pause, he turned back to Janusz.

"The general is busy. I don't know anything about a girl," he said reluctantly.

"Very well, I'll take her back," Janusz said, directing Natalia away from the door.

"Wait, wait, wait," came the stuttering reply. Majid closed the door behind him before stepping out. "Leave her with me, no problem."

Janusz handed her off and walked over to hide in the stairwell. Natalia used the elevator to take the Iranian to the club terrace lounge. She then proceeded to spike his drink as instructed. After waiting several minutes, Janusz returned to an empty hallway. He immediately walked back toward the suite. Using the master key card, he let himself inside. The empty foyer resembled the entrance of a grand apartment. A small leather chair by the wall, opposite the front door, had a magazine and a sandwich on top. He took the SIG P226 from inside his coat and screwed a suppressor over the muzzle. Three separate doors led out of the foyer. He opened the middle one. In front of him was a long hallway with cabinets. He searched through a few without finding anything of significance. At the end of the hallway, he opened a set of double doors leading to another room.

The lights came on, and he was standing in the master bedroom. It resembled a museum. Against the wall in front of him was a dark mahogany cabinet with gold accents around the edges. A large Ming Dynasty vase had been placed on top. Embroidered chairs created a cozy feel for two separate seating areas to his right and left. Beyond the chairs to his left was a sumptuous king bed perched against the wall on the far end of the room. The bed was messy. He walked over for a closer inspection. It was empty. To his right, Red Square was visible through the large window.

He walked back to the foyer. This time he opened the second set of doors. It led to an empty piano room. Behind the piano room was a living room with a grand view of the Kremlin. Back to the foyer he went. He opened the last set of doors. It led to another hallway beyond which was an elegant dining room. There was another set of double doors in this room. Based on the map of this suite Roman had provided, he was certain the other set of doors led to the study. Janusz held the weapon tightly in his right hand while his left grabbed the knob. Time stood still as he pushed slowly against the lever. With the door halfway open, General Kalantari was visibly seated facing away from him.

Images from a crackling fireplace reflected off the mahogany desk on which his feet were perched. Janusz walked in as quietly as possible, holding the pistol in front of his face. This was the mastermind behind the deaths of hundreds of American soldiers in Iraq, not to mention his own brother. Janusz's heart pounded with excitement. His index finger itched to hug the trigger, but that was not an option. Not yet at least. The general had valuable information to be exploited. As the adrenaline coursed through his veins, Janusz felt the sweat greasing his grip on the SIG. The general was so engrossed in his paperwork that he had not yet detected the presence of the intruder behind him. It was 1:20 p.m.

"*Haj Kalantari Ahest-e Pasho,*" Janusz demanded in Farsi. *Get up slowly.*

The general brought his feet down to face Janusz. The intruder's pistol prompted General Kalantari to gently drop the documents on his desk before speaking.

"Where's Majid?"

"He's with Natalia."

"Who?" When he realized what Janusz meant, General Kalantari cursed Majid under his breath. "Are you with the Monafeghin?" The Iranian opposition group MEK. "No, I don't think so, an internal enemy, perhaps? A reformist faction in the MOIS?"

Janusz laughed at the irony. "Wrong. I'm the American angel of death. I've come to avenge my brothers."

The general raised his brows at the bold proclamation. "Impossible. The godless Americans would never risk killing me in Moscow. They don't have the balls for it. You're with Mossad," he said.

"Take it however you like. Either way, we have some business to discuss."

"I'm only going to discuss business with your mother's pussy," the general said derisively.

"That'll be quite difficult. My mother's pussy does not speak Farsi," Janusz said. The general raised his brows again as he reached slowly for something while he maintained eye contact with Janusz.

"I wouldn't recommend that, Haj Kalantari. I don't want to have to shoot you accidentally." Janusz walked up to the QF chief.

"We both know you're not going to kill me. Why don't you just leave unless you—"

Janusz popped him in the mouth with the butt of the SIG before he could finish his thought. The Iranian bled over his papers on the table. He seemed surprised as he used his hand to wipe his mouth.

"Fuck your mothe—"

Janusz hit him so hard this time that he fell out of his chair. "Don't push your luck. I have *gheirat* just like you." *Honor.* "Playtime is over. Tell me about the Marburg attack on America. Choose your words wisely. I don't want you to lose any more teeth."

The general immediately placed a finger over his mouth. As he checked around, his finger stayed over a spot where a front tooth had fallen out. The QF chief instinctively searched the floor on his hands and knees before he spotted what belonged to him. He picked up the tooth, examined it, and threw it back down.

"The Marburg attack, where, when, how, and the code name of the operation?" Janusz insisted.

"You can't make me talk. Torture is against the Geneva convention. America would never do such things. Allah protects us from the likes of you."

"Whoever said I worked for the American government?" Janusz said. He stomped on the general's right hand, which was holding him up against the floor. The cracking sound of broken bones was distinct. The general cried out in pain as he held the mangled hand up to his face. Several fingers dangled out of place as white bone protruded through his palm.

"I'd say wiping your ass will be more of a challenge from now on," Janusz observed casually, then picked him up off the floor. The general was barely able to stand. Janusz proceeded to gut-punch him. General Kalantari laughed as he spat blood all over the floor. Janusz then grabbed him by the collar and placed him on his back over the mahogany desktop.

"Let's see if you think this is also funny, Haj Kalantari." Janusz unbuttoned his pants and pulled the zipper down.

"What are you going to do, you infidel?"

"You have no idea what pain is. Pain was Rome in 1995. You approved a Hezbollah attack that killed a bunch of American schoolkids. My brother was one of them."

"You?"

"Yes, I've been waiting for this moment for a long time," Janusz said as he unscrewed the suppressor on his pistol. He made sure the general was watching.

"Why are you doing that?"

"Because the tip won't fit in your asshole otherwise," Janusz said as he put the suppressor away. He then turned the QF general on his stomach and jammed the muzzle of the SIG in his anus. "Lying will cause me to squeeze this trigger. That'll open up a second orifice so you can experience the joys of womanhood firsthand."

The general put his mangled hand up to indicate surrender. "Operation Devil's Vengeance. It was my suggestion to avenge the sabotage of our missile program."

"Because you never caught the man responsible, right? He escaped from the warehouse in Sharjah?"

"How would you know?" General Kalantari said, bewildered.

"Because that man is standing behind you."

"You again, it can't be, it just can't. Who are you?" General Kalantari cried.

Janusz pressed the SIG against his anus as he cocked the hammer. "Where, when, and how?"

"A tiny town called Pine Valley, California. It's isolated to allow your CDC to quarantine the region."

"Go on, keep talking."

"An elite QF assault team is headed there as we speak. They're driving up from Mexico City, where they'll cross your border from Tijuana."

"Brilliant! No one will question them once they're inside

California," Janusz said sarcastically.

"California was ideal for many reasons," the general agreed. "From Tijuana, it's only an hour's drive to Pine Valley, where there are no biological agent detectors. The attack will take place on your heathen holiday of 'haloveen.'"

"Halloween, that's tonight!" Janusz said in a panic.

"Six p.m. local. Another fifteen hours in Pine Valley to be exact."

"Where are they staying?"

"The Pine Valley Motel."

"Why Halloween?" Janusz asked, using a thumb to press the general's testicles.

"Because it allows my men to use biohazard suits as Halloween costumes. They can spray the targets with blood using an aerosol. Your Dr. Simmons taught us that. Our own experiments perfected the data. Each time we see a kid on the street or knock on a door for food, we intend to spray them with what they'll assume to be fake blood."

"Very clever. Where do you keep the data?"

"What data?"

"The research and results of your Marburg experiments."

"It was with our field team in Idlib, Syria. The Russians accidentally blew it all up. I'm here to convince the Russians to give us their data, since they destroyed ours."

"It was lovely meeting you, Haj Kalantari. I've got a plane to catch."

"You'll never make it. We did our research. California authorities won't cooperate with your federal police to find my men. You're out of luck," General Kalantari cried.

"You're quite right. I don't need cooperation from California, however. I'll take care of this myself as soon as I finish with you."

"You must be joking?"

"You let me worry about that. See you in the afterlife, Haj Kalantari."

"In the name of Allah, you can't do this. The Russians will never let you leave this hotel alive."

"Haj Kalantari, you forget that I'm also an FSO colonel," Janusz said with a sinister laugh as he flashed his badge. The Iranian general pushed himself off the desk and lunged unexpectedly. Janusz ducked as he clutched the pistol. He quickly reattached the suppressor over the muzzle and pulled the trigger, pointing at General Kalantari's groin. The QF chief crumbled to the floor with his pants around his ankles. Placing the suppressor against General Kalantari's head, Janusz pulled the trigger once more. Blood rushed out the exit wound. Janusz moved close to observe the life drain out of his mortal enemy.

He spent the next five minutes cleaning up. After wiping down surfaces and picking up the shell casings, he walked to the foyer and out the suite. It was exactly 1:35 p.m. On his way to the elevators, the FSO guards pounded on the conference room door. They shouted for assistance intermittently, but there was no one else on the floor. They would not escape for a while. At the terrace lounge, Janusz quickly found Natalia. Majid was resting against the back wall in a dark corner.

"I take it you gave him the sedative?" Janusz asked.

"Fifteen minutes ago. He's sleeping like a baby."

"Is there anything keeping you in Mother Russia?"

"What do you mean?"

"You should come with me to America. You're no longer safe in Russia after what we've done here today."

"Just my mother and sister. They live here in Moscow."

"I'll arrange for their extraction later. The FSO will not hurt them. The jet is waiting at Vnukovo. Let's go."

She took a second to think things through. She pushed Majid out of the way, then grabbed her red purse and stood up to hold his hand.

"Lead the way," Natalia said confidently.

"Act naturally in the lobby. We can't seem nervous. I'll tip the bartender to let this idiot rest here until closing time," Janusz said, pointing at Majid.

"Where are we headed?"

"San Diego," he said as they made their way toward the lobby.

Out the elevators, they made a beeline for the revolving doors while holding hands. Janusz tipped the valet another Benjamin in return for the car keys. An hour and fifteen minutes later, they ditched the Mercedes on the tarmac. Still no sign of the FSO. It was 2:50 p.m. The FSO would be outside the general's door any minute now. Janusz grabbed the suitcase with Roman's equipment along with the two duffel bags full of cash. Natalia only carried the clothes on her back.

"Don't worry, I'll take you shopping in California," he said as they boarded and buckled in as quickly as possible. The flight time was projected for twelve hours. With any luck, they would land in San Diego by 4:30 p.m. local time on October 31. They waited with clenched jaws and tight fists for the control tower to clear them for takeoff.

50. PINE VALLEY, CALIFORNIA

October 31; Halloween

J anusz pushed the accelerator against the floor, heading east on Interstate 8 at over a hundred miles an hour. At these speeds, the California Highway Patrol was sure to catch up sooner or later. It was a risk he had to take. In half an hour, it would be too late. He considered bringing Natalia along to save time but decided not to risk exposing her to Marburg. Instead, he dropped her off at the Sheraton behind the airport.

Exit 45, Pine Valley, was up ahead. Veering right to exit, he turned left on Pine Valley Road. The sun had yet to surrender. Its rays were fighting hard to keep the darkness at bay. On Old Highway 80, the GPS guided him to make a right turn. The town seemed deserted, with the exception of few cars turning into Pine Valley Park. He spotted the local fire station before passing Major's Coffee Shop. There was even a bike lane on this road. He made a left turn into an outdoor parking area, driving past a supermarket all the way to the parking lot of the Pine Valley Motel. He did not expect to find them there, but it was the best place to start his search. A soda vending machine sat next to the motel check-in entrance. He pushed the door open and walked inside.

The place was empty. A small flat-screen mounted on the wall opposite the receptionist's desk was set to a news channel. Janusz froze in place, instinctively immersed in the story. Reports from Moscow indicated an Iranian general by the name of Vahid Kalantari, along with his personal assistant, had vanished. A reporter standing outside the Ritz-Carlton Hotel asked bystanders how a foreign general could disappear in their city. One man suggested searching for the general in the brothels. Another proffered that the Iranian general had run off with a Russian wife. Others suspected foul play. The program suddenly cut to a news conference by Russian President Putin. The Kremlin boss expressed his regret about the incident, vowing to utilize the full powers of his office to track down all leads. President Putin then offered his personal observation. "No matter how capable the Russian security services are, no country can find a man who does not want to be found." It was comedy hour in Moscow.

The report mentioned numerous complaints from the Iranian Foreign Ministry and its embassy in Moscow. With Putin's denials and pleas of ignorance, there was nothing anyone on the planet could do to change the outcome. The Russians were not about to admit failure in protecting a visiting Iranian VIP across the street from the Kremlin. Nor would they incur the cost of investigating the incident on behalf of bearded clerics. Janusz felt safe the matter was closed.

He banged his palm against the countertop. "Hello, anyone home?"

It took another minute before a woman walked behind the reception desk from a back door. She was blond, with a puffy face and quite overweight. She took a doughnut out of her mouth long enough to ask what he wanted.

"Can I help you?" she asked sarcastically with an annoyed expression.

Janusz flashed a fake FBI badge. His credentials did not change her demeanor.

"Have a group of Middle Easterners checked into your motel within the past day?"

"Listen, mister, you're in California now. State law frowns upon our cooperation with federal authorities in tracking down illegals. Oh, wait, I meant undocumented residents." She had a slight drawl, definitely not local.

"Those laws only apply to the police, dear lady. You're a private citizen. Your cooperation is greatly appreciated to track down these men."

"I got nothing to say to you. Come back when you have a warrant," she said annoyingly.

Janusz reached across the desk, pulling her by the collar. They were eye-to-eye now. He pressed his thumb against her throat just hard enough to make his point. "I'm through playing Mr. Politically Correct with you. The sons of bitches I'm after are about to carry out an attack. I know they checked into this hotel. You need to tell me which room!"

"Rooms eleven and twelve, all the way down the hall." Her voice was shaking.

"Lovely, let me see your ledger for those rooms," Janusz said. She ran to the computer. When the information hit the screen, he read the names, most likely aliases. "Are there only five of them?"

"As far as I know."

"Do you have keys, or should I break my way in?"

She reached under the counter and handed him the keys.

"Thanks, you can call the cops now if you like. I'd appreciate their help," Janusz said, knowing full well she would not do anything to help him. He stepped outside and down the corridor, keeping his pistol tucked behind his back. When he reached room 11, he took two deep breaths and inserted the key. Janusz turned the knob and gently opened the door. Two queen beds covered with junk sat unoccupied against the wall. Janusz walked in to find food strewn about the floor. On the bed was an empty sandwich wrapper next to the Quran. A bottle of water sat on the dresser.

BANG. Something fell on the bathroom floor. He could see the light under the door as the sound of bare feet moved to and fro. He made his way over, ever so gently cracking the door open. He placed four fingers against the wood to give a gentle shove. The bathroom door flew open, and a naked man locked eyes with him. They stared uneasily at each other for what seemed like an eternity.

"Inja cheekar mikoni?" the man said in Farsi, *what are you doing here,* before charging like a bull. The naked man closed the distance before Janusz could react. His opponent pushed him from the bathroom straight onto the bed. Punches connected with his head as Janusz brought his guard up to absorb the blows. The strikes hit their mark before he was able to mount a proper defense. Janusz kneed the naked man in the balls. The man screamed in pain, allowing Janusz to throw him off. Janusz then grabbed a lamp from the nightstand and smashed it on the man's head, causing him to go limp. Not wanting to hurt an unconscious man, Janusz left him there as he poked through the room. Next to a flat-screen facing the bed was a duffel bag. Janusz opened the zipper to browse inside.

A small notebook contained details of a flight from Mexico City to Paris along with the address of a house in Tijuana. A box of condoms was perched on top of a Colt .45 semi-automatic pistol. Janusz took only the notebook. He was about to leave when a shiny object in the bag caught his eye. He dug in to pull it out. It was a metal cigarette lighter, but this one was special. On the front was the insignia of the IRGC, an extended arm holding a Kalashnikov rifle. The last one of these he had taken was in the snow in Iceland. It was given out to members of the QF. He placed the trophy in his pant pocket, the fourth QF lighter in his collection.

"Fuck you, American," the voice came from behind. When Janusz turned, the naked Iranian was holding a serrated combat knife.

"Where's the rest of your team?" Janusz asked in Farsi.

The man froze momentarily. "You're late. My team is already in the park." Then he attacked once more.

Janusz instinctively moved aside as the man's hand plunged directly into the TV. Janusz wrapped an arm around his neck and pulled the Iranian toward a closet. The knife-wielding hand came at him out of nowhere. Janusz released his grip, grabbed the knife, and pushed it into the Iranian's abdomen. His guts ripped open, and blood gushed down his legs toward the carpet. The Iranian collapsed as Janusz watched him writhe in pain.

Janusz exited the room and ran parallel to Old Highway 80 through several parking lots. He spotted the park not too far in the distance. He gasped for air as he passed by the post office in full stride. When he arrived at the park, there were families with children all around wearing costumes. Janusz walked the crowd in search of the QF assassins. No one paid attention as he wiped the blood from the side of his face. It was the perfect night to kill or be killed. It was ten past six, and the community Halloween party was under way beneath the bright lights of the park. General Kalantari had placed the time of the attack at 6:00 p.m. For all Janusz knew, someone might have been sprayed already. He searched among the crowd, wondering if the dead Iranian in the motel had misled him. A young boy came forward, extending a half-empty bag of candy.

"Trick or treat?"

"I'm sorry, kid. I don't have anything to give you," he said to the disappointed boy dressed up as Spider-Man. Out the corner of his eye, he spotted two men standing side by side. They were wearing yellow plastic suits, blue gloves, white head covers, and breathing apparatuses around their mouths. Each man had a spray bottle in his hand with a picture of Dracula on the front and the words *blood spray* written on the side.

Janusz approached with caution, bracing for the worst. Tapping one of the men on the shoulder, he flashed his badge. "Excuse me, may I see your blood spray?"

Before he could finish speaking, the man in the yellow suit tried to spray him. The nozzle jammed. The man threw the can at his face and drew out a knife. Janusz ducked. The knife was an exact replica of the one he had just plunged into the abdomen of the naked Iranian. Screams rang out as bystanders ran in every direction. Janusz placed the badge in his pocket as a second man approached holding another spray can in front. Janusz delivered a spinning hook kick, knocking the can out of the second man's hand. As the first man with the knife charged, Janusz moved out of the way, allowing him to pass by. A third voice emerged in the background, speaking Farsi.

"Finish him and come with me," the voice commanded. Janusz's glance revealed the third man to be dressed in the same yellow biohazard suit. The two yellow-suited figures now flanked Janusz to his left and right simultaneously. That's when Janusz remembered the object tucked in the back of his pants. As his opponents charged from their respective corners, Janusz turned left, squeezing the trigger of his SIG P226 just once. The perfect head shot dropped target number one. Janusz immediately fell to the floor and turned his arms toward the sky. The second Iranian was standing above him with the knife pointed down. Before the Iranian could plunge, Janusz fired two rounds straight into his chest. The Iranian fell forward still holding the knife. Janusz's extended arm deflected his limp body, guiding it safely to the side. He immediately stood up as screams came from all around. The third Iranian ran across Old Highway 80 into a residential neighborhood. Janusz ran after him, wondering if there were any police officers in this town. Galloping at full stride, he did not detect the masked man behind the tree in front of him. A jagged knife blade sliced his right biceps and made him drop the SIG.

"Motherfucker, where did you come from?" Janusz blurted. The only good news was that he'd finally located the fifth man. With his pistol on the ground and his upper arm injured, Janusz needed to even the odds. He searched hastily for something, anything. The Iranian lunged several times, slashing the air with his knife. Janusz leaned over to pick up a large branch lying against a tree. In one motion, he smashed the branch against the Iranian's head, forcing him backward. Janusz followed up with a roundhouse kick that dropped his opponent to the ground. He picked up the branch, now broken in half. After tearing off the broken piece, he jumped on top of his opponent.

Placing the thick branch under the Iranian's chin, Janusz pushed down with all his might until he heard the crackling collapse of his opponent's windpipe. He continued pushing until he was sure the man was dead. There was only one QF operative left. Janusz glanced at his arm. Although it was bleeding, the cut was not too deep. He removed his belt and wrapped it around his arm as a tourniquet.

Janusz crossed Old Highway 80, running as fast as he could with his injured arm. Wailing sirens of some sort finally came to life from behind him as he entered Deodar Trail, a residential street across from the park. The sirens moved in the opposite direction toward the park. He wondered if the local authorities had been afraid to come earlier. After all, the sheriff's office was right next to the park. Janusz passed several fenced properties as he ran up the street.

A woman's voice was crying out for help. As soon as he spotted the driveway, Janusz approached the house. The front door was open as he walked up the stairs to enter. A woman and two young children, a boy and a girl, all had red spray over their clothes and faces. The remaining Iranian assassin, in his yellow suit and mask, held the aerosol can in his right hand. Janusz stared at all of them with the leather belt dangling from his arm. On any other night, this would be a strange scene, but on Halloween, the woman and her children did not seem the least bit startled by his presence.

"This man barged through the door and sprayed us. He grabbed my phone and won't leave," the woman pleaded with Janusz.

"Everything will be all right, ma'am," Janusz said as calmly as he could.

"You're too late, I already sprayed them. Now I vill spray you," the Iranian said, and took a purposeful step forward. Janusz surveyed his surroundings. The living room was not that big. There was a small couch, a TV stand, a bookcase, and a recliner but not much room to move around. He was not about to abandon this family. He would stay and fight regardless of the risk of his own exposure to Marburg.

Janusz motioned the Iranian forward. "Let's get on with it, you son of a bitch."

His opponent moved closer and pressed his finger against the nozzle. Janusz held his breath and rushed forward like an NFL linebacker. Grabbing the Iranian by the torso, Janusz pushed him all the way back against the nearest wall. Janusz slammed the Iranian several times against the wall until the spray can fell out of his hand. Janusz then turned and threw his opponent against the couch. Janusz could not be sure if he had been exposed to the virus, but it did not matter anymore. The homeowner and her kids gazed wide-eyed as if watching an ultimate fighting cage match. Except this was truly a match to the death as the Iranian stood back up.

"I'm commander of an Iranian Qods Force Unit. Do you know the Qods Force, Mr. vimpy American?" the Iranian asked as they circled each other in the living room.

Janusz reached into his pant pocket to pull out the lighter. "Do you mean the little bitches who leave these behind?"

The Iranian's eyes opened wide in recognition of the QF lighter. As Janusz jostled to place the lighter in his pocket, the Iranian struck without warning. His punch landed right on the belt around Janusz's biceps.

"Son of a bitch," Janusz cried out. He felt bad about cursing in front of the children and bit his lip. The Iranian landed another punch. It hit Janusz on the face, forcing his head back. The Iranian maneuvered for a third strike. This time Janusz's kick crushed his balls. The Iranian hunched over reflexively, and Janusz grabbed his head and pulled his mask off. He then smashed the head against the side of the wooden coffee table. With a loud crack, the Iranian's forehead split open. As his opponent's body went limp, Janusz reached up to untie the belt around his arm. He grabbed the belt around both ends and placed the leather strap under the Iranian's neck. Janusz pulled back as hard as he could. He choked the man for several minutes, squeezing every ounce of life out of him. Suddenly, he looked up as three men rushed through the door with guns drawn.

"Police! Put your hands up," they yelled. Janusz raised his arms. The Iranian's head fell to the floor as the cops maneuvered to cuff Janusz. At that exact moment, his thoughts transitioned to Marjan.

51. ESPINAS PALACE HOTEL, TEHRAN, IRAN

November 07

He gently caressed her arms and tried to kiss her as she sat next to him. It was the perfect opportunity for her to finally get that glass of tea on the dining room table. From there she walked over to the large panoramic windows overlooking the entire city. Perched at the foot of the Alborz Mountains, the Espinas Palace was considered the only five-star hotel in the Iranian capital. The suite was booked to consummate their Sigheh, the temporary Shia marriage allowing a man and woman to have sex within the confines of the law. As she looked out the window at the iconic Milad Tower to the south, her body shivered when he called her name. She dropped several lumps of sugar in the tea and stirred.

"Zohreh, come here, honey," he said as Mrs. Salehi tried to ignore him. "What's the matter? Don't you want to sit next to me?"

"I'm sorry, Dr. Nader. I've got a lot on my mind."

"Please, now that we've made this official, you can call me Nader."

She felt like vomiting but forced herself to sit next to the abominable man once more while placing the glass of tea on the coffee table.

"Zohreh dear, I know this is hard for you. You should try to relax so we can—"

"It's been barely two weeks since Mohsen died," she protested.

"I know, I know. How about the view from this room?"

"You're right, Nader. This is very thoughtful of you. Did you bring some dirty movies like I suggested?" she asked.

"I searched far and wide to find something for you. I think you'll like what I got. Let me just get my laptop," he said as he lunged toward a nearby end table.

"Nader?"

"Yes, dear."

His response made her nauseated. "Before we get to that, I need to hear the truth from you," she said as he walked back toward her. "I will only give myself to you if you tell me what happened to my husband, I mean Mohsen. You know what I mean," she said.

He threw his head down and sighed as he sat next to her. "What do you want to know?"

"Was that him in the room when they dragged me out?"

He kept his eyes down as he took a deep breath. "Yes."

"What was the cause of his death?"

He hesitated, almost pleading with his eyes to be let off the hook. "We're not allowed to discuss that. I could get in serious trouble."

"Do you want to consummate the *Sigheh* or not?" she asked firmly while gently caressing his leg with her hand.

Looking around the room for several more minutes, he finally turned to her. "Your husband was working with the deadly Marburg virus. He had been infected during an experiment. Since the IRGC Qods Force was running the show at the hospital, I presume it was their program."

"Was it his fault like they said?"

"I don't think so. He was involved in a rather unusual experiment with chimps. They were cutting lots of corners. He did as he was told."

"Was this part of the government's effort to develop a new biological weapon?"

"I'm fairly certain that it was."

"How do you know all this? How can you be so sure?"

"As head infectious disease doctor at Vali-Asr Hospital, I was privy to some details on what happened. I filled in the rest by myself. I was sworn to secrecy with the threat of severe retribution. If any of this ever—"

"Don't worry. By the grace of God, I will make sure you're rewarded for telling me the truth," she said as she moved to kiss him on the lips. He immediately pulled back, holding on to her with trembling hands.

"Don't be so nervous. Here, have some tea. It'll help you relax," she said as she handed him the glass from the coffee table. She then maneuvered behind him to rub his shoulders as he drank his tea. Ten minutes later, he was sound asleep on the couch. She impatiently dug the phone out of her pant pocket to play the recording. When she was satisfied with what she heard, she got up to grab her bag. She then called a friend who had agreed to drive her and the kids to Imam Khomeini International Airport. The appointment was set for the next morning in Dubai, UAE, with the general manager of Al Arabiya News and several reporters. The network had promised to pay her one million dollars for verifying rumors about Iran's deadly new biological weapon. She knew her tape was much more valuable to the Gulf Arabs than what they were paying. She would use the money to start a new life for herself and her children in France.

52. UNIT 81 SAFE HOUSE, MCLEAN, VIRGINIA

November 21

Peering out the window, he was focused on the kids. If not for them he would have done this differently, a lot differently. He shifted his body to avoid touching the window. His arm still hurt from the attack in San Diego. After a three-week quarantine at the Nebraska Medical Center in Omaha, he had passed the incubation period for Marburg with a clean bill of health. The family he rescued in Pine Valley had become infected, but with round-the-clock care by the professionals in the Nebraska Center's biocontainment patient care unit, they were expected to fully recover.

"Here we are, dear, fresh lemonade." Marjan entered the living room with a tray.

"You shouldn't have," Janusz said, walking over to grab a drink.

"It's the least I can do."

"I finally caught up with the men who ordered the murder of your husband. You don't have to worry about them anymore," Janusz said, watching her hand tremble slightly as she almost spat out the lemonade.

"Oh dear, how can I ever thank you? But the Iranian regime has many agents around the world. If they're determined to find someone, they'll eventually succeed."

"I don't think that'll be a problem in your case. Life is full of so many surprises, wouldn't you agree?" he said sarcastically.

"What do you mean?"

"Have you gotten settled in yet?" he asked, avoiding her question.

"I don't have any friends here. Roozbeh's parents live in Maryland, but that's about it."

Her reply caught him by surprise. "Really, where exactly?" he asked.

"Let me think. Oh yes, a town called Annapolis. I took the kids there several times. Always lots of traffic."

"Well, perhaps I can help change that. Will you excuse me for a minute? I need to use the restroom," Janusz said.

"Certainly."

He returned five minutes later to find Marjan sipping her lemonade on the couch.

"Sorry, I had to make a phone call."

"I was still in shock when we met in Brazil, you know?" Marjan explained.

"Yes, that seems like so long ago now."

"I didn't get a chance to thank you for coming to the morgue with me."

"Oh, that's not necessary. You've thanked me and the Unit more than you can ever imagine."

"I've tried my best at work, but—"

"Oh, you've done more than try. You practically handed me over on a silver platter," Janusz said.

She stared at him with wide eyes. Her face turned pale as she shifted uneasily on the sofa. "Oh dear, I hope I've not offended you," she said in a voice that was almost apologetic.

"At first, I thought it was a coincidence that Dr. Ahvazi showed up in France. It was right after you started working with us, right?"

"I'm not sure I understand."

"I kept wondering how you could've known about my weakness," he continued.

"You're scaring me, Janusz. What weakness? What's going

on?"

"It finally hit me when I looked through my wallet. I'd pulled out the wrong card by mistake. Instead of the contact card for the Unit, I'd handed you the card to my addiction specialist."

"What's an addiction specialist?"

"You know exactly what it is. Heather saw you holding the card your first day on the job. You told her you were looking for a therapist, but she read the doctor's name on it and did a little digging. No more lies, Marjan. Why did you do it?"

"This is crazy," she continued to protest.

"If you think that's crazy, you'll get a kick out of this. Immigration service, otherwise known as ICE, is coming for you now."

"But why?" she asked while fidgeting on the couch.

"Because the Unit is no longer sponsoring you. As far as our government is concerned, you're here illegally. The kids, however, can stay with their grandparents in Annapolis."

She put her face in her hands and began to cry when he cut her off.

"Why did you betray me to the Iranian regime, Marjan?" he demanded, unfazed by her antics.

She wiped the tears away and straightened up. Her demeanor changed instantly; now she stared at him with a serious expression. "Because the MOIS was blackmailing me. Before Roozbeh bought the tickets to Brazil, I got a call from a man asking me to meet him at an apartment in Tehran. The man identified himself as MOIS. He explained I had no choice but to work for them if I cared about my parents. They promised a house, nice cars, the best medical care, and vacations for them. Once Roozbeh gave his press conference, they pressured me to help find him."

"And me, why did you tell them about me?"

"I wanted to do a good job. I thought it would make me look competent in their eyes. It wasn't personal. I had to do it for my family," she said with a stone-cold face.

"The good news is, I got my money back from your government plus interest for my pain and suffering. The bad news is, you won't be around to watch your kids for a few years unless you find a brilliant immigration lawyer. There was no way I could let you get away without some sort of punishment."

"Please, John, there's got to be another way. I don't want to leave my children."

"You should've thought of that before you got your husband killed and then betrayed the people who helped you. Believe me, if not for those kids, I would've asked Kim to kill you already. They've suffered enough, and I didn't want them to lose another parent. We'll hand them over to their grandparents in Annapolis unless you want to take them with you."

She stared daggers at him before speaking up. "That'll work. They can stay with their grandparents for now."

The doorbell rang as two ICE agents walked in to arrest Marjan on charges of living in the US illegally. At that moment, Janusz realized that she already knew too much about the Unit.

53. DULLES AIRPORT, VIRGINIA

November 22

J ennifer glanced at the departure board to check the status of their FIJI-bound flight. There was another thirty-minute delay. She faced her husband, squeezing his hand tightly. She seemed happier now. They were taking a well-deserved vacation for a month. Their most immediate plan was to start a family. The sound of Janusz's phone startled them both.

"Oofta, do you have to get that?" Jennifer asked.

"One last time, darling. I promise you won't see this phone until we return."

"Well, at least put it on speaker so I can hear."

"Fine," he said before picking up.

"Janusz?"

"Speaking."

"It's Jason Osborne from the SSCI. Do you have a minute?"

Janusz put the phone against his ear. "Jason, why are you calling me directly? We have channels for that. I'm definitely not in those channels."

"Something terrible has happened."

"What are you talking about?"

"There was a shooting on Route 28. Tony and Stan were coming to meet me at our facility. The car was shot up on the road."

"How are they?"

"Sorry to tell you this, Janusz. Stan is dead."

His words stunned Janusz. Jennifer just stared at him. "What about Tony?"

"He was transported by helicopter to Inova Fairfax. It's not looking good."

"I'm heading out to the hospital now. Thanks for the call."

He held his hand out. "Come on, Jennifer."

She grabbed on as they hurried out of the terminal.

TO BE CONTINUED

GLOSSARY OF TERMS AND NAMES

Akbar Shadi: Iranian Deputy Assistant Health Minister responsible for monitoring the activities of Dr. Ahvazi and RCERID.

Ali Ansari: Chief of Iranian MOIS.

Arnaud: French police officer that temporarily detains Janusz in Lyon, France.

Ayatollah Mashhadi: Supreme Leader of Iran.

Ben Soltani: Janusz's younger brother killed during terrorist attack in Rome.

Bill Turner: Head of Operations at Unit 81.

Brad Paisely: Political consultant and Jennifer's ex boyfriend.

Claude: French police officer that temporarily detains Janusz in Lyon, France.

David Schultz: Director of National Intelligence.

Directorate General for External Security (DGSE): French foreign intelligence agency performing same function as the American CIA.

Directorate General for Internal Security (DGSI): French internal security agency performing same function as the American FBI.

Donald Patrick: Chairman of the Senate Select Committee on Intelligence (SSCI).

Farhad Soltani: Janusz's father.

Federal Protective Service (FSO): Russian security agency concerned with the protection of high-ranking state officials.

General Anatoly Zelnikov: General in charge of Russian war effort in Syria.

Guy Devereaux: President of France.

Iman Vakili: A microbiologist working under Dr. Ahvazi at the RCERID. Iman is sent to Geneva to find a cure for the Marburg Virus after defection of Roozbeh.

Iranian Ministry of Health: Similar to US Department of Health and Human Services, the Iranian Ministry of Health is the top level executive authority responsible for administering the country's health system.

IRGC Qods Force (QF): A branch of the IRGC with the mission to support and train Iran's foreign proxies and to carry out intelligence operations outside Iranian borders.

Islamic Culture and Relations Organization (ICRO): Institution responsible for coordinating the Iranian government's foreign influence operations around the world. Located at Iran's embassies in foreign capitals.

Islamic Revolutionary Guard Corps (IRGC): A branch of the Iranian military founded after the Iranian Revolution to safeguard the Islamic Revolution.

Janusz Soltani: Operative working for Unit 81.

Jennifer Soltani: Janusz's wife.

Jason Osborne: SSCI senior staffer/intelligence analyst who liaises with the Unit.

Javad Ahvazi: Dr. Ahvazi is director of RCERID as well as the chief scientist responsible for the weaponization of the Marburg Virus.

John Kellerman: Director of the CIA.

Karl Sanders: Chief of Staff for US President Robert Adkins.

Kimberly (Kim) Jennings: Janusz Soltani's partner in the Unit who accompanies him on the mission to Brazil and Europe.

Marburg Virus: A member of the Filoviridae family of viruses similar to Ebola Virus that causes hemorrhagic fever and bleeding.

Michele Camus: Director of DGSE.

Mohsen Salehi: A technician infected with Marburg virus during experiments with the chimps in RCERID.

Zohreh Salehi: Mohsen's wife.

Morteza Karami: A career Iranian Ministry of Intelligence (MOIS) counter intelligence officer. Morteza is head of counter intelligence operations for Operation Devil's Vengeance who tries to recruit Janusz.

MR-191 Human Monoclonal Antibody: This is the cloned antibody of an individual who survived a Marburg infection in 2015. This antibody has shown promise as a treatment for those infected by Marburg Virus.

Natalia Kalinskaya: Russian escort who assists Janusz in Moscow.

National Security Agency: US Government agency responsible for the interception and decoding of foreign communications.

National Security Council: Coordinating body where senior US policymakers discuss national security threats to the US and formulate policy for the President.

Omid Reyshahri: RCERID technician who is killed during Russian air strikes in Idlib, Syria.

Pasteur Institute of Iran: Parent body of RCERID, Iran's Pasteur Institute is responsible for advancement of public health in such areas as disease monitoring, pharmaceutical research, and production of vaccines.

Paul Upman: US National Security Advisor.

Peter Beck: Air Force General and Chairmen of the Joint Chief of Staff.

Protovax: French pharmaceutical in Lyon, France developing a Marburg treatment of interest to Dr. Ahvazi.

Ray Simmons: American scientist in charge of Marburg viral research for USARMIID. Dr. Simmons and his wife are killed in their Leesburg, VA home.

Connie Simmons: wife of Dr. Ray Simmons.

Research Center for Emerging and Reemerging Infectious Diseases (RCERID): RCERID is a national laboratory located in the town of Akanlu near Hamedan, Iran. RCERID monitors the spread of infectious diseases and conducts related research for a cure.

Robert Adkins: US President.

Roman Tomchenko: Russian Federal Protective Service (FSO) colonel who assists Janusz in Moscow.

Roozbeh Navabi: A microbiologist specializing in viral vaccine research at RCERID who defects to Brazil to warn the world about Iran's new biological weapon.

Marjan Navabi: Roozbeh's wife.

Ryan Irving: US Secretary of Defense.

Sergei Petrov: Russia's top scientist for biological weapons.

Shahram Sabeti: Iran's Cultural attaché in Brasilia, Brazil.

SOCOM: aka US SOCOM is the Special Operations Command. SOCOM is a US combatant command responsible for the operation of US Special Forces.

Stan Roth: Tony's deputy in charge of Unit 81.

Supreme Council for National Security (SCNS): The SCNS is Iran's national security council, a forum for the discussion of national security threats.

Tony Volpe: Director of Unit 81.

Unit 81/High Risk Capital: Unit 81 is a private intelligence agency set up in 1981. High Risk Capital (HRC) is a private equity firm that serves as the cover for Unit 81. Unit81/HRC is located in Herndon, VA.

US Army Medical Research Institute of Infectious Diseases (USARMIID): US Defense Department's main institution for defensive research of biological weapons, located in Ft. Detrick, Maryland.

US Centers for Disease Control and Prevention (CDC): Located in Atlanta, Georgia, the CDC is responsible for protecting the public health of Americans.

Vaccigen: Pharmaceutical Company in Northern Virginia that works with Unit 81 and is knowingly serving as a cover organization for Janusz's assignment.

Vahid Kalantari: Major General and chief of the Qods Force.

Vali-Asr Hospital: Affiliated with Tehran University of Medical Sciences, this center maintains wards for infectious diseases where Mohsen Salehi is hospitalized.

Velayat-e Faqih: System of government in Iran where an Islamic jurist (senior cleric) is the most powerful individual in charge of society as both commander-in-chief and final arbiter of all domestic and foreign policy.

World Health Organization (WHO): United Nations agency responsible for the monitoring and coordinating of global health emergencies.

YPG: The People's Protection Units, a Kurdish militia organization opposed to both the Syrian Government and Islamic Jihadists.

BOOKS IN THIS SERIES

Janusz Soltani Series

The Buraq Project

Operation Devil's Vengeance

The Billionaire's Conspiracy

IF YOU ENJOYED THIS STORY, PLEASE PROVIDE A REVIEW ON AMAZON